Your Sad Eyes
and Unforgettable
Mouth

EDEET RAVEL

Your Sad Eyes
and Unforgettable
Mouth

VIKING
CANADA

VIKING CANADA

Published by the Penguin Group

Penguin Group (Canada), 90 Eglinton Avenue East, Suite 700,
Toronto, Ontario, Canada M4P 2Y3 (a division of Pearson Canada Inc.)

Penguin Group (USA) Inc., 375 Hudson Street, New York, New York 10014, U.S.A.
Penguin Books Ltd, 80 Strand, London WC2R 0RL, England
Penguin Ireland, 25 St Stephen's Green, Dublin 2, Ireland
(a division of Penguin Books Ltd)
Penguin Group (Australia), 250 Camberwell Road, Camberwell, Victoria 3124, Australia
(a division of Pearson Australia Group Pty Ltd)
Penguin Books India Pvt Ltd, 11 Community Centre, Panchsheel Park,
New Delhi – 110 017, India
Penguin Group (NZ), 67 Apollo Drive, Rosedale, North Shore 0632, New Zealand
(a division of Pearson New Zealand Ltd)
Penguin Books (South Africa) (Pty) Ltd, 24 Sturdee Avenue, Rosebank,
Johannesburg 2196, South Africa

Penguin Books Ltd, Registered Offices: 80 Strand, London WC2R 0RL, England

First published 2008

1 2 3 4 5 6 7 8 9 10 (RRD)

Copyright © Edeet Ravel, 2008

*Publisher's note: This book is a work of fiction. Names, characters, places, and incidents
either are the product of the author's imagination or are used fictitiously, and any resemblance
to actual persons living or dead, events, or locales is entirely coincidental.*

We acknowledge the support of the Canada Council for the Arts which last year invested
$20.1 million in writing and publishing throughout Canada. Nous remercions de son
soutien le Conseil des Arts du Canada, qui a investi 20,1 millions de dollars l'an dernier
dans les lettres et l'édition à travers le Canada.

Canada Council   Conseil des Arts
for the Arts   du Canada

Manufactured in the U.S.A.

Library and Archives Canada Cataloguing in Publication data available
upon request to the publisher.

ISBN: 978-0-670-06867-8

Visit the Penguin Group (Canada) website at **www.penguin.ca**

Special and corporate bulk purchase rates available; please see
www.penguin.ca/corporatesales or call 1-800-810-3104, ext. 477 or 474

For Larissa
kindest of souls,
brilliant and wise

*There is a name for us now: we can, if we wish, call
ourselves the second generation. We have websites;
books have been written about us. But back then we
were alone with our parents, and they were alone with
their survival. Limping and stunned, they returned
from the Nazi camps. How does one reconcile that
world and this one? No one has the answer. It seems
impossible, and yet they forged new lives; but even
those who had not lost their minds had lost their
orientation.*

*One way or another, we, their children, inherited
fragments of their memories. We were the children who
came to reclaim the world, proxies for ghosts. Hovering
always between resistance and compliance, we did what
we could.*

SHIRI ARYEH

Yes, it's been a boozy evening. Patrick's back in Montreal for his mother's funeral and I suggested we meet at a downtown brasserie. He was already there when I arrived, but I didn't notice him at first; the place was crowded and dimly lit, and he was seated at the far end, facing away from the door, his hair thinner now. I almost settled down at the bar to wait for him, but then I spotted his wife, whom I recognized from a photo his mother had shown me— glasses, delicate features—and I made my way to their table. Patrick scowled slightly when he saw me, and introduced his wife in a distracted way, as if he'd only met her a few minutes ago. Her name is Adar and she works for an academic publisher, translating Hebrew and Spanish texts into English.

Adar wasn't very talkative, but she was watching us closely, and I felt she was trying to extract clues from what we said and how we said it. Clues about what? About Patrick, I think.

Patrick's profession intersects with mine: his work at the university library includes curating, and he's interested in art history—or art reception, as I prefer to call it. Instead of catching up, we clung to the present; we discussed document preservation, current trends in teaching or not teaching theory, climate change. The three of us were hemmed in on both sides by tinted mirrors that allowed us to see kinder versions of ourselves; as the evening progressed and the vodka flowed, the mirrors became increasingly co-operative.

I'm back at my Plateau triplex now. Holding on to the cold, wrought-iron railing, I negotiated the spiral staircase to my front door. The triangular steps are treacherous in winter, but we're all attached to this architectural quirk for which our neighbourhood is famous, are quite proud of it, in fact—even though keeping the stairs clear of ice and snow is an ongoing challenge.

It's late, but I'm not at all sleepy. I checked my email: no new messages. And then, in that post-alcoholic surrender to fate, I opened a blank page and stared at it, as if waiting for a sign from above—or below—to appear on the screen.

Does Adar know our story, I wonder. Has Patrick broken the pact, now that his mother has died? Or did he tell Adar when they first met, in spite of his admonition that Rosie and I never tell anyone, not even our lovers?

Our story—that's what I want to write about. A tale of love: my love for Rosie, Anthony's fleeting love for me, Patrick's love for no one. As I gazed at the mirrors in the brasserie, it seemed to me that the people we weren't talking about were hovering there, behind our reflections, waiting to be acknowledged. Or was it seeing Patrick's casual cruelty towards Adar that sent me somersaulting back in time?

I may change my mind tomorrow and abandon this project. I may not have the stamina—which is a sly way of saying I'm half-afraid. I have the time, if I need it. It's Friday night, and since I'm only teaching two courses this semester, a four-day weekend looms ahead. The women whose ranks I swell at Sororité—our city's last surviving lesbian bar—will manage, somehow, without me. I'm being facetious, of course—though I don't know exactly how I feel about my dependence on that laid-back neverland, where we are indeed growing older, but in a cloistered haven of our own. *Let all who are hungry* ... Even if I do not find at Sororité whatever it is I hunger for, I do find distraction from hunger.

In any case, I will stay at home this weekend and embark on this phantom-laden voyage. I will try to write out, write down, an account of our star-crossed saga. I've even pulled out of a back drawer the diary I kept long ago, when I was a teenager.

This diary of a young girl not in hiding, not heroic, consists of twenty-three spiral Hilroy notebooks, $8^1/_2$ by 11 inches, sixty lined pages each, though I rarely stayed in the lines. The first notebooks have cheap, mud-brown covers, rough to the touch. Then Hilroy noticed that the times they were a-changin' and the covers were redesigned to attract flower children: three Canadian geese against a grey and orange sky; a skier, illuminated by a flash of blinding sun, spraying snow crystals as he swerves down a hill; the feet of six hikers resting on the ground, their legs raised on backpacks.

Everything is here, inside these pages: our shifting and shuffling, our small victories and elaborate blunders.

In I go.

1968

I lived back then with my courageous mother and, luckily, my grandmother, in an upper duplex on Bedford Street, in the Côte des Neiges district.

A pretty name, Côte des Neiges, evoking images of snow angels and silver skates, but to Montrealers the words suggest an immigrant population, neighbourhoods running to various stages of seediness, small shops. Forty years ago, there were fewer seedy stretches, and Jews newly arrived from Europe or seeking escape from the noisy Plateau chose to settle on the more respectable streets: Kent, Linton, Bourret. We liked the worn-out witticism: God gave Moses Canada because he stuttered; he'd meant to say Canaan. All that has changed; these days, other immigrants live on Linton and Kent.

The rooms of our Home Sweet Home were arranged in a claustrophobic ring around a central foyer. The living room faced the street, my bedroom came next, then the kitchen—with a door leading to the back balcony. A bathroom and my mother's bedroom, which she shared with my grandmother, completed the asymmetrical circle. The hapless architect had left the foyer for last, and it was oddly shaped, a by-product of the five unevenly spaced rooms.

But the floor plan was the least of it—the entire building was doomed by its white-tile facade, low ceilings, plywood doors. These paltry efforts aroused my sympathy: I felt sorry for the aluminum windows, the stippled taupe-and-white linoleum in the kitchen, the unloved and unlovable wall-to-wall carpets. They were doing their best.

Here, then, on a rainy Saturday in April—April 15, 1968, to be exact—I, Maya Levitsky, daughter of Fanya and the late Josef Levitsky, could be found soaking in a scrubbed and sterilized lavender-blue bathtub, after a windy, drizzly journey to the

Atwater Library and back. I was in love with the Atwater Library, in love with the majestic reading room, polished pine tables, vaulted ceilings, enormous arched windows, and the skylight of diamond panes surrounded by garlands in low relief—yes, garlands! Someone had gone to all that trouble, just for a ceiling. And of course the books, shelves and shelves of art books, shelves and shelves of novels. That's what I did on weekends: I read at the library, and when I grew tired of reading I leafed through folio-sized reproductions of famous paintings. The art prints held as much intrigue and drama as the novels: Venus and Cupid in erotic embrace, angels and weeping mothers, village squares, sunsets and nightmares, a lone woman in a red hat waiting for a train ...

I sat up in the bath and submerged my legs, then slid back down as my knees went up. Maya, the human accordion. I never did mind my overly long, overly freckled body, and I felt protected by my Pre-Raphaelite red hair. Right now, though, with my head immersed up to my ears, I felt like Millais's floating Ophelia. That very morning I'd read the story behind the Ophelia painting: Millais's docile model, Elizabeth Siddal, had posed in a tub in the dead of winter and, not wanting to interrupt the artist at work, said nothing when the lamps heating the tub went out. As a result she contracted pneumonia, and her father sued. All in all, I preferred Waterhouse's Ophelias, eager and sensual in white-and-gold and blue-and-gold. Waterhouse, like us, craved an alteration of the sad plot, wanted to keep Ophelia alive and well.

Here I am, then, in the water, in the house, neither posing nor drowning, twelve years old and already nearly six feet tall. How did I come by my height? Both my mother and Bubby Miriam, who was my father's mother, barely reached my shoulder, and according to them, my father was also on the short side. Someone in the lost and distant past must have been tall—an aunt, a second cousin. I imagined my giant ancestor, swinging in a rocking chair somewhere in Eastern Europe, knitting herself a shawl for the winter. On and on it trailed, past her knees and along the floor.

At school they called me Beanstalk. We owned a hand-me-down copy of *Jack and the Beanstalk*, donated by one of my mother's card-playing friends. I'd read the story to Bubby a hundred times; she never tired of it, and neither did I. *Fee fi fo fum, I smell the blood of an Englishman*, I said in a deep, hollow voice, and we both laughed like goofs. It was never entirely clear whether my bubby understood English, but there were illustrations to help us out.

The beanstalk in the story grew and grew, exactly like me—*like a Cossack*—my mother liked to say. She touched me as if I were an amulet, kissed my arm because she couldn't reach my face unless I hunched down. I didn't hunch down—not for her. I bent down for Bubby but not for Fanya. Yield to my poor mother's unfeasible demands, her gluey woes, and you could end up like Elizabeth Siddal—or Ophelia.

So there I was, with or without Cossack blood, steeping in a bubble bath. When the water began to cool, I used my toes to rotate the faucet with the faded red dot. Through the thin walls I could hear Bubby clattering in the kitchen. That was the only sort of noise my grandmother ever made: she wore cloth slippers over her bumpy bunions, and she usually crept soundlessly through the carpeted rooms, but when she baked, a tin-pan racket filled the apartment.

It was quiet, apart from that. My mother was out; she worked on Saturdays and sometimes on the way home she stopped at Steinberg's to buy groceries. In the Fanya-free stillness—even the furniture seemed to breathe a sigh of relief when my mother was away—I contemplated my body. I approved of it, on the whole. Like the apartment, it was doing its best, though in addition to being excessively long, it was angular, disproportionate, my shoulders too broad, the rest of me bony. I'd found a replica of my naked body at the library, in a painting by the fifteenth-century illuminator Belbello da Pavia. Belbello—what a divine name!—left us an Adam and Eve who look as if they've run into each other accidentally at the pizzeria (the cute red-and-green building on the left) and are trying to decide between the all-dressed and the double cheese. Adam's body resembled mine; maybe Belbello couldn't find a male model. Or maybe I had a man's body. All in all, I was lucky that my nickname at school was Beanstalk and not Frankenstein.

I leaned forward, pulled out the plug for a few seconds, then replaced it and added more hot water. My baths were typically drawn-out affairs, especially in winter. Not that the apartment was cold—heating was included in the rent, and my mother and Bubby preferred a tropical climate. But we were mostly house-bound from December to March, and baths provided a diversion. My mind wandered as I sank under mounds of bubble bath. I loved the foam—the snow-white dips and towers, the weightless solidity, the soft, soapy sound of tiny bubbles popping in unison.

Bubby continued clanging in the kitchen. She would have been baking her intricate European pastries: little rolls and squares and triangles filled with cinnamon, jam, chocolate cream. The door to the bathroom was unlocked, in case my mother came home while I was still in the bath. Closed doors made her frantic; she'd fling them open like a blast of wind in Kansas. My mother's free access to the bathroom, regardless of circumstances, resulted in a rather lax—one could even say bohemian—attitude to nudity in the all-female Levitsky household.

The Levitsky household: Bubby Miriam, Fanya, Maya. Three mad women. Mad, mad, mad.

Take my mother's bedroom. Had I lived in a sane house with sane people in it, my mother's bed would have stood at one end of the room, Bubby's at the other. But along with many other phobias—some of which were probably unique to her—Mère Levitsky was averse to alterations in the placement of furniture. The result was a Mondrianesque composition, with Bubby's narrow bed extending at a right angle from halfway along the footboard of my mother's double bed. The reason for this peculiar set-up was my mother's refusal, when Bubby joined us, to move her bed from the

centre of the room to the wall; the only other option was the L-
shaped arrangement, though why the new bed was pushed right up
against my mother's footboard, I couldn't say. Bubby didn't mind,
as far as I could tell.

But Bubby was also strange. Here's how my bubby washed
herself: she carried an empty pail to the bathtub and filled it with
hot, soapy water, then removed her clothes, climbed into the bath,
and scrubbed herself with a sponge. Her body was thin and
misshapen, because of *there*. That is, misshapen because her back
was broken *there*, and thin because that was the way she was.
When she finished washing, she rubbed herself dry with a
facecloth and called to my mother to help her out.

Then there was the fully mobilized laundry campaign. Bubby
was in charge of laundry, and no one was allowed to interfere. She
took care of the entire journey, from hamper to washing machine
to clothesline or rack, back to laundry basket, and finally to the
ironing board. She didn't mind about other things, she was
compliant and oblivious in every other way, but if my mother or I
tried to reclaim a single item of clothing while it was en route,
Bubby would wrest it from our hands.

As for my mother—I wouldn't know where to start. There was
no beginning with Fanya Levitsky, and no end. No middle either,
come to think of it. Her brain was jumbled and jammed, and everything was bouncing around in there, like the bobbing needle of her
sewing machine. Hard to believe, in view of her general state of
emotional strain, but my mother was a dressmaker, with a particular
fondness for lace collars, tinted glass buttons, velvet ribbons,
flounces, and filigree. Her feet swelled out of high-heeled shoes, her
elbows were dimpled, her neck was powdered, her hair had been
sprayed into layers of stiff waves, as if in imitation of a wig.

But despite the trouble she went to, despite the perfume and
mascara and white nylon slips, at the drop of a hat she would fall
apart, all wails and weeping, railing and ranting—not at me, that
would be unthinkable, but at department stores and pickle

manufacturers, can openers and leaky faucets. As for the relentless unveiling of shreds and scraps from *there*, I'd stopped listening when I was six years old. Body parts, kapos, electric fences, attack dogs—what could it all mean? I preferred to focus on *B Is for Betsy*; I was trying to read all the Betsy books, if I could find them. There were five libraries that carried children's books in English, and my mother and I travelled across the city in search of *Betsy's Busy Summer*, *Betsy's Winterhouse*, *Betsy's Little Star*.

So much for Bubby and my mother. That left me. Actually, I wasn't sure whether I was mad or not. I was merely play-acting, which meant I was deflecting, not absorbing, the lunacy—or did it? At mealtimes, for example: though I piled food on my plate, I never managed to sample all the dishes spread out before me. One day I forgot the green beans, glistening under clumps of margarine; another day I neglected the kasha and bowties, flavoured with tiny black tendrils of fried onion. My omissions did not go unnoticed by my mother, who wrung her hands and tried to guess the food's fatal flaw. Exasperated, I'd plunge my face into the spurned bowl and, imitating a predatory animal, gobbling and snorting and growling, I'd scoop up the beans or kasha with my teeth.

My mother, half-laughing, half-whimpering, brought both hands to her cheeks and rolled her head—*ai ai ai mamaleh even a crumb of bread we would look for in the mud*—

Not that she sat with us—she was too busy running back and forth between table and stove, checking pots, adjusting the heat, fretting over culinary setbacks. As for eating, she squeezed it in before and after the meal, tasting bits of food straight from the pot or nibbling leftovers.

Bubby was also hard to pin down: you had only to glance away for a few seconds and every last morsel on her plate would be gone. She ate each of my mother's offerings separately: first the rice, then the tiny pieces of chicken my mother had chopped up for her, then the *Canadian Living* quiche. Every Sunday my mother meticulously copied out what she called Canadian recipes from her magazines, unless they involved alien ingredients such as asparagus or zucchini. When Bubby was done, she quickly removed her plate, hobbling to the sink and depositing it there. Then she returned to the table and watched me with fixed absorption, as if witnessing a complex operation—someone assembling a clock or repairing a radio.

I wanted to help out with the meal, if only to diffuse my mother's attentions, but she wouldn't hear of it. Bad enough I didn't have a father, cousins, uncles, aunts, more grandparents; bad enough that we were poor—at least I would have an easy life. An easy life meant, apparently, being waited on. It seemed to me back then, and still seems to me now, that my mother often imagined that her own sufferings had transferred themselves to my life, and that she had to find a way to compensate me for our shared misfortunes. And then there was her needy surplus of love, love that had nowhere else to go. I was the love sponge. It was good and not good.

In short, I definitely didn't belong to one of the families featured in our English reader: the children raking autumn leaves before dressing up as pumpkins for Halloween, the mothers in tidy brown hats and skirts, the fathers a little remote but always jovial and reliable as they sat at the wheel of their black cars.

But Bubby Miriam had sailed into our lives like a lifeboat. She found us, with the help of the Jewish Agency, when I was six. The war had dispersed families; no one knew who was alive. The lists of missing people were too long to be ordered, and locating lost relatives was frequently a matter of chance—a familiar candlestick, for example, glimpsed in a shop window.

We spent several weeks preparing for the miraculous incarnation of my father's mother. When she first heard the news, my mother seemed to fall into a semi-trance, and for once she sat with me at the kitchen table as I ate, hands folded in front of her, staring at the ceramic frogs that clung with outstretched legs to the sides of the napkin holder. At regular intervals she chanted *living living living*, and I joined in, for in spite of the dramatics I understood that this development was auspicious. I was acquiring a grandmother.

Practical matters soon roused my mother from her daze. My bubby was in Chicago; she had to cross the border; there were documents to be signed. Anything could go wrong along the way, my mother warned me. But she went ahead and bought a bed and a feather pillow from a friend whose husband had made a fortune on the stock market and who was redecorating her entire house, actually hiring an interior designer—*such things they have here*—

When the big day arrived, my mother, who had been cooking and baking for days, set all the cakes and buns on the table and plumped the pillow of the new bed half a dozen times. At the prescribed hour, she took my hand as if we were the ones setting out on a journey, and as we stood waiting in the cubist foyer of our flat, she drew me close to her and made tiny, mewling sounds, like someone encountering calamity and trying, not entirely successfully, to remain silent.

The doorbell rang and my mother swung her free arm in imitation of an airplane about to land. The runway was her chest.

—come in come in—

She opened the door and there they were: the man from the agency and, standing beside him, my grandmother. "Well, Mrs. Levitsky." The man smiled weakly. "Here she is—your mother-in-law, Miriam Levitsky." He turned to me: "Your bubby." Shyly, he lowered his eyes and dug his hands into his pockets. He must have expected a tearful embrace. Instead, my mother stared at my grandmother for a few seconds, then began to wail—*Yossi my Yossi*—but my grandmother was apparently hard of hearing. She lifted her suitcase, shuffled past my mother, and shut herself inside the bedroom.

My mother offered the agency man a glass of tea, and without waiting for an answer she scuttled off to plug in the electric kettle. The man sat down uneasily on the living-room sofa. He wore a dark suit and a striped tie. The tie looked borrowed, somehow, and seemed to be on the verge of strangling him, and his trousers had inexplicable vertical creases running down the front. I wondered whether I'd want him for a father and decided I wouldn't. You could tell he was unlucky. His own relatives, I assumed, were still missing.

My grandmother emerged from the bedroom wearing a flowered dress with brass buttons. Her white hair was held neatly in back with a shiny metal clasp. She beckoned to me with her arm and handed me a piece of chocolate wrapped in foil.

"Is she staying?" I asked hopefully.

"Yes," the agency man replied quickly, glancing at the door. Twenty minutes with my mother and he's pining for freedom.

As soon as he'd left, my grandmother walked slowly to the kitchen, opened the back door, and gazed out at the yard below. She nodded in approval, and my mother and I dragged three kitchen chairs to the balcony. We called it a balcony, but it was really a landing from which a flight of stairs spiralled down to the lawn. The stairs were made of wood, and when my mother and I went down to the yard to pick daisies the boards sagged under our weight with disquieting creaks, and we gripped the railings with both hands.

There was exactly room for the three of us on the landing. I sat in the middle, between my mother and my new grandmother, sucking on the chocolate so it would last a long time. In the yard, a neighbour's beagle was digging and running and wagging his tail, and we all laughed. My mother began reminiscing—*the sun the sun was shining on the dead bodies*—

My grandmother took my hand, squeezed it, and winked at me. I looked up at her and, with what seemed like an almost supernatural feat of translation, I gathered that it was possible to ignore my mother. I smiled at my bubby, and she smiled back. We continued to hold hands, complicit in our dismissal of my mother's extraterrestrial commentary.

Ai, ai, as my mother would say, was it any wonder I had no friends? Not real friends—not friends you met outside of school. Fanya would never let me visit just anyone; she'd insist on coming with me, inspecting the premises, meeting the parents. And what would they make of her garbled snippets of horror-history, her prophetic alarms?

Surprisingly, I wasn't one of the outcasts either. I was invited to birthday parties, I sat with the popular girls at lunchtime. One boy, Neil Charles, slipped me a folded note when the teacher's back was turned: *I like you.* A quiet boy with a poetic face and dramatic ears. I smiled at him, but he flushed and looked away quickly. Too complicated for me.

The bubbles in my bath had gone flat. I ran my fingers through the white islands and watched them separate like amoebas in science films. *Alas, my love, you do me wrong*, I sang, *to cast me off discourteously.* I was imitating Jane Hathaway, the yodelling secretary on *The Beverly Hillbillies.* I hated that sitcom, really hated it. In its various manifestations, life in Canada proved daily that my mother's overwrought, splintered world was not real. But here was a TV show that echoed her distortions. I was baffled. Who were these people? What exactly was funny about them? The laughter was canned, I knew, but everyone at school seemed to agree with the studio's cues. My classmates recapped each scene at recess with shrieks of delight.

Only Jane struck me as comical, and I half-watched the show in hope of seeing her. I was exactly like her: tall, hopelessly wayward, blissfully hopeful, and possibly the only competent person in my immediate surroundings.

I began feeling hungry, and I was wondering whether the pleasure of stuffing myself would be worth the trouble of getting out of the bath when the front door flew open. Huffing and puffing, eulogizing and exclaiming, my mother entered the house, safely delivered from her pilgrimage to Steinberg's.

—*Maya Maya my mamaleh*—

Her coat was wet and she rushed to the bathroom to hang it over the tub. And there I was, soaking in the bath, ruining her plans. She didn't mind—she didn't mind anything I did. I was the daughter who could do no wrong, the daughter who would show

the way. That was one of my several roles in the family circle: New
World liaison. Pointing at a word in one of her magazines, my
mother would ask me what it meant. I deciphered advertisement
slogans, television dialogue, comments overheard on the street. If
necessary, we consulted our bible, *Webster's New English Dictionary*,
paperback edition. Sometimes I had to explain the explanation.

Bubby came to my mother's rescue with a hanger, took the coat
and toddled off. I drew the shower curtain, leaving only my head
exposed to my mother's scrutiny. I noticed that she was waving a
long skirt of pink reward stamps in one hand and her even longer
grocery receipt in the other. The groceries themselves would arrive
later; my job would then be to tick off each item on the receipt as
my mother darted from brown-paper shopping bag to cupboard,
breathless with suspense. Never once, in all the years, had
anything gone astray, but my mother enjoyed the ritual and so did
I. Stocking up. The cupboards refilled with the things we liked.

—mamaleh look look what I found—

Crammed between sink and wall, tucked into a satin yellow
dress she'd made for herself, trailing clouds of Ben Hur perfume,
she brandished the supermarket receipt. She often copied down
notices from the bulletin board at Steinberg's: a bride needed a
seamstress to alter a wedding dress; a McGill student was offering
violin lessons; someone was selling a ten-piece camera set. My
mother would painstakingly transcribe the entire text onto the
back of her receipt so she could consult me when she came home.
I reached out to see what she'd dug up this time, but she jumped
away, clutching the precious scroll to her satiny bosom—*no no if it
gets wet and smudges—*

Instead, she knelt by the tub and held it up for me to see:

*This summer, send your children to Camp Bakunin, where the
campers make the rules, improve their minds, and learn humanitarian
values. Ages 10–14. Reduced rates for the proletariat.*

My mother's neat handwriting always impressed me. I would have expected a congested scrawl, but even her shopping lists were written in elegant script. *Butter* was a tiny drawing; *pineapple in a can* looked like a garden. She'd been taught penmanship, she explained, when she was a schoolgirl. She wasn't "from some shtetl"—her parents were educated, they went to the theatre, they read Homer on Sunday afternoons. Though I blocked out most of my mother's torrential reminiscences, I was familiar with a few manageable strands: her father had been a respected photographer and amateur astronomer; famous people had come to the house to have their portraits taken by her father and their clothes sewn by her mother; professors and artists had joined them for dinner. Over prolonged meals of borscht and baked fish they discussed every topic under the sun. Palestine, yes or no? Séances, real or sham? Pavlov, good or bad?

—*see what it says here you you make the rules if only Yossi*—

Yossi, my father, had died before I was born—before he even knew I was an upcoming human. My mother invoked his name at random, as far as I could tell.

As for making the rules, we both knew what that was about. I was terrified of sports, terrified of flying objects, high jumping, and above all the evil vaulting horse! Every Wednesday my mother wrote a note for the gym teacher—a grumpy, tyrannical man who with his impregnable torso and belligerent beard resembled Popeye's nemesis, Bluto—and asked that I be excused from gym class. I was "in a certain time of month," "suffering from a terrible cold," "dizzy," "faint," or (my favourite) "low with iron." The gym teacher had stopped reading these notes; he'd toss the envelopes I handed him on the windowsill and, giving me a dirty look, motion me to sit on the bench. From the sanctuary of the corner bench I watched the girls in my class running and jumping in their blue shorts. I enjoyed myself, though I never stopped wondering: how was it humanly possible to enjoy volleyball?

My aversion to sports was an insurmountable obstacle when it came to any summer camp project. What if they wanted me to swim? This was before the days of science camps, art camps, music camps; the barbaric assumption back then seemed to be that all children were athletic. I felt fortunate that at least my mother never forced me to do anything. In some instances—for example, if on a rainy day I refused to bundle up like Nanook of the North— she begged and wept, but she never coerced. Every trait or resource a person might need in order to rule by decree, Fanya lacked.

"I need a towel, mother dear," I said. "I'm getting prune fingers."

With a flurry of signals my mother indicated to Bubby that I needed two clean towels—one for my long hair and one for the rest of me. Bath towels were used only once in our home; Bubby snared them before they had a chance to dry and sent them off on the laundry tour.

At least my hair was no longer tangled when I came out of the bath. Earlier that year, my mother had come across an ad for conditioner in one of her magazines: *Nobody knows like a hairdresser what a ground-breaking new product like this can do. Watch your husband's eyes when he greets you that night!* My mother rushed out to buy the ground-breaking product, and our post-toilette scenes were instantly transformed. I no longer had to sit on a chair for an hour, reading Gogol while my mother grappled tearfully with knots and bird nests. Now the brush slid effortlessly through my wet hair— *see see how this works it's mindboggling—*

"Mindboggling?" I was amused. But looking back, I'm impressed; impressed that my mother, for whom language was a fraught enterprise, was determined to take on English. She'd more or less discarded her other languages, now that we were Canadian, and she spoke English even to Bubby.

Swaddled in towels, I took the grocery receipt from my mother and shut myself in my room. The only mother-proof door in the house was the one leading to my bedroom. When I was much younger, my mother would run to my bed every second or third night. Crying and quaking and muttering what sounded like voodoo incantations, she'd take me in her arms, her bouncy body heaving under her nightgown. I can't say why I wasn't frightened, or how I knew her distress had nothing to do with me—a child's unerring intuition, I suppose; or maybe I didn't find these night-time episodes all that different from the usual wringing of hands that went on during the day. But I didn't like being jolted from sleep, and one night, shortly after my eighth birthday, I came up with the idea of pushing my desk against the door.

My mother, as usual, took a catastrophic view—what if there was a fire and she couldn't wake me? She shared her apprehensions with her card-playing friends, who were more than happy to be of service: "Make an appointment with Dr. Fine. He gives out sleeping pills like nobody's business." My mother was not one to spurn a helping hand—*yes yes I will do*—

Sedation, in the form of Seconal, put an end to Fanya's nocturnal peregrinations, but I liked the new system, and whenever I wanted privacy I pushed my desk against my bedroom door. My mother soon developed a worshipper's awe of the barrier, and the desk became superfluous. All I had to do now was shut the door and my mother walked quietly away. Oh, *ma mère, ma mère.*

Like a midwife of home decor, my mother had plunged me, by way of matching bedspread and curtain, into a rayon explosion of purple and blue chrysanthemums. She'd become enamoured of the set while browsing through an Eaton's catalogue and had saved up for it. I was happy because she was happy; that's the way it is with children. If the chrysanthemums made her heart swell with pride, I had to admire them for their uplifting properties.

But the notice in my hand was pulling, like the Pied Piper, in another direction. I stared at the invitation—or invocation, as it seemed to be. My mother had not caught on, I thought with a rush of excitement; she had definitely not caught on. Camp Bakunin must be a hippie camp.

The currents that were travelling from south of the border were made to order for me: this was who I was. At school, I had a reputation for irreverence, though my objection was not to our teachers but to the rules and the way authority figures clung to them. I'd been the first in my school to pin a *Make Love Not War* button onto my lapel. I was told (more rules) to remove the button; instead, I kept it hidden like a secret banner under my sweater. Not that I followed the news, or knew exactly what was going on in Vietnam, but political awareness had strayed into the sphere of popular culture and permeated everything.

Outside of school, my education was being furthered by Esther, the young, dreamy librarian at the Atwater Library. She smiled even when no one was looking, and her two bulky, straw-coloured braids hinted at counterculture allegiances. Under her guidance, I'd read *The Grapes of Wrath* and *Cry, the Beloved Country*. Injustice in those books was abstract, inspirational. A more tangible rebellion was moving our way, even though we weren't the ones sending soldiers to kill and be killed in Vietnam; we were the ones helping them defect. On the radio, Peter, Paul, and Mary sang about a draft dodger fasting in jail, dying.

I lay down on my bed and stretched my toes. I was too long for my bed—like Dr. Seuss's Ned, who had to poke his feet out of two holes in his footboard or else push his head through a hole in the headboard. If I went to Camp Bakunin, I'd sleep in a bunk bed, a bunk bed in a cabin filled with girls. I'd been out of the city only once in my life, on a field trip: in fifth grade we were taken to see the Plains of Abraham. The park was pretty, but I remained detached; it was all too nebulous, too structured. A few hours away from the classroom, then back to Coronation Elementary School on rickety yellow buses. And why were our teachers so cheerful about hundreds of luckless men stabbed, shot, and clubbed to death? It would have been more appropriate, I felt, to gather solemnly and sing "Where Have All the Flowers Gone."

This would be different: this would be the real thing. When I was small, I would hide behind the sheer, floor-length curtains in our living room and pretend that Harry Belafonte was coming to take me to Kingston Town. Our life there would be one endless street party; skinny women in crimson dresses would ask me to hold their matching crimson purses as they danced. Or else it was Tintin who would arrive at my door with his little fox terrier in his arms. He'd tell me I was urgently needed in Turkey; I'd have only minutes to pack while a uniformed chauffeur waited by the limousine. My hair was nearly the same colour as Tintin's optimistic little tuft and would look as picturesque against the blue sea, the deep blue sky.

As if to dispel any lingering doubts, "Strawberry Fields" came on the radio. Oh, lovely Beatles! John also wanted to take us with him on his languorous, psychedelic voyage. I rose from my bed, opened the door to my room, and announced, "Okay, Mrs. L, I'll go."

My decision set in motion nine weeks of shopping and packing, warning and lament. I didn't mind; my mother's focus on the great event coincided with my own impatience. I daydreamed more than usual at school; I drew log cabins and pine forests in the margins of my notebooks. The school year dragged on, until one fine morning our teacher, a tough little mouse of a woman, marched into the classroom with a stack of report cards, handed them out, and sent us home.

The next day my mother packed the last three items on her list: toothbrush, hairbrush, a tin of Bubby's pastries. The Camp Bakunin pickup spot was a side street in the St. Henri district, just south of downtown; from there a bus would take us to the campgrounds. I kissed Bubby goodbye and extracted from my mother a promise to translate my letters home into Yiddish. Bubby was happy for me, and she waved from the window as we set off.

Lugging our new four-piece green nylon luggage set, my mother and I boarded a city bus. My mother grabbed the sideways seats up front, retrieved the address from her purse, and harassed the driver with continual reminders to let us off at the right stop. He finally turned around and asked her to be quiet. Fanya wasn't offended—*such little lambs these Canadians*—but she mistrusted people in charge, even if they were little lambs. When we reached our stop, the driver suggested we leave by the back door, and as we struggled with our suitcases my mother called out for all the world to hear—*wait wait mister don't close don't close—*

Sweaty and out of breath, we made our way towards the meeting place. There were large sections of Montreal I'd never seen, and I was enchanted by the little clapboard houses, with their skewed stairs and toy shutters, all happily sinking into decline. This was exactly what I wanted for myself, I thought. I wanted to live here, or at least know someone who did. The shutters and doors were cobalt blue, cherry red, sun yellow, or had been left to weather, and the layers of peeling paint had faded into a montage of floating colours.

The counsellors were late, and we all stood in awkward silence with our awkward parents. We were an odd lot. A heavily built boy whose eyes were nearly invisible behind the thick lenses of his glasses was singing "Yesterday" to an imaginary audience. He spread his arms in that old-fashioned Paul Anka way, a showy display of humble magnanimity. His friend, who seemed to be his mirror opposite—skinny, with a sharp, clever face—urged him on with a peculiar mixture of mockery and affection. A wisp of a girl dressed in black sat on the sidewalk reading *Thus Spoke Zarathustra*. Her twin sister straddled their navy aluminum trunk with a bemused expression on her face; for some reason, she was wearing a tiara and a superhero cape. Across the street from us, a frail boy held his mother's hand and muttered advertisement slogans to himself: *Try it, and see for yourself. A few extra pennies, a lot more value.*

My mother was no less conspicuous. When the bus arrived, she changed her mind and clung to my shirt, begging me not to go. It was too late. I hopped onto the bus and blew kisses through the open window as she wiped her eyes.

Our counsellors stood at the front of the bus and introduced themselves. Just as I'd thought, they were hippies. You could tell by their long hair and extravagant hats, their bead necklaces and leather wristbands. Olga had drawn sunflowers under her round, earnest eyes; Bruno was nervous but kind; Sheldon had Arlo Guthrie hair and a Bob Dylan smile. Jean-Marc, bearded and headbanded, was the oldest (forty-two) and in charge—if anyone could be said to be in charge. Until recently he'd been Jonathan Markowitz, but he'd taken up the Québécois cause and had changed his name in an act of solidarity. Two more counsellors, Anthony and Mimi, had stayed behind to prepare snacks and keep an eye on things.

I fell in love instantly; I think we all did. As soon as the introductions were over, Sheldon led us in song: *Oh when the saints! Go marching in! Oh when the saints go marching in! Oh Lord, I want to be in that number. Yes, when the saints go marching in.*

By the time the bus pulled up in front of the camp, I was sure the saints had already marched in and transported me to heaven on earth. No one on the planet could possibly want to be anywhere but here. We climbed down and hauled our luggage towards the grounds.

Camp Bakunin had taken over an abandoned campsite; a carved wooden arc supported by two posts welcomed us to Cedar Hills. The name rang a bell—girls from my school must have spent their summers here. But Cedar Hills had either folded or moved to another location. In its current state, the place had a museum look: pilgrim efforts in the wilderness. Since the plumbing was no longer functional, the cook would be bringing canisters of drinking water in from town. As for the call of nature—this, our counsellors assured us, was a precious opportunity for breaking down bourgeois barriers as we all tramped together into the forest, comrades in our common pursuit of bodily relief.

Though Camp Bakunin had permission to use the grounds, we felt like conquerors revelling in the spoils of victory. The size of the camp contributed to the fantasy—Cedar Hills had been built to accommodate at least two hundred campers; we were a group of forty-seven, with twenty cabins and log houses at our disposal. During the first few days we came across assorted odds and ends: a Mickey Mouse watch in the art room, a lone sandal buried in the sand, a baby-blue disc on which tiny white contraceptive pills were arranged in a circle. These paleological remnants made me think of a world swept away by glaciers or drought; maybe we weren't conquerors after all, but time travellers.

We were free to move into any bunk house we liked. The *Thus Spoke Zarathustra* girl wandered off to the edges of camp and appropriated an isolated cabin for herself, the boys split up into two groups, and the remaining girls, including me, chose to congregate in the bunk house closest to the kitchen. We dumped our belongings on the saggy mattresses and made our way to a snack stand set up on the lawn. Leaning against the back of a chair was a large poster on which our counsellors had written: *Welcome Campers! When we can no longer dream, we die.—Emma Goldman.* Next to the poster, like ministering angels at the gates of paradise, Anthony and Mimi presided over the milk and cookies.

Time for a break. I feel almost limp with fatigue, as if I've been climbing mountains. A long soak in the bath should help. A long soak with sweet-smelling, skin-soothing elixirs, followed by a steeping of my senses in forgetfulness, i.e., sleep.

I'll be back. The past, it turns out, exerts a supernal force of its own, compels me to continue.

The late November sun is bravely casting its pallid light. I've made myself a pot of spaghetti and answered two emails from students— *hi miss, i can't finish the paper by tuesday on account of a microeconomics exam / Hi miss, I really truly don't feel very well* ... I gave them both a five-day extension.

I was about to carry on with my story when the doorbell rang. I knew it was Mr. Jamal, my tenant, from his ringing style: a brief, timid buzz followed almost immediately by a longer one, in case the first didn't go through. Mr. Jamal and his family live on the ground floor. I keep the middle flat of the triplex empty, for in my circles there are always transient women, drifting between affairs or countries, looking for a place to stay. My motive is not entirely altruistic—I don't want anyone directly below me, running the washing machine when I want to sleep, sleeping when I want to listen to Franck's Sonata for violin and piano.

But I rent out the ground-floor apartment; for the past fourteen years, an Afghani family of indeterminate size has been living there. I never know, at any given time, how many people are actually staying in the flat. Relatives turn up, leave, come back; or maybe new branches keep arriving. Maybe the Jamals are a kind of depot, and newcomers stay until they find their own way or get into a fight and disperse—sometimes I hear angry shouts at the doorway.

The core family consists, I think, of Mr. and Mrs. Jamal, a grandmother, and three or four boys. Mr. Jamal pays the rent punctiliously, in cash, on the first of every month. He hands me the envelope furtively, as if executing a dangerous or illegal transaction, and runs away with a guilty air. Maybe he's afraid I'll engage him in conversation; maybe he's ashamed that his English is still so poor after fourteen years in Canada. His wife, Gharsani, is faring better. She's a brisk, attractive woman in perpetual good spirits, even though she was a doctor in Afghanistan and now works behind a counter, pouring coffee into plastic cups.

Financially, the rental is something of a disaster. I pay for heating and hot water, and since there are frequently large numbers of people bathing and washing clothes in the Jamal flat, the rent barely covers my bills. I never could muster the nerve, however, to raise it, even when I noticed the Jamals' new van parked outside or the expensive electronic equipment making its way into their place—no doubt on the instalment plan. But my spinelessness doesn't end there: too many comings and goings have taken their toll on the building, and every few months I have to call a plumber to extract a diaper that's been accidentally flushed down the toilet or repair a faucet that was shut too assiduously, and if a window breaks, I'm the one who replaces it. On the other hand, Mr. Jamal's jumpy efficiency comes in handy when the stairs and landing need to be cleared, especially after an overnight snowfall. I can sleep in without worrying about dereliction of duty; I know Mr. Jamal will be up early in the morning, shovelling away.

I assumed when I trotted down the stairwell to my front door— the entrances to the middle and top flats are both on the first-floor landing—that the toilet had flooded again or a pipe was leaking, but Mr. Jamal had come to tell me that he and his family are moving back to Afghanistan. I think the creditors have finally caught up with him.

I didn't have a chance to ask when they're leaving. I'll need to fix the place up before I advertise for new tenants.

This Plateau triplex is almost a stand-in for a partner, as shrines tend to be. I worked at creating this shelter from the storm by scavenging regularly through junk shops, church bazaars, even the occasional garage sale, in search of treasures: old French-Canadian furniture, hand-embroidered fabrics, sundry *objets d'art* and antique oddities—such as my nineteenth-century apple peeler, a G.M. Hopkins wonder of cogwheel, spring, clamp, and crank. My prized collection of Victorian illustrations, disinterred from discarded books, hang on the walls. The captions say it all: *"Things are bad, but not hopeless," remarked Dr Keith. / I was only a slip of a girl, badly dressed, and with no presence whatever. / She rose from her seat, and began to pace up and down the room.*

I'm also on the lookout, always, for slide projectors. I'm the only teacher in our Cégep who still uses slides, mostly because I enjoy handling the shiny, miniature squares of film, their shadowy colours hinting at the revelation that light and magnification will produce onscreen, but also because our PowerPoint equipment inevitably breaks down somewhere between *The Turtle Dove* (Sophie Anderson, 1857) and *The Wounded Dove* (Rebecca Solomon, 1866). One day the university's antiquated slide projector will break as well, but I'm not worried—I have five backups stored in the empty flat. Projectors crop up fairly regularly at my haunts, next to the ancient round-keyed typewriters.

But it isn't only what I've brought into this flat that makes me feel safe here, it's the house itself. These ornate red-brick triplexes, which lie at the foot of the great green mountain at the heart of our city, were built for the aspiring middle class of the early twentieth century; the owners would live on the ground floor and rent the upper flats. Remarkably, rents were low enough to attract impoverished Jews and other destitute immigrants. Rich and poor ended up sharing the same neighbourhood—not to mention the same hardwood floors, detailed oak panelling, stained glass, and high ceilings from which plaster angels look down with chubby benevolence.

Today such features have become rare, and we're drawn to them. I was lucky, finding this seven-room flat thirty-five years ago, when rents were low—I was a tenant back then. It's classic Plateau: a long, wide corridor with the kitchen at the end and a small storage/laundry room beyond that; bedrooms and double living room on either side of the corridor; bay windows in front.

At the centre of this domestic scene is its canine protagonist, Sailor, an irresistible St. Bernard. He's getting on, my Sailor, and these days he mostly sleeps between walks. When I first brought him home, he headed straight for the shelter of my eight-sided oak table, and as this continued to be his favoured resting spot—I understand the attraction—I created a little bed for him there; four-poster, you could say. He likes to settle his warm chin on my bare feet as I eat or grade papers—a perfect example of mutualistic symbiosis.

And so we return, Sailor and I, to the snack stand at Camp Bakunin, some four decades ago—

Anthony, first view of.

Lean and a few inches taller than me, aquiline nose, Kafka ears, though otherwise nothing like Kafka, for he was neither lopsided nor haunted—his face was symmetrical, tanned, composed. Composed but lively: his blue-grey eyes looked at you with curiosity, and you could see that he wasn't telling you everything, not because he was secretive but out of consideration. His dark hair, damp with sweat, clung to the top of his high forehead, and his navy T-shirt was splotchy in front. That's all he had on, jeans and a T-shirt; it was a minimalist look, without the hippie trappings. He was as easygoing as the other counsellors, but he had more physical confidence; he seemed ready, even impatient, for new experience.

"Bonjour, bonjour," he said, pouring milk into small glasses. "Je suis Antoine from *Paris*, where we make the big riot." A moment later he was Antonio, director of *401 Blows*, a new wave movie about a handkerchief, and then Anton, Russian physicist and inventor of the weightless space knish.

I noticed him staring at me as I munched on a cookie. "Who are you?" he asked.

"I'm Maya," I said, crumbs falling from my mouth. "Sorry."

"This poor waif hasn't eaten in weeks. Who's in charge here? Haven't they heard this child ask for more?"

"Actually, I eat a lot," I said. "My mother cooks a lot of food."

"But who are you?" Anthony asked a second time.

I liked the playful attention, but my inability to come up with an original or interesting response made me self-conscious. "I don't know. Sorry."

"I forbid you to be sorry. Now or ever."

I almost apologized for apologizing but caught myself. "All right," I said, giggling.

"Promise me."

"I promise."

He turned to Mimi, who was in charge of the cookies. She had steel-wool hair and granny glasses, and she wore a peasant dress, as they were called then—flowery cotton, ankle-length, puffed sleeves. Several long strings of amber beads were trying to decide whether to settle between or around her breasts. I thought she might be my favourite, if I was going to have one.

"Don't tell me you haven't noticed," Anthony said, turning to Mimi. "Have you ever seen a more striking resemblance to Joan of Arc?"

Mimi smiled. "Let's hope not."

I wondered whether Anthony was teasing me because I happened to be standing there, or whether he really had a particular view of me. That year I'd been singled out for the first time by someone other than my mother and grandmother, and possibly Esther the librarian: one of my teachers, Miss Lariccia, had taken a liking to me. She lent me *The House in Paris*, *The Sound and the Fury*, stories by Flannery O'Connor. In return, I wrote a composition that had the entire staff humming with approval. There was talk of entering it in a competition, but in the end the subject matter was deemed inappropriate. *How My Grandfather Was Shot in the Forest*. Fiction: I knew only that he was shot, the rest I invented. A secret race of mutants, born without hearts, heartless, dangerous. My mother saves herself by climbing a tree. There she is cared for by an eagle, dines on sunflower seeds. In the end, darkness, the sun shrinking to the size of a dolphin, then an egg, then a grain of sand.

Anthony shifted his attention back to pouring the milk and seemed to have forgotten all about me. But as I turned away, he called after me: "Joan Malone! Don't forget to send a postcard!"

"I'll write every day!" I called back.

Looking back at that summer, it still seems to me that a perfect falling into place, a lucky convergence, had brought our counsellors together. Mimi, Anthony, Sheldon, Olga, Bruno, Jean-Marc—they were all good-humoured, affectionate, kind.

This may have been partly due to drugs. In the privacy of their own cabins, our counsellors swallowed and inhaled a variety of substances. We knew because we peeked in through their windows, because Bruno told us, and because we caught whiffs of the exotic smoke when they opened their cabin doors.

But they took their role as our protectors seriously. Every evening we gathered around a blazing campfire and listened, wide-eyed, as Sheldon, true to the Camp Bakunin mandate, improved our minds with stories of martyrdom: Sacco and Vanzetti, Ethel and Julius, the Scottsboro Boys. Marshmallows were bourgeois and hot dogs upset Mimi, who was vegetarian, so we passed around bags of chips instead. After the stories Sheldon played guitar and taught us songs. *Go down, Moses! Wa-a-y down in Egypt Land. Tell old Pharaoh, to let my people go*.

I, too, had been liberated. Though I hadn't imagined this setting for my new life, the long-awaited event had taken place: I'd left my mother. At mealtime I would make the rounds, moving from camper to camper and throwing my arms around them. I was half-joking, half-overflowing with love. And that was the motto of the day: all you need is love, love is all you need. The underlying eccentricity of the entire Bakunin project camouflaged my kooky behaviour, and the hugs became routine, solicited as soon as I appeared by the chanting of my name, *Ma-ya, Ma-ya*, accompanied by a rhythmical drumming of spoons or feet.

In order to prevent the days from slipping by too quickly, I tried to hold on to every detail. Sheldon played sixteen instruments. Bruno had been born with the vestige of a tail at the small of his back. Mimi took midnight walks. One time I tagged along with her, and we ended up in the deserted infirmary. Mimi stretched out on the bare mattress and told me that she'd given birth to a baby girl who was adopted by an aunt in London. Would she ever see her daughter again? She didn't know. Maybe, maybe not. I was tongue-tied with Mimi, even though she was the one I most wanted to like me.

In our eyes they were all beautiful, but I think it was our counsellors' attentiveness that accounted, more than anything else, for our infatuation. We weren't accustomed to so much courtesy—not from our parents and teachers, not from one another.

Should we follow Olga to the art room, Mimi to the beach, or Bruno on the hiking trail? We wanted to be with everyone. Anthony did the hard work: took out the garbage, drove the cook to fetch water, helped her peel potatoes. He would show up at odd times in odd places; as soon as we saw him we stopped what we were doing and waited to be entertained. His jokes were often incomprehensible, at other times inane. He was the one who taught us the *Hitler has only got one ball* song, to the tune of the "Colonel Bogey March," and we sang it as we trooped into the dining hall.

Moral instruction around the campfire was sometimes enhanced by skits. One night, Sheldon read aloud Shirley Jackson's terrifying story, "The Lottery," and we had to act out the plot as he read—collect stones, choose slips of paper from a box. All our slips were blank. The counsellors began circling Mimi menacingly and hissing: *We know you have it, we saw you hiding something, hand it over, Mimi.* And Mimi pretended to become more and more frightened. Then, as Olga and Bruno held her arms, Jean-Marc removed her sandal, and the paper with the black dot fluttered out. And Mimi began to wail, "Why me, why me?"

"Now, would anyone here stone Mimi?" Sheldon asked. Of course we wouldn't, even if—the idea made us giggle—we'd found out that Mimi was a serial killer. It was only when an authority, seen or unseen, created fear—it was only then, Sheldon explained, that people behaved badly, instead of following their hearts.

Having arrived at that satisfactory conclusion, we proceeded to a few rounds of traditional slave songs. *Poor Howard's dead and gone, left us here to sing this song ...*

Later, after we'd all gone to bed, I found myself unable to sleep, not because of the disturbing story but because my stomach was growling. Supper had not been a success—soggy grilled-cheese sandwiches, soggier mashed turnips—and no one had eaten very much. I strolled to the kitchen in search of bread and peanut butter. On the way back to my bunk house, I heard voices coming from behind one of the counsellors' cabins; there was a wooden bench there that was a favourite hangout. The voices belonged to Anthony and Mimi, and something about their tone made me stop. I don't recall feeling guilty about eavesdropping; if anything, I think I felt lucky that I'd stumbled on a snippet of grown-up life. Mimi wasn't exactly crying, but she sounded distraught. I caught only a few words here and there: "He promised ... I wish ... when I came here ..."

But I had no difficulty hearing Anthony's response. "You're expecting too much, sweetheart. Think of the story we read tonight. They practically stoned Jackson for writing it."

Then: "Yes, Mimi, yes, I know—it's the dawning of the Age of Aquarius. Meanwhile, napalm bombs are falling on children—and for what? Some manufactured fear ... Back where we began, or rather back where we've always been."

And finally: "In six months you're not even going to remember tonight. Or you'll remember, vaguely, but you won't care. In five years you'll be amazed you ever cared. One has to admit, angel, our humble fare left much to be desired. I'm famished, are you?"

A silence followed. I assumed they were setting out, like me, for the kitchen, and I hurried off before they caught me spying. But now, when I think back to that moment, it occurs to me that what I heard was the silence of a kiss.

A week later, I, too, had a late-night, or rather early-morning, encounter with Anthony. I'd been stirred from sleep by the sound of sobbing, and before I was fully awake, I thought my weeping mother had come to take me home. I imagined myself clinging to the bedpost, refusing to budge.

But it was Sheila, my bunkmate, who was crying quietly into her pillow. I remember being puzzled: why would anyone cry, here in Shangri-La? Lily, who was only ten, had famously wept for an hour when Sheldon described Ethel and Julius Rosenberg saying goodbye to their children before being led to the electric chair, but that was different.

Sheila had an oval face, nearly translucent skin, and black eyebrows that rose like twin mosques over delicate eyes. Her parents were religious and would never have sent her to Bakunin had they known anything about it. But they were poor, and couldn't afford an ordinary Jewish camp like B'nai Brith. Sheila refused to apply for a scholarship—"They'd kick me out of there within hours," she told us. Instead, she'd convinced her parents that Camp Bakunin was both ordinary and Jewish. It wasn't hard to do; they were afraid of their own shadows, according to Sheila. "I earned this break," she said with languid defiance. "Talk about exploited workers. I have to do everything at home."

I was surprised to see her in tears; she'd seemed far too world-weary and aloof to take anyone's problems very seriously, including her own. "What is it?" I whispered. "What happened? Are you sick?"

She shook her head; she didn't want to tell me. "Did something happen?" I persisted. "You're sure you're not sick? I could call someone."

Arming herself with self-deprecation, she told me that her period had started and she couldn't face washing her underwear. At home her mother performed the odious task; if she had to do it herself, she'd faint. But throwing the panties into the garbage was out of the question: she'd bought three pairs, light blue lace with a border of tiny lace flowers, especially for camp. They had cost $2.49 each.

Her distress interested me. My own periods were unimpressive, and it was only with great effort that I succeeded in preventing my mother from following me into the bathroom in order to applaud my small output.

"I can wash them for you," I said. "I don't mind."

Sheila shook her head again. I couldn't tell whether she was being considerate or whether the thought of involving me embarrassed her.

"It's no big deal for me," I repeated.

Reluctantly, she handed me the rolled-up towel in which she'd concealed her panties. I found my flashlight and a bar of laundry soap, patted liquid mosquito repellent on my pyjamas—a trick Mimi had taught us—and headed for the lake.

Walking outdoors in my flannel pyjamas in the middle of the night made me feel cosy and adventurous at the same time, as if I'd been parachuted into enemy territory with an urgent message, but inside a story I knew would end well. This was the witching hour: around me the disembodied odours of sand and pine seemed to lift me out of my body as well. I could be anybody, anything, in the transient night air.

The lake under moonlight was alive, friendly, mysterious. Any moment now a mermaid, or Neptune himself, would rise to the surface. I knelt down and washed Sheila's underwear with the rectangular bar of yellow soap. I wondered why anyone would be squeamish about the body's foiled quest for reproduction. She didn't have to touch the stain, or even look at it—but the whole idea made her sick. Why?

I got soaked, kneeling in the water. When I'd finished, I spread the panties on a large rock and sat on the cool, gravelly sand so I could watch the sun rise. Pale gold light gradually seeped out of its blue prison. It lit up the sky and unfurled on the water its trembling jewels. I thought of my father, who had been buried at sea. *Those are pearls that were his eyes.*

I stood up, rolled up the legs of my pyjamas, and stepped into the chilly water. The sand stirred under my weight and the small pebbles pushed against my feet like a greeting. For the first time, I was sorry I didn't know how to swim. Why had I not inherited my father's talents? He'd been, according to my mother, a champion athlete once upon a time, as well as a star student and talented comic actor.

I was so absorbed by these meditations that when a voice broke the silence, I thought that I was imagining things, and that my father's ghost was calling to me. But the voice was real. I turned around and saw Anthony sitting on the sand.

"I didn't know you were here!" I exclaimed. "What did you say?"

"I was asking whether you were washing away our sins."

"I didn't see you."

"I was making my way back to my humble cell when I saw a tall, shadowy figure in pyjamas heading towards the lake. My curiosity aroused, I stealthily followed."

"I smell something," I said. "Hash?"

"Possibly."

"I'm never going to take drugs. I could end up like my mother."

"Ah, the famous mother. I don't think you're in any danger. So what exactly are you doing here, Joan Malone?"

"I was just washing someone's underwear."

Anthony gazed at me impassively—or so it seemed to me—for a few seconds.

"One of the girls was crying," I explained. "She got her period, and she's squeamish."

"Ah, I was right about you. Didn't I say from the start?"

"But it doesn't mean anything, because it's easy for me. So it doesn't count."

"Yes, who would not leave their warm bed in order to solve another person's delicate predicament?"

"It's fun being out at night. I love when it's dark but also hot. Anyhow, I thought anarchists believed in people. That we're all good, if we get a chance. That's what Sheldon taught us."

"You have a point," he said, bored with the subject. "Do you think Olga likes me?"

"I think she likes Sheldon," I said. I'd seen Olga and Sheldon kissing in the forest, when I went to pee. It was a short kiss, a kiss in passing, but it hinted at things to come, or at something that had already happened.

"Yes, you're right. Mating rituals of the ruling class."

"Are you in love with her?" I asked.

"No, how can I be? I love you. Come here, Rapunzel, I'll braid your golden hair for you."

"It's not gold," I said. "It's sort of orange." I usually wore my hair loose or tied back with an elastic band; I associated braids not with flower children but with the oppressive sentimentality that accompanied my mother's depictions of life before the war—*such happy girls we were baking bread laughing laughing*—it gave me nausea, that sort of oppression, that sort of sentimentality.

But it was all right: Anthony would ensure that I was shielded, at least for now, from my mother's past. He divided my hair into strips with difficulty. "My God, don't you own a hairbrush?"

"Sorry."

"Joan Malone, I thought we had an agreement about that. You promised. And already you're betraying me."

"Why Malone?"

"'In Dublin's fair city, where the girls are so pretty, I first set my eyes on sweet Molly Malone,'" he sang softly.

"I don't know that song."

"'As she wheeled her wheelbarrow, through streets broad and narrow, crying "Cockles and mussels, alive alive-oh."'"

"What are cockles and mussels?"

"Non-kosher seafood."

"What exactly is that?"

"What exactly is what?"

"Kosher. I'm never really sure what it means."

"What kind of Jew are you anyhow?" he asked. "Kosher as in religious law permits you to eat it. Non-kosher as in pork, lobster, snails, itsy-bitsy spiders."

"I wouldn't mind having a brother like you," I said.

He squinted at me. "A brother, huh?"

"My father died and my mother didn't remarry, so I'm stuck being an only child."

"What do you think, Joan—shall we take up arms against a sea of troubles?" Anthony asked, and suddenly he was himself. I was taken aback: he'd never spoken as himself before. Even when he was being Anthony, he was acting. Now he'd dropped the stance, and I felt privileged. Maybe it was wrong of him to hide all the time, even if we derived pleasure from the theatrics. His uncensored voice was vaguely wistful.

"Hamlet," I said. "'To be or not to be.'"

"Yes. A braid in back suits you, and you'll have fewer tangles."

"I use conditioner. Can I ask you something?"

"Yes, but turn around so I'm not talking to your shoulders. Your braid's done, though the end is going to come loose without an elastic."

I turned towards him and absently scooped up a handful of sand, sifted the pebbles between my fingers. "Do you ever feel mean?"

"How mean is mean?"

"Very mean."

"That's exactly the question the Maid of Orleans asked. Exactly what she couldn't figure out. Was she mean? And if so, how mean? And did being mean to her mother count?"

"I *am* mean to my mother," I confessed, hanging my head. "I call her Mrs. L, I make fun of her, I do things on purpose to shock her, like barking or mooing."

"Barking and mooing, huh? That is serious. But, really, I don't think she notices. As long as you don't put frogs in her bed, you're doing fine."

"Do you get along with your mother?" I asked.

"Ah. That's a hard one, Joan," he said, and I lost him again. He'd gone back to his impersonations. "It's difficult to say. I would say that it's impossible to get along with her, and impossible not to get along with her. She is who she is." He yawned. "You can turn off your flashlight. Waste of batteries."

"Oh. Thanks."

"So, who are your friends, Miss Malone?"

"I don't have any real friends," I said. "The problem is I can't invite anyone over."

"Of course you can. No one cares."

"You don't know my mother."

"Everyone's parents are *meshuga*. Parents are *meshuga* by definition. Believe me, no one will notice. When's your birthday, Joan On Her Own?"

"January. I'm twelve and a half."

"Do you think you can wait for me?" he asked.

"Wait for what?"

"For me to come and rescue you, and myself."

"I've been rescued already," I said. "For the summer, at least."

"I've never met anyone like you," he said. "Everything comes from inside with you—you never do or think things just to make an impression, or so someone will think about you in a certain way. You're on a whole different plane, my love."

"Isn't that bad?" I asked. It seemed to me that it was important to care about how you were seen.

"No, it's very good. Very good and very hard."

"I wish I knew more. But I hate reading facts, unless they're about, you know, colour and all that stuff."

"Tell me what you like," he said. He stretched out on his back and drew one arm over his eyes.

"I like everything about being here. I wish the summer would never end."

"You're going to go places, Maya. Your artist's soul will take you far."

"I'm not an artist," I said. "I can't draw at all."

"Loving art is the same thing. It's lonely, though. I hope you'll let me come along. Will you? Will you let me come with you? Say in four years' time?"

In some recess of my mind I understood what Anthony was saying. But when you're loved by someone—loved *that* way—and you can't respond, love slides from you like water sliding from flippers. "I'm not going anywhere in four years," I said. "Except maybe university."

"You'll get married one day."

"No, I'm never going to marry," I said.

"And why is that?"

"I'm just not. I can tell."

Very abruptly, Anthony stood up. "I hear the bells tolling," he said. "They toll for me." And he walked away in the direction of the dining hall.

I'd almost forgotten about Sheila's underwear, which I'd left drying on a rock. The delicate blue lace looked like the reflection of a bird on the rough granite, and I sat down next to it, hugged my knees. The world around me was suffused with silent light, as if newly created and waiting to be claimed.

A series of unfamiliar sensations came over me. I knew my life was a tightrope act, with my mother's nightmares perched at either end. Like her, I'd taken on a fugitive existence. I'd wanted to be a sparse person; I was hoping to keep my balance by shedding perspectives.

But Anthony's faith in me had left me with an addict's yearning for more. If I were part of the hustle and bustle, if I let myself loose among the crowds—the possibilities stretched out like a beanstalk to the clouds. My mother would wait below, anxious but hopeful, as I climbed up. And each branch of the beanstalk would lead me to another chattery group of people. I would have friends.

Friday, late. It's been two weeks now since I began this incursion
into the distant past. The days, like all my days, passed mysteri-
ously in a sea of trivia that demanded my attention. I prepared for
class, met with students, bought food, cooked it, ate it, cleaned up,
walked Sailor, did laundry. There were memos, emails, even a
semi-love letter from a small city in Peru. Someone I met last year,
through one of those wild coincidences that but for the flap of a
butterfly's wings might never have occurred at all.

It was February, the middle of the night, and I woke from a
recurring dream I've been having for decades, a dream about
searching for a place to live, perhaps temporarily, and then moving
into or considering strange, rundown rooms and houses and
wondering how to fix them up. Sometimes I can only reach the
rooms by hoisting myself up through the narrowest of tunnels or
funnels, with nothing to hold on to—a dreadful ordeal, but in the
dream I have no choice.

What if I'd not had that dream, not turned on the light at
that moment? But I did, I turned it on. Sailor, who'd been
snoring at the foot of my bed, wagged his tail; it's always a treat
for him, company at night. It was warm under my duvet and cold
in the flat, but I was hungry, so I dragged myself out of bed,
turned up the heat, and plodded to the kitchen. I made myself a
lettuce and tomato sandwich and strolled over to the front
window, as one does in winter—partly to ward off cabin fever,
partly to check out the snow situation. It was very cold out,
close to minus ten with the wind chill, and yet there on the
sidewalk, next to a car, was a young woman shouting at a man
who was shouting back at her.

The man held on to the hood of his car. The engine was
running, the door was open, and the man was trying to persuade
the woman, or girl, to go with him. I could see by the sweeping
movements of his arms that logic was on his side, but she refused
to budge. Exasperated, protective, foiled, he grabbed her jacket
and pulled. She tried to kick him and missed—the cold makes us

all a little klutzy. That was the last straw for the man. He threw himself into the car in disgust and drove off, leaving his companion alone on the street. She clasped herself and frantically looked around for some place to duck into. No hat, no gloves, an inadequate jacket—like my students, who even in the midst of blizzards dress as if they lived in California.

I hurried downstairs, opened my front door, and called out to her, but the wind swallowed the sound of my voice. I called again, urgently, because I was in my bathrobe and in precisely two seconds I'd be dead of hypothermia. She heard me this time, looked up. It didn't immediately occur to her that I was inviting her in, because when, in real life, do fairy godmothers actually show up when you need them? "Do you want to come in?" I yelled in English, then in French. "You must be cold!"

She nodded vigorously and climbed the icy helical stairs, grasping the rail so as not to slip, then followed me up the stairwell to the flat, then to the kitchen, and then to wherever I moved in the kitchen, as if she were attached to me by a short cord. When I walked to the sink, she walked with me; when I went to the cupboard to fetch two mugs or to the fridge to take out a lemon meringue pie, she stayed close behind. She kept her coat on, and I had a fleeting image of one of those cartoon sleuths shadowing a suspect.

"I'm Maya, by the way," I said. "I teach art."

"I'm Tyen. I was doing a graduate degree in biochemistry at UBC," she said. She was older than I'd thought at first, in her late twenties at least.

"Who was that guy?"

"My cousin. He's mad at me. My family wants me to go back to Vancouver. I can't go back. I'm mortified!"

I'm used to second-language English, and I assumed Tyen had meant to say something else—*fed up*, for example. "I have a spare flat below," I said. "You can stay there if you like—it's empty right now. I just need to heat it. It takes about half an hour to warm up."

Tyen smiled and took my hand. One of the clan—what were the odds?

"You have nice eyes," she said. "They show what you're feeling."

"Sugar? Milk? It's skim …"

"And your hair is the colour of the earth in Egypt."

"You've been to Egypt?"

"Only for one day. My father took us all in a plane from Vietnam to Montreal when I was ten, and we stopped in Egypt. The earth there is exactly red."

"Is he a pilot?"

"No, he's a doctor. My mother's brother was the pilot. My mother died when I was three—she stepped on a landmine, left over from the war." She yawned. "I'm having jet lag. I flew in from Vancouver this morning."

"Why don't you want to go back to UBC?" I asked, trying to slice the pie without making too much of a mess.

"I was caught stealing," she said, pouting. "It was mortifying."

"What did you steal?"

"I filled in that I worked five more hours than I really worked … Your arms are so long. And your legs. Next to you I'm a shrimp."

"You know, probably no one cares about those hours, apart from you."

We spent the next three weeks talking about the fabricated worksheet, Tyen's future, the respective lengths of our bodies. In the end she decided to complete her studies, but only if I promised to email her every day. I kept my promise, though I haven't been able to reach her recently, because she's been doing fieldwork in some Peruvian bog, miles from anywhere.

But yesterday a letter arrived, filled with long descriptions of vein necrosis in leaves, period cramps, cravings for ice cream. In a PS she added, *I can't wait until I see you again. Stock your freezer with B&J organic chocolate-fudge ice cream. Next time I come I'm not leaving so be warned. Love me. Your Tyen.*

That's all I have to report. I've been occupied, I've been busy, with nothing to show for it. Yet all the minute tasks that take me through my days seem important—crucial even—at the moment I perform them. Another kind of fabrication.

Things are amiss with me. I know that. Things are not as they should be. Reliving that morning by the lake at Camp Bakunin, I feel exiled, almost, by the collapsed bridge between those hopeful stirrings and this land of nowhere, this coalition of no one, to which I've been relegated—have relegated myself. But at my back I always hear—something. Not time's wingèd chariot, something else, just as rumbly and threatening. Not the future. The past.

1969

I left my heart at Camp Bakunin. School, now drearier than ever, held me prisoner, and I counted the days to my release. But in mid-April Jean-Marc phoned to say that the Bakunin group had disbanded. Mimi was leaving for a kibbutz in Israel, Anthony had moved to New York, Olga was running an artists' colony, Sheldon would be touring with a rock band, and Bruno had joined a Jesus cult. In any case, the campsite was no longer available—the insurance company had discovered that there was no running water on the premises, and without coverage Jean-Marc couldn't get a permit.

I wept with frustration and disappointment. As if he knew how I'd take the news, Anthony called an hour later. I was sulking in my room, but I dutifully trudged to the telephone when I heard the ring. My mother and Bubby were superstitious about the phone, which they associated with dire news—though only if they picked up the receiver; I was exempt from the Curse of the Phone. I was therefore the only one who could take calls, and when I wasn't at home, the rings went unanswered. If I was the one calling from somewhere, I had to use the secret code: ring once, hang up, call back.

"Hello?" I said bleakly.

"Yes, hello and hello again. Am I speaking to Miss Malone?"

"Anthony!" I cried out. Maybe he'd fix everything, find a way to revive the camp. Maybe he was calling with the good news.

"How are you, Joan?"

"I just heard about Bakunin. Jean-Marc says we can't go back. Isn't there some way?"

"Alas, I fear not. A good time was had by all, but—life moves on."

"I can't believe it."

"Neither can I. I was hoping to see you again, Joan. Are you all right, otherwise?"

"I guess ..." I said reluctantly. "Jean-Marc said you were in New York."

"I'm tripping the light fantastic as we speak. Ready to snap my fingers at poetry readings. Seems I'm too late, flower power has taken over."

"I know that song! 'Me and Mamie O'Rourke, Tripped the light fantastic on the sidewalks of New York.' That's where the title of that book comes from. You know, *Boys and Girls Together*."

"Ah, yes. The illustrious William Goldman. I came across him only the other week, at a party. At least that's who he said he was. He may have been an impostor."

"Really? You met him?"

"New York is small, if you exclude the down and out."

"How come you're there?"

"Ah, who knows, Joan Malone. Who knows why we do the things we do?"

"I was really counting on going back to Bakunin this summer," I whined—with Anthony, as with my mother, I could whine as much as I liked. "Now I'll be moping around in the city, with nothing to do and nowhere to go."

"Actually, I need you," he said. "I need an assistant and you might be just the person, avid reader that you are."

"You mean, like a job?" For some reason the first thing that came to my mind was Miss Pride, in *Boston Adventure*, hiring Sonia Marburg to be her amanuensis—a word I'd had to look up.

"Yes. Are you interested?"

"I'm not sure I can do anything."

"You can do this. I've written a novel, I need you to read it and comment."

"Okay, though I don't really know anything."

"I detect a theme here."

"I just mean ..."

"I know exactly what you mean—don't I?" The question began as banter but wavered midway into uncertainty.

"This call is costing you a fortune," I said.

"Is it? Well, money is no object when it comes to friendship. But you're right, it's time to say au revoir. I'll be in touch. Take good care of your mother."

"Thanks for calling," I said awkwardly, or at least that's how I felt—awkward, inadequate. There was something Anthony wanted from me—cleverness, for example—and I wasn't up to it.

Two weeks later, a package from New York arrived in the mail, but it didn't contain Anthony's manuscript. Instead, he'd sent me a copy of *Middlemarch*, bookmarked with a postcard of a sweetly solemn group of Jewish black congregants, circa 1929, photographed in their Saturday best in front of the Moorish Zionist Temple. On the back Anthony had written, in minute print: *Alas, the novel has gone up in flames. Following the example of that sad creature Mme Mozart one cold night I tossed whatever paper was at hand into the fire, for a few moments of warmth. I send you instead this cautionary tale, though not as a caution to you, Joan. You would never fail to recognize pretension. Take it easy. Who knows what the summer holds for us all, and especially for you?*

Who knew indeed? Anthony's hopeful speculation proved to be prescient, for that was the summer I met Rosie.

My mother was convinced that my continued existence depended on her being in the house when I came home from school, and she'd arranged to work on Saturdays so she could leave the dry cleaners early on weekdays.

But this morning I had only to pick up my report card and empty my locker and I'd be free to go. I'd finally graduated from Coronation Elementary School. This break in routine was creating havoc in the Levitsky domicile—or rather a focus for havoc. My mother wouldn't be at home when I returned from school, and Bubby had strict instructions not to answer the front door.

—mamaleh don't forget a key my sunshine where are you—

I emerged from my bedroom and Bubby handed me a clean towel, in case I was seized by a sudden urge to shower. I bowed, flung it open, and spread it around my shoulders like a cloak. "Meet me at dawn, and I shall have satisfaction," I declaimed. My mother laughed, and panting with the exertion of being manic she raced past us, first one way, then another. She had to set aside Bubby's lunch, a stew, and fill three glasses with juice and soda water—the soda bottles were too heavy for Bubby to lift.

My mother placed an empty pot on the stove and repeated instructions my grandmother had heard, or not heard, every day for the past seven years. How to turn on the stove, how to turn it off, what to do if there was a fire, who to phone if she felt faint. The glasses of juice and soda water, protected from the elements by Saran Wrap, were lined up carefully on the bottom shelf of the fridge. Saran Wrap! What would we do without it? Our lives were held together by Saran Wrap.

Bubby nodded patiently. She often spent the day baking, and had evidently mastered the finer points of turning the stove on and off without burning down the house. But in all the commotion of juice and stew and projected fire, in the commotion of trying to help my mother unfold the Saran Wrap as it stuck to itself, I did forget the key.

In class, I waited for my name to be called. Laurie Leahy, Maya Levitsky. I'd miss Laurie's euphonious name, our alphabetical proximity. I walked up to the desk and with a silly grin I accepted the report card that seemed to fill everyone but me with holy, or unholy, dread, as if it were somehow more than a piece of blue cardboard folded in half.

With a blind animal sense, children grasp the basic principles from the start. I knew, for example, that my mother wanted me to be a parent as well as a child. This was partly because she believed that anyone born in Canada automatically had access to privileged information denied to immigrants, and partly because of *there*. My poor mother had lost her confidence *there*. This might have unsettled me, had Bubby Miriam not arrived just in time. With my bubby to hold the fort, I didn't have to worry about poor Fanya's deference to me.

I expected the same latitude in school, and so did my mother, on my behalf. When the time came to enrol me in first grade, my mother found herself in a quandary. She'd heard that teachers were allowed to hit children in Canadian schools—*sooner I would die than allow such a crime*—Tears flowed down her cheeks, smudged her mascara. The solution was to send me to a Hebrew school; I'd be safe enough there from teacher brutality. There were four or five Jewish schools in the city, and the children of my mother's card-playing friends all attended one or the other.

But my mother had had enough of being Jewish. What if *they* came again? *They* would go to those schools first. She agonized for weeks, until one of the many casual acquaintances and passersby whom she accosted with her dilemma informed her that the Protestant School Board had recently banned corporal punishment. My mother rushed home with the good news. She tried to hug me, but, as always, I squirmed away from her embrace; even when my mother was happy, I was afraid of vanishing inside the vortex of her helplessness. All the same, I was relieved. No one could lay a finger on me, no matter what.

So much for discipline. In school, as at home, I felt free to sift through the rules, select the ones that suited me. I didn't pay attention in class, I didn't do my homework, I lost textbooks. I asked to be excused and was found loitering in the yard. Sometimes I was rude. And when my teacher's back was turned, I slipped my hand into my schoolbag and surreptitiously ate soda crackers.

Attempts to induce me to change my ways failed. I didn't mind being kept in after school: I read the violet/olive/lilac fairy books in the peace of the detention room. Nor did I mind writing out lines: my mother had bought me a calligraphy set, and I worked on perfecting flamboyant scripts as I copied out promises to improve. I was particularly fond of swashes.

After four years of impasse, they decided to hold me back. My report card was a sad sight: *unsatisfactory* in every subject except English, which came easily to me, and Geography. Geography was my favourite subject because of Miss d'Arcy, a shy woman with teary eyes and tortoiseshell glasses attached to a neck cord. She wore a cross, and there were rumours that she'd once been a nun. At first everyone jeered, pretended to pray: *Ave Maria, Ave Maria.*

I strode up to the front, taller than my classmates, brazen as usual, and roared, "QUIET!" There were rough and tough students at Coronation, but they saw me as a fellow reprobate, and if I was on Miss d'Arcy's side, they decided that they would be as well. I returned to my desk and Miss d'Arcy returned to exports and imports. "Fisheries," she said. I was in love with that word, with the lilting way Miss d'Arcy said it: "fisheries."

But in spite of an *excellent* in English and *excellent+* in Geography, it was felt that I ought to repeat fourth grade and the principal wrote to my mother to inform her of the board's decision. They didn't know what they were up against. My mother marched into the school office, fanning the air with the offending letter.

—*who who here is in charge Chekhov she's already reading*—

Followed by a lengthy excursus on dead relatives, lice, husbands lost at sea, and various other topics.

The secretary, then the vice-principal, and finally the principal tried, unsuccessfully, to calm her down. And possibly out of concern for my personal welfare, the principal reversed his decision on the spot. I would be allowed to advance to fifth grade.

It was all over now. The ageless building, with its embedded odour of old salami, decaying peanuts, and wet wool, would be gone from my life for good. Miss Kenny, my homeroom teacher, returned my smile; teachers were always in a forgiving mood on the last day of school. Giddy with relief, I left the classroom and began emptying my locker. Goodbye, Coronation! I tossed my report card into the garbage, along with the empty soda cracker boxes, broken protractors, and leaky pens, and ran outside. I waved to the girls who had tolerated me, waved to Neil Charles, the boy who liked me. As usual, he looked away, embarrassed.

And then I realized I'd forgotten my house key.

I had no choice but to make my way to the Sparkly and Shine Dry Cleaners, where my mother, keeper of the spare key, worked.

The sun was a summer sun, finally reliable after indecisive springtime spurts, and the sky was a splendid blue. I decided to walk the entire way, sixteen blocks. I wish I still had the dress I wore that day: thin grey-and-white stripes on soft, crinkly cotton, black pea-shaped buttons all the way down the front. The dress had come with a bright red patent-leather belt and matching purse, lingering remnants of the Doris Day look. I gave the purse to my mother: "Just right for you," I said ambiguously. But the belt I kept—I liked its silly flirtatiousness, its coy puerility.

My new white sandals clicked on the pavement. I fell into a reverie in which it seemed to me that the clicks were linked by an invisible mechanism to the sun, and the wild buttercups scattered on patches of creased grass were bits of liquid sun that had fallen to Earth. With their impossibly deep glow, the buttercup petals were as beautiful, as thrilling, as any work of human art. If only I could do more than pluck one and stare at it.

The Sparkly and Shine Dry Cleaners was the only successful enterprise in a row of small shops. Bambi Children's Apparel promised *Quality Clothing for Boys and Girls*; a sample of their goods was displayed on two child mannequins that must have been rescued from a *Twilight Zone* episode. A nameless store sold footwear for the entire family: red high-heels for women, black party shoes for girls, brown-and-white men's loafers, tiny white baby shoes speckled with holes. Dusty and usually empty, these stores were unbearably depressing. If only I were rich, I thought, I'd go in and buy everything.

I slipped the buttercup into my suede shoulder bag and entered the Sparkly and Shine Dry Cleaners. Mr. Hirshfeld, the owner of the shop and originator of its lopsided name, had apparently not grasped the intricacies of English grammar—or any other grammar, as far as I could tell. Trapped in an inexhaustible, throttling rage, Mr. Hirshfeld was never heard to utter human sounds. Instead, he barked at anyone who came near.

Nevertheless, business thrived. Mr. Hirshfeld was multilingual; he could bark in several languages. His customers brought him their droopy clothes and Mr. Hirshfeld, who knew how things were done in Europe, silently swept the disgraced items out of sight. And returned them the following day, all shiny and clean, as promised.

Generally I avoided Mr. Hirshfeld, who was, I felt, particularly ill-disposed towards me, but now I entered his store without a second thought. Even seeing my mother, with her damp forehead and solid mountain of curls, working away at her sewing machine amidst the heat and steam and barking, deflecting compassion by unleashing her catalogue of persecutions—even seeing Fanya didn't ruin my mood.

"Hey," I said.

She looked up and flagged me with a fluster of arms—*mamaleh mamaleh my only child my heart my life*—

"I need the key!" I finally managed to interject. "Key!"

—*ai ai ai the key I told you I told you*—

She reached for her black alligator purse and snapped open the big bronze buckle. The small red purse I'd given her was for going out in the evening to play cards. Mr. Hirshfeld was already barking at us, he wanted her to get back to work. My mother dismissed him with a truculent guffaw.

—*to work to work he is the whip I am the horse*—

Her perfumed chin wobbled as she laughed at her joke. Canadians, the little lambs, didn't frighten my mother. Like my teachers, like bus drivers, Mr. Hirshfeld could do us no harm— that's what it came down to. There was trickery everywhere: carpet cleaners damaged her carpets, the makers of cereal boxes deceived her with air, but they had no clout, and this safety catch gave my mother courage. With her pink nail polish and fishnet stockings held up by fat garter clips, she was armed to the teeth.

—*he is the whip I am the donkey*—

My mother laughed, Mr. Hirshfeld barked, I shouted "Key!"—it could have been an avant-garde performance piece—and in walked Rosie.

In walked Rosie, lost inside a cloud of white nylon curtains, the kind that smelled of rust and made a small zed sound when you rubbed one fold against the other. The kind you hid behind when you were waiting to be carried off by Harry Belafonte.

She unloaded the curtains on the counter and Mr. Hirshfeld barked, "Curtain! Two-ninety-nine!" Then, re-evaluating as he tugged at the fabric and found more than he'd anticipated, "Three-ninety-nine! Tuesday!" He took hold of the curtains in his strong arms: Mr. Hirshfeld and his bodiless bride.

"Hi." Rosie smiled. "I'm Rosie Michaeli. Are you Mrs. Levitsky's daughter?"

Hypnotized, I nodded. Not that I minded owning up, but right now any mention of my mother seemed intrusive. Luckily, she had returned to her machine at the back of the shop, where the suffocating heat enveloped her like a malevolent balloon.

"Maya, right? Your mother's talked about you. Do you want to come over?"

Come over. The words dislodged me, as though an enormous celestial map were spread out before me, a map sprinkled with shooting stars and new planets and dotted lines. *Come Over* would be the name of the bridge that led there.

Two black braids, large dark eyes, black eyebrows, heartbreaking mouth. Skin that glowed like the skin of red-cheeked children in coloured frontispiece illustrations, carefully preserved under a sheet of onion paper. *Ted and Ellen flew downhill in the sled.*

I saw at once—anyone could see—that Rosie was a hybrid: beauty queen and do-gooder. I had thought that popularity and charity were incompatible; the leading girls in elementary school were shrewd, vigilant, and deliberately coarse, and their good looks had more to do with authority and a sense of privilege than with appearance. They sucked in available rewards like plants curling towards light, and their occasional handouts were self-serving. Rosie, for all her glamour, was on the alert for opportunities to rescue—not conspicuously but incidentally. It made no difference to me, knowing that I was only another hapless delegate of need. I didn't mind that Rosie was indiscriminate in her invitations. I smiled and nodded.

And yet I was filled with grief. In the beginning of all love there is grief, because at that moment you're closest to the ghost of parting. You know how easily it could all slip away, how easily it could evaporate into eternal, never-to-be-consummated longing. "Sure," I said.

"Great. I live on Coolbrook—we just have to take the 161 to Decarie, and we can walk from there. It's such a nice day."

"I walked all the way from Victoria," I said. "It didn't even take that long."

"We can start walking, and then if we see the bus, we'll run for it … I love your dress. And I love your hair! It must have taken you years to grow it that long."

"I'm thinking of cutting it all off."

"Oh no, please don't ever cut it!"

"All right," I said, secretly imposing on my consent the immutability of a sacred vow. A vow would bind us.

"We always bring our things here. Your mother's really good. She fixes stuff for us all the time."

"Her mother was a dressmaker too. I guess it runs in the genes."

"Does she make you dresses and things?"

"She tries. I don't always like what she makes."

"You're lucky for that, at least," she said, divining it all: Maya and Mrs. Levitsky, a tense and tipsy acrobatic act.

Though I was a head taller than Rosie, we fell easily into step: I was a slow, lackadaisical walker, and Rosie was light and quick, so it evened out. She was wearing a navy blue skirt, an ironed white blouse, black penny loafers. There was an alluring inevitability about this Spartan outfit, like the ruby flash on the wings of a blackbird, or the immortalized gown of the cloak-bearer in Botticelli's *Birth of Venus*. Later, when I had a chance, I would casually touch the navy skirt, feel the cotton fabric for myself.

"What school do you go to?" I asked Rosie.

"Eden. Well, Mei-Eden really. We call it Eden for short. It's a Hebrew school—my father teaches music there." She pronounced *Eden* so it rhymed with *heaven*.

"Like Paradise? Adam and Eve?"

"Don't get the wrong idea! It's just a dumb old school. You're so tall—how old are you?"

"Thirteen and a half. What about you?" I asked.

"I'm fourteen, but I just finished grade seven, same as you. I missed a lot of school in grade five, so I had to repeat."

"How come you missed school?"

"Daddy was sick—I had to help out."

"I almost had to repeat too. Not because I was away, though. I just got bad marks."

"What are you doing this summer?"

"I wanted to go back to the camp I went to last year, Camp Bakunin. I loved it there—but it doesn't exist any more. So I'm just staying in the city."

"Me too. I can't leave Mummy and Daddy."

"Where will you go to high school?" I asked her, trying to conceal the urgency of the question.

"Same place, Eden. They have a high school too. Daddy teaches grades one to five. He's the music teacher."

"Could I go to Eden?" I pronounced the word the way she had.

"But you'd have to know everything they've taught us up to now! You know, Hebrew and *Tanakh* and all that."

"What's *Tanakh*?" I asked, struggling with the third consonant.

"Oh, Bible and stuff."

"I could catch up this summer."

"Well, it would be hard in one summer ... I'll ask Daddy. I'll bet if you just learn Hebrew it'll be enough."

Because she assumed responsibility for everyone, Rosie didn't sound like a teenager, or even an ordinary adult. She roped you in with her solicitude, and when she spoke, her intrepid, cheerful tone and careful constructions made me think of a tourist guide in a foreign city. *Here is the canal, where Vittorio de Lima nearly drowned in 1782. Please watch your steps, everyone, as we board the gondola.*

We caught the bus at Pratt Park and sat together on a double seat. Rosie's arm touched mine, white skin against freckled, as the bus bumped along. "That was my school," I said when we passed Coronation. "I'm glad I don't ever have to go back."

"I heard bad kids go there," Rosie said, worried for me.

"I was one of them," I assured her, and we both laughed. It was an intimate, conspiratorial laugh, the kind that excludes the rest of the world. Oh, bliss!

"Here's our stop," Rosie said, and for a second or two my heart pounded as if I'd been running—the body's involuntary passion alert. We crossed the Decarie expressway, and even the concrete overload and the blare of cars zooming below us grew softer in the aura of anticipated pleasures.

Coolbrook. You know how it is, with love—all at once, the mundane, arbitrary details of the beloved's life arouse every emotion you've ever felt or will feel, and a street name you hardly noticed before will never be the same. There were duplexes here too, but instead of yellow or white imitation-brick exteriors glued onto cube frames, the houses on Rosie's street were old, heavy, built of red bricks or coarse grey limestone set in irregular mosaic patterns, and they had overhanging roofs and charming little entranceways.

Rosie lived on the ground floor, even though her parents were tenants. Owners usually took the bottom units, renting the upstairs to poorer families like us—I'm not sure why. Maybe the lower flats were favoured because they came with a basement, or (this was before the fitness craze) because there weren't stairs to climb. Living downstairs meant less income from rent, but in this high-strung community of refugees and war survivors, esteem and comfort were the precious commodities.

My mother, as usual, brought her own unique perspective to the subject and preferred living upstairs: she was convinced that if robbers or murderers came to the building, they'd be much more likely to maraud the lower units. There would have been continual clashes between my mother and any landlord unlucky enough to be saddled with her. By a stroke of good fortune, however, the owners of our duplex had migrated to Florida. They left the building in the care of their nephew, a law student who strongly resembled a turtle. His duties were to collect the rent and keep an eye on the property. Instead, he had developed ingenious strategies for avoiding my mother.

"We live on the ground floor because stairs are hard for Daddy," Rosie explained. "Our landlord doesn't mind living on top—he's really strange. He takes cold baths, and he looks through our garbage. And every three days he tries to raise the rent."

"What's he looking for, in the garbage?"

"He thinks maybe we threw out something useful. The whole basement is full of his junk. Poor guy."

Rosie opened the tall arched—arched!—door, and I followed her in.

This was the house my giant ancestor lived in. Or else I'd crossed the ocean and reached Brobdingnag. "Out of sight," I said. "Literally. You can't tell from the outside how big it is—like one of those optical illusions."

"I know," Rosie said. "Daddy can't bear small spaces, he has a thing. We used to live in a house on St. Hubert, but it was too noisy."

Oddly, apart from its size, the apartment was as insipid as ours; the same plywood doors, aluminum windows, flecked linoleum, dismal wall-to-wall carpets. I imagined the draftsman going about business as usual, intending to write forty on the blueprint and accidentally adding a digit, or maybe one night someone got fed up and decided to try something new: space, more and more space.

There were two living rooms, one adjacent to the entrance, its windows facing the street, and an even larger one at the end of a wide corridor. Both could have accommodated—and, as it turned out, did accommodate—concerts or a dance party. Rosie led me down the hallway, and like a passenger on a train, I felt the scenery was passing by too quickly: a kitchen and den to our left, two bedrooms to the right. If only time would freeze for an hour, so I could take everything in.

Rosie's parents were seated at either end of a sofa in the back living room. Mrs. Michaeli was negotiating an unwieldy newspaper and her husband was absorbed in a paperback. They made me think of penguins or swans: silent and alike, at home in their chosen habitat, entirely benign, but essentially untouchable. They rose when they saw me, first Rosie's mother and then, with the help of a cane, Mr. Michaeli.

"Mummy, Daddy, this is Maya, Mrs. Levitsky's daughter—from the dry cleaners."

Rosie's mother was Rosie with the charm drained out of her, and with blonde hair, now streaked with white, instead of black. Her skin was papery, her undefined body curved softly under her dress, her eyes were misty. "How do you do," she said.

Mr. Michaeli steadied himself on his cane. If he were a painting, there'd be only a few tremulous outlines on the canvas, filled in with hasty strokes. He wasn't exactly gaunt, but it was as if he'd been pieced together in a last-minute, makeshift effort. And sure enough, Rosie and her mother immediately closed in on him with concern as they walked to the kitchen. I tagged clumsily behind them.

"Here, have a seat," Rosie and her mother both said, and I didn't know whether they meant me or Mr. Michaeli.

The kitchen table had been pushed to the corner of the room, and I slid into the narrow space between the wall and the table. I felt like an astronaut in a capsule, an astronaut whose deeds of bravery were about to be honoured.

"So you're Mrs. Levitsky's daughter ..." Mr. Michaeli looked at me and smiled. For all his fragility, there was a faint suggestion of recklessness and subterfuge in his smile. His eyes resembled tiny watery stars, for like a drowsy cat he raised his lids only slightly.

"Yes," I answered nervously.

"She for us has fixed many things. And always so fine the stitch, you can't even see. Presto."

"Mrs. Levitsky's mother was also a dressmaker," Rosie said proudly.

"And from her she learned?" Mr. Levitsky asked me. Beneath his question lurked a chasm I could not begin to fathom.

"I'm not sure," I said. "They were separated when my mother was thirteen. But, I was telling Rosie, it probably runs in the genes." I was talking too much, and soon I'd get on their nerves. "But I don't sew at all," I added desperately.

"No, no, in modern times it's different. Ready-made. Ready-made everything."

I was afraid that if Mr. Michaeli overexerted himself, the slender mechanism holding him together would give way and he'd collapse. It seemed amazing to me that he was a teacher, that he stood in front of a class and raised his voice to a roomful of children.

"Maya, Maya, Maya," he said. I need not have worried about making a fool of myself. Mr. Michaeli's covert intransigence could have been intimidating, but it was countered by informality—an informality that went hand in hand with his retreat from the tenets of the world the rest of us inhabited. I could trust him. As for Mrs. Michaeli, she was only tenuously connected to her surroundings, though not because of a surfeit of preoccupations, as with my mother, but because she was absent-minded. I sank back into my astronaut seat and waited to be served.

"Would you like juice, milk, or tea?" Rosie asked me.

I was witnessing a tribal ritual. In this anthropological scene, no other options existed: when guests arrived, they were led to the kitchen, ushered to the seat against the wall, given a choice of juice, milk, tea. Something admirable about them or their family was brought to notice; a plate of homemade poppyseed cookies and a bowl of apples and bananas were set at the centre of the table.

"Tea, please—thank you—I'm sorry," I said inanely.

"Do you want your pillow, Daddy?" Rosie picked up a shabby cushion from one of the kitchen chairs. We had the same chairs—sturdy, framed by curved metal rods, upholstered in some kind of transparent laminate—but theirs were marbled grey and white, while ours were a plasticized marvel of cornflowers and blue leaves.

"No, no, me I am fine. Hunky-dory." Mr. Michaeli chuckled with private despair.

"Please, help yourself," Rosie said, passing me the cookies. Her mother put on the kettle for tea. She smiled at me, but her smile was distant and somehow unreliable. "Mummy used to be a nurse," Rosie informed me. The biography—or hagiography—was, like the drinks, a part of the ritualized hospitality they were offering me. "She met Daddy that way, when she was working with the Red Cross, taking care of people who came out of Auschwitz."

Auschwitz, Red Cross—the words were familiar from my mother's mangled monologues. But what exactly happened during the war? The only clear image I had of the war was one I'd invented myself: my mother and I are trapped in an immense windowless museum: sterile, brightly lit, and bare, with endless serpentine corridors. On exhibit, under glass globes, are worms, happily squirming. We want to ask one of the barrel-bellied guards for directions, but they turn out to be wax figures, and my mother seizes my hand, scurries this way and that, searching for an exit.

Where did these images originate? Possibly from a nightmare I had when I was small, back in the days when my mother ran to me at night, weeping with terror. But the dream, if that's what it was, took hold. For months at a time I forgot about the museum, and then, for no reason at all, a phantom memory of being trapped in the windowless labyrinth would come over me, accompanied by nausea and a piercing headache, and I'd have to stay in bed. My mother would hover over me with mugs of hot milk and honey. As I sipped the milk, she swished a bar of Pears soap in a basin of warm water, dipped a towel in the fragrant solution, and rubbed my back and arms and legs. Eventually the worm museum receded, and in its place I resurrected Monet's brimming poppy fields. There an ordinary girl trailed alongside her ordinary, umbrella-twirling mother, their heads protected from the sun by ribboned hats that replicated the colour of the clouds.

"I'm not very good at history," I said apologetically, and the Michaelis burst into laughter, all three of them laughing in the exact same way, as if this was the best joke they'd heard in a long while, or maybe ever. They didn't mean to exclude me; their laughter, almost deliberately prolonged and hearty, was affectionate, and for a minute I hoped I'd said something witty. But I knew my comment was ridiculous. I also understood, in a flare of lucidity, that the Michaelis were inseparable, and more impenetrable, as a trio, than any clique I'd encountered at school.

The laughter subsided and Mrs. Michaeli prepared the tea. Rosie's family, like ours, drank their tea in glass cups with slivers of lemon floating on top. I dropped two cubes of sugar into my cup and stirred. Rosie went on: "Mummy was lucky, she managed to work in a hospital the entire war, and no one found out she was Jewish—but everyone else in her family died. She called Daddy the humming patient because he didn't tell anyone his name at first, he just hummed tunes. She didn't know he was famous. Daddy was a violinist before the war."

There was no avoiding it now: the Michaeli household was as mad as my own. Even the form of madness was the same. Like my mother, Rosie's parents were both holy and unappeasable; in this home, as in mine, the persistent echo of absence and horror made way for fantastic claims on us, the progeny.

Rosie, intuitively grasping my silent verdict, nodded at me and shrugged helplessly. Yes, this was how it was, for better or worse. Yet she held the strands together with her serenity. It was a feat I was in a position to admire.

"My parents met on a ship," I said. "Or rather, they were reunited."

But the Michaelis already knew the story: my mother never missed an opportunity to ply captive audiences with the full range of her misfortunes. It was this trait that led to her dismissal from Solomon's Kosher Butcher; customers complained about the stress of buying a chicken from Fanya Levitsky. She wasn't sorry to leave. Raw livers disgusted her, and she also disliked Solomon, whom she called King Solomon or, when she'd had a particularly hard day, Slaughterman Sol.

"Daddy, do you think Maya could go to Eden next year? She really wants to. What if she studies all summer?"

Mr. Michaeli nodded, smiled, nodded again, considered. Imagine someone always on the verge of recoiling with fear. Not actually afraid but on the verge, at the edge. The second before terror. Imagine someone frozen into that moment forever. "Maybe, maybe ... the main thing would be to learn to read Hebrew. We'll find for you some books, yes?"

"I could get them from Mr. Lewis." Turning to me, Rosie explained, "The janitor. I'll get him to open the cupboard. He's still at school, cleaning up."

"What will we sing for our guest?" Mr. Michaeli asked no one in particular.

I thought he meant a singalong around the table, and I was about to suggest "Michael Row the Boat Ashore," but the three of them rose and made their way back to the living room. I had somehow missed seeing or had not paid attention to the upright piano in the corner. Mrs. Michaeli and I sat on the sofa,

Mr. Michaeli perched himself on the piano stool, and Rosie stood beside him like an attendant, facing her audience of two. Snacktime was over, storytime was over—now we were ready for the music recital.

The piano was the only thing of beauty in the room—or in the apartment, as far as I could see. In my own home, my mother's personality declared itself in every ceramic shepherd and plastic apple, every snail-shaped soap dish and skirted tissue-box cover. The Michaelis, on the other hand, seemed opposed to the entire idea of ornamentation. There were no paintings or prints on the walls, and even the sofa seemed devoid of colour, as if it had come with the place and through some process of progressive invisibility had faded from notice. The floor lamps, with their stark metal stems and yellowing shades, were merely serviceable, and the only movable object in the music room was an overflowing ashtray on the armrest of the sofa—Mrs. Michaeli was a heavy smoker. The house was a variation on Rosie's navy skirt and white blouse: a form of stalling, a way of keeping something, though I didn't know exactly what, at bay.

But the walls in this room weren't altogether bare: fourteen framed photographs of Rosie had been arranged in sequence above the piano. An annual celebration, starting when she was a year old.

I gazed at the portraits and mourned. I was not there when Rosie wore a sailor dress, I was not there when she'd had a Christopher Robin haircut. Rosie beaming for the camera, six years old, eight, eleven: I'd missed it all. At the same time, I absorbed this iconography with famished gratitude. At least those lost years weren't hidden away, at least they were on display.

"*Les Nuits d'été*, by Berlioz," she announced, then added, for my benefit, "Except we call him Berliozo. We have crazy names for all the composers—Mozartino, Lord Ludwig ... This isn't real singing—I'm only faking. Daddy says you can't start training for opera until you're eighteen." She nodded to her father, and he began to play.

Though I hadn't been in many homes, I knew these family traditions were idiosyncratic. Whoever heard of Miss Popularity offering her beleaguered parents to her friends, or singing arias for their entertainment? But beyond that, there was an exigency in the Michaelis' behaviour that clashed with their casual style, as if they were involved in some ongoing ceremony which an onlooker could only partly understand.

Rosie sang, her father accompanied her, the two of them exchanged meaningful glances.

> L'ange qui l'emmena
> Ne voulut me prendre
> Que mon sort est amer
> Ah! Sans amour s'en aller sur la mer!

Extraordinary talent takes us by surprise, when it emerges from someone we've met in ordinary circumstances. *Here, let me show you my secret wing.* I was hoping when the song ended that no one would speak for at least an hour. But Mr. Michaeli had long since renounced reverence, and deliberately broke through mine. "What say you, Maya, to that G? You do not expect it, and there it arrives. Unfortunately, such things in life don't last. A whole octave and one-half you must go to get back to Earth."

Rosie hugged her father, folded him into her embrace as he sat at the piano, and Mr. Michaeli said, "Yes, yes, love we definitely have." He didn't exactly return Rosie's embrace, and to compensate he mocked himself, mocked his own inadequacy. Rosie didn't mind. She and her father had come to an understanding.

"Would you like to hear another song?" Rosie asked.

"Oh, yes! Yes," I said, and the three of them laughed again, briefly this time.

Mr. Michaeli played a few notes and Rosie's voice, effortlessly bearing its sensuous, incorporeal sadness, slowed down as she invoked the lowering of a coffin into the ground—

When I am laid, am laid in earth
May my wrongs create
No trouble, no trouble in thy breast
Remember me! Remember me!
But ah! forget my fate.

Rosie asked for her fate to be forgotten for the fourth and last time, and as Mr. Michaeli struck the final funereal notes, his body seemed to droop with sudden fatigue. I was afraid it was my fault and, wanting to help, I quickly asked Rosie: "What other names do you have? I mean, of composers."

"Oh, they're crazy." Rosie smiled. "Moony Mahler … Bachanova … We even have a dance called the Bachanova."

"A dance?"

Rosie giggled and Mr. Michaeli nodded. He began playing a piece by Bach in a boppy, syncopated rhythm. I didn't know at the time what he was doing exactly, for I had only the vaguest notion of Bach or his music, but I recognized the frivolity of it. Rosie swung her arms with simian abandon as she tap-danced on the faded carpet. She danced until she was flushed and out of breath.

"You must think we're nuts," she said, holding on to the piano to regain her balance.

"Oh, no—it's funny. I don't know much about classical music. I didn't even know there was a composer called Berlioz. But those songs you sang, I never heard anything like it in my life."

Mr. Michaeli examined me through his half-closed eyes. "At school here they teach only the important subjects, what is grown in Manitoba and what fish to catch in Newfoundland. Music, who so much cares?"

"I'm going to start listening to the classical music station on the radio," I said.

"Oh, Maya!" Rosie came over to me and looked into my eyes, as if apologizing for what she couldn't give me. "Do you want to get the books from Mr. Lewis now?"

This is not who I am, this person who is worthy of the Michaelis' hospitality—and what will happen when they discover their mistake? But Rosie bent down and whispered in my ear: "Mummy and Daddy really like you."

We left the Michaeli mausoleum and walked towards Eden. "I hope Daddy doesn't forget that Patrick cancelled today," Rosie fretted.

"Who's Patrick?"

"One of Daddy's private students—he's really funny, like you. Only more ... sort of dark."

"I once had a piano lesson at the house of this friend of my mother, Mrs. Blustein, on Linton. We couldn't afford a piano, so Mrs. Blustein said I could come over any time to practise on hers. I learned to play 'The Farmer in the Dell,' but my teacher quit after one lesson—I guess my mother scared him away."

"Poor you! Too bad you didn't come to Daddy. 'The farmer in the dell, the farmer in the dell, hi ho the dairy-o, the farmer in the dell,'" she sang. "I love nursery rhymes. I have a whole collection at home, I'll show you. 'See-saw Margery Daw, Jenny shall have a new master. She shall have but a penny a day, because she can't work any faster.'"

"I had a book of Mother Goose rhymes when I was a little kid," I said. "One of those square books with the gold edges?"

"I have that one. Also a record. 'Wynken, Blynken, and Nod one night, Sailed off in a wooden shoe—Sailed on a river of crystal light, Into a sea of dew,'" she sang, and her voice sailed like the crystal light in the song. "Do you know it?" she asked.

"I don't have a record player."

"Oh, you'll come over and listen to ours, it's stereo. We found it at a garage sale and Daddy repaired it. He's good at things like that."

We passed through a park and there was Eden, across the street. I'd seen the building before, had noticed its ornate, alien letters carved like code into the stone wall. I would never have guessed that one day I'd be going through those doors.

The school was deserted and the halls smelled of old bubble gum and mildew. Our footsteps echoed on the wood floor.

"Mr. Lewis!" Rosie called out.

We set out to find the janitor. The search doubled as a tour of the building. "This is the elementary side," Rosie said. "It connects through that corridor to the high school. This was my locker."

Rosie's locker. I wanted to fall to my knees, wrap my arms around her legs. That's what love is—the anguish of knowing the person you love has a locker, a handwriting, a favourite scarf. I tried not to look at the green metal door.

We found Mr. Lewis in the library, stacking chairs. He was an odd man—tiny, ancient, sinewy.

"Mr. Lewis, I'm Rosie Michaeli, the music teacher's daughter—remember?"

He stared at us with blank eyes.

"We need some schoolbooks."

"For who?" he wheezed.

"For the music teacher."

We followed him down the hall. He walked with short, uneven steps, like an elf on stilts, but he was strong—I was sure that if I touched him, my fingers would find a surface as firm as rock. He opened the door to the supply closet and watched us suspiciously as we entered the small room. Under a bare light bulb, the crammed shelves and tall stacks of shabby books looked long abandoned; a perfect set, I thought, for an art-house film about the end of civilization. I recognized a few of the titles—*Our Nation Proud and Free. Our Living Language. Math Is Fun!* All of them silenced now by the fall of the empire.

"Here, why don't you take these?" Rosie handed me three books, their ripped spines curling at the ends. She gathered another three or four for herself. "You'll also need a special notebook. I think I have one at home."

"How is it special?"

"It has the alphabet on the back, and thin sort of lines. Thanks, Mr. Lewis. Sorry we bothered you."

Mr. Lewis locked the door and returned to his janitorial duties.

"Let's bring these to your place," she suggested. "Mummy will drive us."

Carrying our loot, we headed back to Rosie's. We set the books down on the hood of Mrs. Michaeli's car, and I watched over them while Rosie went in to fetch her mother and pick up the special notebook.

Mrs. Michaeli's car smelled of lilac and Elmer's glue and menthol cigarettes. I'd only been in a car a few times, when parents drove me home from birthday parties, but I settled into the back seat as if I'd been chauffeured all my life. Rosie described our small excursion for her mother, made it sound funny and quaint. She did it even though she knew it wouldn't help. Rosie's fatalistic generosity was not very different, in the end, from my acts of evasion.

Using the key my mother gave me, I opened the door to our flat, and Bubby crept towards us like the tide.

"Hello, there," Rosie said.

It didn't matter, after all, what Rosie encountered in my house, not only because her home was as odd as mine, or because she wouldn't hold anything against me. It turned out that I'd been wrong about friends; I'd always assumed that you started off by inviting someone over, and out of that gesture a friendship evolved. But it wasn't like that. Once you had a friend, that person was part of your life and everything in it.

I bent down to receive Bubby's whiskery homecoming kiss. "This is Rosie," I said. "I met her today."

I led Rosie to my bedroom. Bubby, as always, had tidied up. Her tidying was efficient if unpredictable: today my navy loafers were arranged end to end on the windowsill, with my hairbrush tucked inside one of them.

We sat on the bed and I spread the books out on the blue-and-purple bedspread. "Your eyes remind me of a painting I like," I said. "I'll take the book out of the library and show you."

"You know so much. What a cosy room!" Rosie said. "I can see how much your mother loves you."

I ran my fingers along the books—my gateway to Eden. The smallest one was a slim blue hardback, almost as thin as the notebook, with thick, shiny pages. I'd never come across such sumptuous paper in a book, paper that made you want to turn the pages just so you could handle it. I stared at the first page: bold, flame-tipped letters seemed to be reaching up to a drawing of lightning and dark clouds.

"That's Torah," Rosie explained, "but for grade one. That's why the print is so big. Torah's just the first part. Then come the Prophets and the Writings. It's called *Tanakh*, when it's all together. Here's the *Tanakh* we used this year."

I opened the heavy book she handed me. Here the flame-tipped letters were surrounded by squiggly marks so minute they resembled the imprints of insects.

Rosie read my mind. "The small print is Rashi. You don't need to know that."

"I'll manage," I said, though I had no idea how. Six years in one summer—it seemed impossible. The script looked impenetrable, more like a cryptogram than a language.

"You read from right to left. The dots are the vowels. Imagine thousands of years ago, when they believed in golden calves and sacrificing children. Here, I'll show you how it works."

What I really wanted to do was touch her braids.

Rosie went through the alphabet on the back of the notebook and explained the final forms of some of the letters.

"I'll practise later," I said. Tonight, in bed, I would begin. My stomach went skidding at the thought, and though I'd never experienced that sort of sensation, I recognized it as sexual excitement.

There was a small crash as my mother, on cue as always, flung open the front door. Her voice, followed by the scent of Ben Hur perfume, filled the house. She'd fought her way through another day, warded off the Cyclops, dropped by Hades.

—*mamaleh mamaleh where are you are you here*—

I slammed my bedroom door shut. Rosie was shocked. "What are you doing?" she asked.

"Oh, all right." I opened the door and let my mother in.

—*who who is this hello hello yes I know you*—

She stopped midway, swayed like a great ship, her face contracted, her bosom expanded. She'd noticed the books.

"Hello, Mrs. Levitsky. These books are from my school, Eden. Maya says she'd like to go there next year—what do you think?"

—*what's that Eden what*—

"Sorry, we should have asked you first."

"Don't pay any attention to her, Rosie," I moaned. "She's always like this. It doesn't mean anything. Mom, leave us alone, please. This is Hebrew—Hebrew, see?" I opened one of the books and, impersonating Reveen the Impossibilist, I swung it back and forth in front of her eyes. "See ... Hebrew ... thousands of years old ... right to left ..."

—*I know Hebrew I know Hebrew don't show me avinu malkenu adon olam ha ha ha*—

"You know Hebrew?" I asked. I'd thought that Fanya had by now ransacked every last corner of her remorseless memory. Hebrew, I was fairly certain, had never come up.

—*the one the one with the father and the leg they sawed off*—

"Don't!" Placing my hands on my mother's shoulders, I steered her gently out of the room. I shut the door firmly after her and rolled my eyes. "My mother and her crazy stories."

"Poor thing. Was she in Auschwitz?"

"Oh, who knows where she was! It's all tangled up there in what she calls her brain."

"Never mind, don't feel bad. I have to go help Mummy make supper, and after that I have a date with this guy, Freddy. But come over tomorrow morning, can you? Maybe you can stay all day, if your mother doesn't mind. There's a party in the evening."

"Party?"

"Yes, Mummy and Daddy spoil me. We have a party every Saturday night, it's fun. We dance, we play games ..."

"What sort of games?"

"You know, charades, stuff like that."

"I won't know anyone."

"Don't worry about that. I'll introduce you to all my friends. You'll like Sheila—I mean, Dominique, that's her new name—she's smart like you. And Dvora, everyone likes her."

"Is Freddy your boyfriend?" I asked, bracing myself for the answer. And yet I wasn't exactly jealous. What I already had—Rosie in my life—was a bounty for which I could only be grateful. But there was more to it: Rosie's availability was a part of who she was, and yielding to it was a way of having her.

"Not really ... he wants to be. He wants to be the only person I date. Poor Freddy!"

"He shouldn't be so possessive, maybe," I ventured.

"I can tell we're going to be best friends. Even though you're ten times smarter than me."

"I'm not. I'm really not."

"Next time I'll tell you more about myself. Will you tell me?" she asked generously.

"I don't have any secrets," I replied, downcast.

"You're a riot."

"I didn't mean it as a joke," I said. "I really do wish I had some secrets, and you were the only one who knew them ... I do have something nice I can show you, though. It's not exactly a secret, but we keep it in a drawer."

Desperation had given me an idea, and with the idea came a sweet surge of anticipation. My mother had a treasured cashmere sweater with pearl buttons which she kept in the bottom drawer of her dresser. It was pale blue, though the usual terms—cloud blue, pastel blue—fail to capture the quality of its colour; it was the sort of colour that, in combination with the cashmere, the pearl buttons, and the simple cut, made you wonder how a piece of clothing could convey such pure innocence. It was nearly unbearable, that innocence, that purity. The story that went with the sweater was as unbearable: when my mother returned home after the war, she found her old apartment empty, not a curtain left, not even a broom, and as she sat on the steps and wept, the man who lived next door showed up with a parcel, left for her by her mother. Inside was the sweater. More likely that he stole it and repented, my mother added with a snort. And who knew what else the neighbours had in their cupboards! Candlesticks, silverware, lace tablecloths that had taken months to sew, hundreds of books— expensive, leather-bound volumes—and, worst of all, her father's entire collection of photographs. The sweater looked bereft even without this Aladdin's story of lost fortune, and I often paid it a visit in the dresser drawer. I'd take it out for an airing, lay it on my mother's white chenille bedspread, press my cheek against the cashmere, then carefully refold it.

Signalling to Rosie not to make a sound, I led the way to my mother's bedroom and shut the door behind us. Luckily Mère Levitsky was busy in the kitchen and didn't see us creeping to her room; it would have ruined everything, had she swept down on us with her account of our solitary family heirloom.

I lifted the sweater from the drawer, held it against my torso, and told Rosie the story of the kind-hearted, or repentant, neighbour.

"They weren't taken away together?" Rosie asked. "Your mother and her mother?"

I shrugged. "I don't know. My mother was at a friend's house or something …"

"It's fabulous," Rosie said.

"Try it on," I implored her. "It's too small for me, but it would fit you."

"Oh, no! I don't think your mother would want that. Anyhow, I really have to go. I have to help Mummy and Daddy … Pretend I died!" And before I had a chance to ask her what she meant, she fell down to the floor and lay there limp and motionless in the nook formed by the two beds.

I bent down and whimpered, "Rosie, Rosie, my only friend, how could you leave me like this?"

She lifted a swan-ballerina's arm.

"She's alive!" I cried. "Call the doctor!"

"There are no doctors in this place," she rasped. Then she laughed and stood up. "You understand things," she said.

"Not really. But I like you."

"I'm sorry I have to go. Will you come over tomorrow?"

"When's the earliest I can come?"

"I usually sleep in until ten or eleven. But don't worry—even if I'm asleep, Mummy and Daddy are always up early. They'll be happy to see you."

"I'll walk you to the bus," I said. "I could ride back with you, to keep you company."

"And then I'll have to come back with you! We could do that all day. Really, I don't mind. I like buses."

"Okay, I'll just wait with you."

We walked to the bus stop and waited together in silence. There was nothing more to say. We both knew that Rosie's benevolence was an equal match to my desire, and that this would be the basis of our friendship. I would give her my need and in return she would give me as much as she could of herself. And if she was enlisting me for reasons of her own, reasons that had to do with her parents, that was fine with me.

The bus arrived and took her away from me. I walked home slowly. Alone in my room, tucked in bed, I let the day's pleasures billow like a sail in warm wind. I had a friend. This was what it was like to have a friend, a friend for life. Rosie's monastic house, the abandoned school, Rosie on my flowered bedspread: with these things in my life, nothing but their disappearance could ever make me unhappy again.

Rosie kept her promise. She drew me into her life, introduced me to everyone she knew. "This is Maya, my new friend. She wants to go to Eden next year, so she's going to learn everything in one summer. She's really brainy."

"I'm not—I practically flunked out," I said, but no one believed me.

The designated centre of the world that summer was the local swimming pool. DJ Doug Pringle with his sexy English accent on the radio, lifeguards with sun-bleached hair, wet feet running on wet cement. It was noisy and crowded, but when Rosie emerged from the dark, dank locker rooms, currents of excitement travelled through the pool crowd. She was beautiful even in her striped navy and zinc-yellow bathing suit, beautiful even in the rubber bathing caps we were all forced to wear. But she was unimpressed by the impression she made, and thought we were only humouring her.

It would have caused my mother no end of anxiety had I removed one of our colour-coordinated bath towels from the house, especially for a venture as dubious as public swimming. With a handful of coins from the money jar in the linen closet, I bought a beach towel at Woolworth's. My mother was convinced that tuberculosis lay in wait for me at the pool: I'd end up spending half my life at a sanatorium. When I came home, she took the towel—on which Rosie had knelt as she spread suntan lotion on my back, on which I had lain as I delved into the mysteries of Hebrew vocalization—and boiled it for several hours in the tub. The oversized image of a sailboat soon faded into a masterpiece of abstract art.

My notion of Judaism up to then had been foggy. At our place, as in a futuristic story in which the last Jew clings irrationally to the single surviving remnant of a forgotten past, we had an aquamarine menorah with a gold Star of David etched in front. Bubby had brought it with her when she came to us, and had set it prominently on the television cabinet. It remained there for the next few days, expanding under my mother's glare. At last, unable to bear its presence any longer, she picked it up by the stem and removed it to a more secluded location, between the toaster and the sugar tin.

Now, as Jeff and Freddy and Kris strolled over and settled themselves along the perimeters of Rosie's towel, I read about the beginning. In the beginning, God created the heavens (plural) and the earth (feminine) and the earth was (feminine form of the verb) chaos, and darkness was (implied verb) upon the void. In Hebrew, it rhymed, alliterated, pulsed. Bone of my bone, flesh of my flesh. A language of abbreviations, blunt and evasive at the same time. The words were everything and nothing.

I worked hard, though there were also days when my brain seemed to be waterlogged. If Rosie were a Catholic, I'd be studying *The Lives of the Saints*—it was all the same to me. But what exactly was Judaism? Clearly it was more than Adam and Eve in the garden, Cain and Abel outside it. I had no one to ask. The Michaelis, like my mother, were removed from the more tangible aspects of Jewish life, and my questions were too vague for my new pool friends. I found a dusty one-volume Jewish encyclopedia at the Atwater Library which I was allowed to check out, and I began to read entries at random. A spiral of festivals and significant food entered my consciousness, and I filled several Hilroy notebooks with complex stories involving miracles and violent death, all of it as foreign as the fat alabaster Buddhas in Mr. Wong's gift shop. I read until late at night, but no coherent picture emerged, and when I put away the encyclopedia and closed my eyes, I had visions of the disparate pieces falling in slow-motion through the air, a shower of plagues and horseradish.

Dvora and Sheila/Dominique came to the pool nearly every day. Yes, Sheila—my former bunkmate! Her memories of Camp

Bakunin were different from mine: "What a pretentious assortment of neurotics," she said, referring to the counsellors. If she
remembered that I'd washed her underwear, she didn't let on.

Along with her new name, Sheila had adopted a particular style
of hippie cool—sombre, skeptical, sophisticated. I rarely saw her
smile, though her comments were often amusing. She wore a long
black skirt and stayed away from the water; she said she was
hydrophobic, but the real reason, I discovered, was her conviction
that kids were peeing in the pool. "You'd have to put a gun to my
head to make me go into that piss-pot," she confided. She couldn't
bear direct sunlight and never stretched out to tan like the rest of
us. "I must be part-vampire," she liked to say.

Sheila—I could never think of her as Dominique—occupied
herself in other ways. In a small black notebook she jotted ideas for
use in a future film or novel. She also knew how to crochet. "I
crochet because I'm high-strung and compulsive," she said, her
arched eyebrows arching even higher. She sold doilies and tablecloths to her parents' friends, and she'd buy us all pepperoni pizza
with the money she made, not because she liked pepperoni, but
because she wanted to prove that God didn't care what anyone
ate. "Have a kid in its mother's milk," she'd say wryly as she
handed us slices. I had read about dietary restrictions in the Jewish
encyclopedia, but the article hadn't mentioned that decisions
about which ones to follow depended on whether you were Very
Strict Orthodox, Strict Orthodox, Religious But Not That Strict
or Not Religious. *Do not eat a kid in its mother's milk:* a moving
directive, thin and exotic, almost a plea.

One day, Sheila gave me a seashell shawl she'd been working
on. "I'll keep this forever," I said, embarrassing her. "Don't
exaggerate," she chided me in her usual sardonic drawl. But in fact,
I still have Sheila's shawl; I've spread it over my DVD. *Study in
Metal and Lace,* by M.L.

In spite of her cultivated nonchalance, Sheila's life was hard.
She could never stay at the pool for more than an hour or two

because she had three younger siblings to look after. Her parents worked long hours at a store, six days a week, and Sheila helped with the cooking and childcare. I offered to lend a hand—we all did—but she put us off. "I like being captain of the ship," she said. Possibly she didn't want us to see the chaos in her home; there were rumours of a cramped, squalid apartment, with diapers soaking in pails.

Dvora in her ruffled bathing suit was round and bosomy; the ruffles matched her Little Lulu curls, which bounced like Slinkies when she moved. An expert on the Top 40, she brought her transistor radio to the pool and always knew who was singing and for how long they'd been on the chart. A flyer from the local radio station helped her keep track, and she ticked off the songs as they came on: "Mrs. Robinson," "Jumpin' Jack Flash," "Angel of the Morning." Between hits she furtively handed us small, individually wrapped toffees she'd snuck past the guards. Sheila broke pool rules as well: we weren't allowed to bring furniture with us, but Sheila sat on her own portable lawn chair. She told the lifeguards that she'd had polio as a child and that her back was damaged. I doubt they believed her (we'd all been vaccinated against polio), but it was easier to let Sheila be. Her Madonna eyes and pale oval face, partly hidden by stray strands of hair, discouraged confrontation.

It seemed as if everyone but me knew how to swim. They'd had lessons, or their parents had taught them, or they'd somehow taught themselves. But I was afraid of the deep end, and there wasn't any marker to show where the floor of the pool dipped—you could be wading in the shallow part and suddenly your footing would be gone. Occasionally I lowered myself into the pool in order to cool off, but I didn't let go of the ladder, and after a few seconds I climbed back out and returned to my towel and books.

My determination to attend Eden so I could be with Rosie transformed the decoding of Hebrew into an impassioned undertaking. I studied amidst an unabating soundtrack of shrieks, splashing, and radio hits. At times a particular song served as a mnemonic. *Stoned Soul Picnic* came to be associated in my mind with the deep abyss of Creation, *tehom*, while "Honey I Miss You" was to be forever linked to God's plan for interminable reproduction, *pru urvu*.

Despite Herculean efforts, by mid-August I had only reached the sixth chapter of Genesis, though I'd skimmed the rest of the Bible in English. And even those six chapters—up to God's instructions to Noah—were only partly intelligible; I was stumped by some of the verses, and no one could help me. Rosie didn't know; Sheila, sighing and looking bored, occasionally agreed to take a stab at the problematic passages, but though her Hebrew was better than Rosie's, most of the time she handed back the Bible with a triumphant "I don't know what the fuck this means." And there was no point asking Dvora, who had never once passed a Hebrew exam.

Like Judaism, though far more hopeless, heterosexuality took shape that summer, summoned not from an inchoate state but from non-existence. Rosie acted as matchmaker: Avi Ozier, the sought-after lifeguard, was taking her out on Friday night, and she invited me and a bony boy named Earl Margolis to come along. Earl, it seemed, had a secret crush on me; he'd confided in Rosie, and she had promised to do what she could.

My fantasies had changed, now that a real-life object of desire had risen from the mist. In my daydreams I'd focussed on the female models who'd posed in studios over the ages; now those anonymous women had been replaced by Rosie, and my passive appreciation by dramas, or rather melodramas, in which I played a heroic role. Rosie was drowning in a lake; I reached out for her, lifted her soaking body onto a boat, bundled her up in a towel. She was wrongfully accused of a crime, and I found the evidence that freed her. Inspired by *Persona*, which I'd seen on late-night television, I imagined the two of us marooned together on a desert island …

I had remained more or less impervious to jealousy; Rosie's Friday-night dates were, I felt, a trivial part of her life, even an aberration, like a cold that comes and goes, or the pool closed for cleaning. I was, however, annoyed that her boyfriends took up time she might have spent with me, and I often wished I could trail along as she and her guy-of-the-evening went roller-skating at the Récréathèque. It had never occurred to me to be interested in members of the opposite sex; vaguely and instinctively, I knew a date with a boy would lead to exactly nothing. But the prospect of joining Rosie on one of her evenings out was, quite literally, a dream come true.

The four of us were supposed to see a movie, but Avi was late, so we bought a large bag of barbecue chips and made our way instead to Earl's place. Earl was the only one of our circle who lived in the Town of Mount Royal, known for its affluence and homogeneous Updike-white population. The basement of Earl's house was more like a clubhouse than a room in a someone's home, with its bar, ping-pong table, beanbag chairs, rows of records leaning inside built-in cabinets, shaggy off-white carpets on a dark red linoleum floor and, permeating everything, the innately nostalgic smell of cedar and mothballs.

"This basement is great," I said.

"Groovy," Avi agreed.

We sprawled on beanbags, and Avi, who was enterprising as well as handsome, produced a small piece of hash, lit it until it burst into flame, trapped the smoke with a glass, and used a hollow Bic pen to toke up. I watched as Rosie and Earl inhaled the delicate smoke but declined when my turn came. What if I got so high I ended up soaring straight into the worm museum?

Nevertheless, I was the keeper of the toking pen, because I was the only one who carried a reliable knapsack wherever I went— you never knew when you'd need soda crackers, tissues, tampons, safety pins, scissors … Every once in a while I come across that dismantled pen at the back of a drawer I'm cleaning out; for years it kept its musky smell, but now only the stained yellow insides of the barrel remain as evidence of its glamorous past.

Avi hung his arm around Rosie's waist. He was brimming with the confidence of recently acquired enlightenment, brought on by readings in Zen that had raised him from ordinary mortal spheres to Olympian heights. Avi: dark curly hair, blue eyes, Jimi Hendrix bandana, purple gossamer shirt, embroidered vest—oh, the eros and esteem one could secure simply by means of an embroidered vest! Breezy with his mind-blowing, consciousness-altering perceptions, he kissed Rosie's hair, and she smiled. Earl sat next to me, wanting to touch me but afraid. "Well, Earl, what do you usually eat for breakfast?" I asked him, trying to make conversation.

"T-toast and jam," he stammered.

"That's *sweet*," I said. What do you do when you're given power over another person's happiness? How is it possible not to sink under the weight? I had so little to offer Earl—barely even friendship.

Earl blushed and ducked his head inside the record cabinet to hide his excitement and misery. "What d-do you want to hear?"

"'Ode to Billy Joe,'" Rosie said.

"What's the thing they throw off the bridge?" I asked.

"Her baby," Rosie said.

"Oh no!" Earl looked horrified. "It's a g-gun. He's killed the man who attacked her and got her pregnant."

"It's her blood-stained clothes. She's had an abortion," Avi said with unZenlike relish, as his hand slowly rotated on Rosie's midriff.

"Anyone see the moon landing?" I asked.

"Yeah. Big deal," said Avi.

"Yeah."

"Yeah."

"Yeah."

"Why did they have to put up that flag?" Avi complained. "No imagination—just ego, ego, ego. Couldn't they have put something universal, like a peace flag?"

"Or Masaccio's *Adam and Eve*," I suggested.

"It ruins looking at the moon, thinking that flag is up there,"
Avi said.

"It won't l-last," Earl assured him.

"It's probably flown away already," Rosie said.

"Yeah, well," Avi grunted. "They're in competition with the
Soviets. So that's more important than schools. You have to give
up desire to reach the realm of the True Self."

"'The ants go marching one by one,'" Rosie sang, and we all
joined in, improvising silly, stoned rhymes.

Meanwhile, back home, my mother was talking to two
policemen in our living room: three in the morning, she wailed,
and not a sign of me, not a word. The policemen nodded. What
did they make of my mother? And what had she told them on the
phone to induce them to pay a house call? I don't know. But they
did have words of warning for her: "She could be on LSD. Parents
are the last to know." For days afterwards, my mother watched me
fearfully, and it took a concerted effort to convince her that LSD
was not being passed around, along with Dvora's toffees, at the
swimming pool.

When you're young and it's summer, time melts away. If not for
Rosie's Saturday-night parties we would have forgotten what day it
was, but the countdown began midweek: three days to go, then two,
then one. The parties were an extension of the Michaelis' distinct
vision of family life: filling the house with teenagers was part of a
larger plan we gladly accepted, though we didn't quite understand
it. Rosie's parents remained in the background, sitting in the
kitchen or paying for the pizza or collecting paper cups; whenever
possible, they tried to direct our focus onto Rosie. But the parties
were a family project, a staged event in which the rest of us had
been cast; and the point was to include Mr. and Mrs. Michaeli,
satisfy a private need of theirs. We didn't care. On the contrary, the
depth and breadth of their need made us feel wanted.

The food never varied. We could expect two large plastic serving bowls filled with Cheezies, four cut-glass candy dishes containing white and pink sugar-coated almonds, and several bottles of soda. Dvora, Earl, and some of the others brought additional drinks and bags of pretzels. At eight o'clock the extra-large pizzas arrived at the door, their cardboard boxes almost too hot to touch and starting to warp from the sogging steam. We ate politely, using napkins, but sometimes tomato sauce dripped onto the sofa or carpets, leaving stains that gradually faded from copper to dark grey.

As we ate, Rosie performed for us. She sang songs by Schubert in her pure, faraway voice, with her father accompanying her on the piano. She sang Mahler's Kindertotenlieder and Pamina's magical aria from *The Magic Flute*—*ach ich fühls, es ist verschwunden. Now I know that love can vanish.*

Classical music! No one else could have got away with it. But if Rosie sang Schubert or Mozart or Berlioz, it was because she was even better than you thought. She wasn't showing off, she was doing it for you, handing you—or her parents, through you—the luminous overflow of what she had to offer.

Occasionally, on request, she also performed the family dance. She must have been fooling around one day in the living room, with her father playing wacky, jazzy Bach to match her odd moves while her mother watched. Over the years, the Bachanova, with its stooped arm-swinging and fake tap-dancing, had evolved into family tradition. No one tried to imitate it; no one would have succeeded.

At regular intervals, Mrs. Michaeli retreated into her bedroom to smoke. She left the door open and I often saw her sitting on the bed with an ashtray on her lap, staring into space. If she happened to glance my way, she'd smile and say, "Will you stay tonight, Maya?"

I did stay. More and more frequently I slept over on Saturday nights. The sofa in the music room opened into a hard, slightly wobbly bed, and Mrs. Michaeli brought me ironed sheets and a pillow from the closet. She would light a cigarette and sit on the piano stool as Rosie and I tucked sheets under the sofa cushions. "Poor Maya," she said. "We have no room for your legs." She was postponing her own bedtime, and we tried to be helpful by talking about the small mating dramas that had taken place during the party. But it was hard going, and as we spoke Mrs. Michaeli stared at the carpet and nodded vaguely. When the bed was made, she would sigh deeply, stub out her cigarette, and say goodnight.

We moved to the bedroom to change. As Rosie undressed, I couldn't help noticing the perfect triangle of dark hair springing like a miniature meadow from the curve of her thighs. Mine, a ridiculous orange, was unruly and wiry; I had not realized there were such variations. She had round breasts while I was as flat as a boy; she was slim but her body curved gently. I felt angular and overly solid next to her, like a child's drawing of a robot next to Titian's *Venus of Urbino*.

"Look at me," I said, the first time I slept over. "My body proves that God has a sense of humour."

"You're a riot, Maya. It's nice to be tall. And everyone loves red hair and grey eyes. I wish I had your grey eyes!"

"I wish—" But I couldn't tell her what I wished. What I wished was to sleep in her bed. I liked to imagine that if I had the same access to Rosie's body as her boyfriends, she'd be impressed, because I'd be so much more passionate and appealing than any boy. In fact I was luckier than Rosie's boyfriends: she never rationed herself with me. I had an open invitation to her place, and when I came over I had her to myself for hours at a time.

"Here," Rosie said unhappily, extracting a pile of letters from a dresser drawer and dropping them on the bed.

The letters were from boys. Avi's large, bold script obediently reproduced the conventions of cursive our teachers had modelled on the blackboard in third grade; Freddy's letters were smudged and barely legible; Kris used a green fountain pen. They all pleaded with Rosie, pledged their devotion. *I can't live without you all I think about is you and if I thought that the future didn't include you I wouldn't want to be part of that future*. The tone was at times accusatory but never aggressive: sensitivity was coming into fashion. See me, hear me.

"What should I do, what will I do?" Rosie looked expectantly into my eyes. "I don't want to hurt anyone ... I just can't give them what they're asking for. They're all jealous of each other."

"Who do you like best?" I wanted to be helpful, but I was also scouting.

"I like all of them, that's the problem."

"But are you in love with anyone?"

"Oh, I don't know. I think I am, then I think I'm not. I guess I'm not, really."

Rosie yawned, switched on her record player, blew on the needle, and placed the arm carefully on the shiny disc. The voice of a wholesome soprano filled the room: *Old Mother Goose when she wanted to wander, would ride through the air on a very fine gander ...*

I made my way to the sofa bed, and Rosie called out, "Don't let the bedbugs bite!"

It took me a while to fall asleep that first night. My sheets smelled of peanuts, the kitchen light had been left on, and the shrill, cheerful warbling of the Mother Goose singer rang eerily through the large room. *Little Bo-Peep has lost her sheep—*

At some point, I slid into one of those dreams you have when you need to pee: I was darting through a deserted beach strewn with transparent blue jellyfish, searching for a bathroom and trying not to step on the pretty but dangerous blue blobs with my bare feet. I woke up and realized that I really did need a bathroom—the salted pretzels had made me thirsty, and I'd helped myself to several tall glasses of lemonade during the evening.

The light was still on in the kitchen, and I heard small, muffled sounds coming from there. On my way to the bathroom I saw

Rosie and her parents sitting at the kitchen table, playing cards. They wore loose, shapeless pyjamas with Miracle Mart designs: blotchy cherries on white for girls, blue stripes for women, a swarm of brown paisley commas on grey for men.

After that I remembered to use the toilet before I went to sleep at the Michaelis'. It turned out that they were all insomniacs, and the nighttime card games—round after round of Hearts—were routine. But though I didn't leave my sofa bed, I was often aware of whispers and footsteps, and once or twice I heard other things, familiar to me from those pre-Seconal years at my own home— weeping, terror, disorientation. But whereas my mother was alone with her nightmares, for Bubby was a deep sleeper and I was only a child, the sounds of distress at the Michaelis' were accompanied by soft voices and gentle coaxing.

My mother accepted my nights away from home with surprising equanimity; she was satisfied that the Michaelis were looking after me. They came, her card-playing friends assured her, with impeccable credentials.

Though the Saturday-night parties continued throughout the summer, Rosie told me they were smaller than usual, since most of her friends were either away at camp or staying in country cottages in the Laurentians. After shovelling snow for five months, Montrealers moved on to the next seasonal ritual, streaming by the thousands to summer cabins that lay scattered across the vast wilderness north of the city. Some of the parents in our circle followed the trend, but they preferred sturdy houses set in neat rows at the edge of a town, with the forest safely consigned to the sidelines. The women socialized on porches while the children attended a local day camp, and the men, who worked in the city, visited on weekends.

Rosie was often invited to drive up with one of the fathers, but she refused to leave her parents, and in the end I was the one who spent a weekend with Dvora at her aunt's country house. I didn't bring my diary with me, and I've retained only a few memories from that visit: scores of ant hills underfoot, the smell of damp sand outdoors and damp carpets indoors, tiny shells that made a fine sound when you rattled them in your hands. On Saturday night, as we played endless rounds of Chinese checkers on the screened-in porch, I was distracted by the thought that I could have been sitting on the sofa in Rosie's music room, playing charades.

Despite our unpromising first date, Earl was still hoping to make some headway with me. He tempted me to return to his basement by placing at my disposal his extensive record collection, along with an endless supply of Black Magic chocolates (his parents owned a pharmacy). He tried to teach me ping-pong, but I was uncoordinated and easily frustrated. At Rosie's parties he shadowed me with glum persistence, and when we danced his bony body made me sad. I kept him at arm's length—literally. The idea wasn't to flaunt my detachment. I wanted to thaw him out of wintry self-consciousness, prod him into understanding me, but he didn't want to see me, hear me.

One evening, lulled by Simon and Garfunkel's "Scarborough Fair," I fell asleep on one of the beanbags in Earl's basement. *Remember me to one who lives there*—in my dream, Scarborough Fair was a vast deserted pool, and I was swimming its length. Earl encouraged me from the diving end—I could barely see him because he was so far away, but I heard his instructions clearly, and his words were more than mere sounds, they were actual pulleys, and they buoyed me up as if I were a marionette. It was wonderful, I thought in the dream, the way words could do that, and I glided with ease through the turquoise water.

I woke up longing to swim, and the following day Earl really did teach me to float. He stood next to me and held my prone body like a magician performing a levitation act. I was weightless on his arms, and when he let go I didn't sink. We'd begun early in the morning, before the crowds arrived, and by afternoon I was doing the frog stroke; it came so easily that I was convinced I'd invented the stroke myself. I dared myself to swim underwater, but as the water closed over my head I panicked and thrashed wildly until I came up. Later that day I tried again; this time I opened my eyes, and had I not needed air I would have stayed underwater for a long time, my arms and legs swaying like seaweed.

Something is happening—there's a difference, I'm discovering, between forgetting and not-remembering. Forgetting is a final oblivion, a relegation to non-existence; no soap opera bang-on-the-head or Freudian couch can bring it back. Old addresses, half the math I learned in high school, the faces of passersby—gone forever.

Not-remembering is different. What did I do last Tuesday? I can't recall, at the moment, but all I need is a jog, and it will be there, safe and sound, like a mitt that turns up in the pocket of last winter's jacket.

Details I'd not-remembered, details I'd left behind, are bobbing up from the handwritten pages of my diary. The Rosie of that first day, the Rosie who sang at parties and brought in the pizza, is the one I've fixed on. Yet here in my teenager's journal is the account of an afternoon in mid-July that I'd conveniently, or deliberately, misplaced.

In the lazy haze of "Summertime Blues" and hidden toffees and the sunny chlorinated smell of the pool's cement floor, we didn't notice a gang of delinquents heading our way—a fox-faced girl and three or four boys with fuzzy moustaches and bleary eyes. The girl's name was Belinda, and I remember that her blonde hair was ragged with split ends, and it seemed to me at the time that this defiant neglect coincided with something lank and ragged about her bullying.

Usually they stayed away from us, but Rosie's popularity must have threatened their sense of supremacy, and with a hunter's instinct they knew that Rosie, if attacked, would not be able to fight back. And so they came over to where she was sitting and, laughing uproariously, pretended to fall on her. As they tumbled down, one of them spit on her face. Before anyone had a chance to react they'd fled, braying like donkeys on speed.

Rosie fled to the locker room, fumbled with the combination of her lock, and pulled her skirt and shirt over her wet bathing suit, all the while sobbing in that hiccoughy way you can't control. I'd never seen Rosie cry—I don't think anyone had. We tried to talk to her, but she'd moved away from us. She ran out of the pool area to the adjoining park and, still sobbing, sat down on the bench of a picnic table. When Jeff tried to put his arm around her, she brushed him off. The only thing she accepted was a tissue, so she could blow her nose.

"Do you want someone to drive you home?" we asked her. She shook her head emphatically. "Don't ever tell Mummy and Daddy," she said, and she made us all swear.

Eventually she calmed down, but she didn't want her parents to see her red eyes. "I need a shower," she said in a fragile monotone, and Dvora offered her house. Dvora's parents had two cars, and every evening at seven either her mother or her older brother Raphi showed up at the pool to pick her up.

Rosie accepted Dvora's invitation. Dvora called her brother from a phone booth, and twenty minutes later Raphi arrived in a station wagon. The three of us climbed into the back and Raphi tore down the street at twice the limit.

Dvora lived in one of the new developments in Côte St. Luc, where new, custom-made houses alternated with barren, as yet unclaimed lots. Dvora's house proudly reproduced a castle's crenellated turrets on all four sides. The doorbell chimed like a harp; you could dim lights gradually by turning a knob; the upstairs bathrooms had two sinks, gold-plated faucets, spouts that released water in a soft spray. I'd heard about these luxuries; most of us were poor, or close to it, and easily impressed. *Did you see the ice crusher, man? Did you see the colour TV?*

While Rosie showered, Dvora and I leafed through *Mad* magazines and romance comic books. Of the pop artists I'd come across at the Atwater Library, the only one I liked was Roy Lichtenstein, who made me laugh—and here was his template: a girl fell for a long-haired artist who drove a motorcycle; he cheated on her; she saw the light and chose the guy in the suit. I could have read these encouraging moral tales for hours, but before I'd finished the second *Young Love*, Rosie appeared in the doorway. Wrapped in a hooded white bathrobe, its belt trailing on the carpet, she looked like the sorcerer's apprentice. "I don't know what got into me," she said contritely. "I'm just going crazy, I guess."

"We're all going crazy in this heat," Dvora said. She meant outside; her house was air-conditioned. "Want some blueberries with whipped cream?"

"I'll just get dressed. You go, I'll be there in a sec."

Raphi was in the kitchen, sitting at a round acrylic table in a noncommittal pose, the chair pushed sideways and one knee up. He wore baggy blue swim-shorts and though he was at least seventeen he seemed small and brittle. But he was good-looking, or maybe it was his nervous confidence that made him attractive. He glanced up at us and began ranting about an article on China in *Time* magazine. He was breathless with contempt as he read the sentences out loud. "Christ, what bullshit. Self-serving propaganda scaled down to the level of the average eight-year-old." With his clever fluency, he reminded me a little of Anthony, but Raphi was on a tangent of his own, while Anthony never said anything that wasn't calibrated against the person he was taking on. Anthony was interested in your response, waited for it, seemed almost to be sustaining himself with what you said, or the way you said it, or even the way you looked at him. Raphi was a self-contained, free-floating system.

Rosie and I watched as Dvora poured cream into the bowl of an electric cake-mixer. Her brother pushed the table away and went to the fridge to get a bottle of Coke. "There's cocaine in Coke," he said. "That's where it gets its name, and that's why I'm addicted. I wouldn't put whipped cream on those blueberries if I were you," he told Dvora. "You're turning into a tub of lard as it is." He plucked the strap of her sleeveless top.

"Fuck *off*," Dvora wailed as Raphi returned to the table with his Coke.

Dvora's mother, who'd been sunbathing on the patio, stepped into the kitchen through sliding glass doors. She was wearing a complicated beach outfit and her tanned arms gleamed with suntan oil. Smiling pleasantly as she clinked a glass of cola with ice, she was immediately recognizable as a non-immigrant: she knew her place was in this house, this country, this life.

"Stop tormenting your sister, Raphi," she said without concern. "I need you outside—the hose isn't working properly."

"I don't know a damn thing about hoses," Raphi said irritably, but he leapt up and darted outside like a skittish alley cat.

"Hello, Rosie. Who's your new friend, Dvora?"

"Maya," Dvora said vaguely.

"How do you do?" Dvora's mother said just as vaguely, and before I had a chance to answer—not that I had any idea how to respond to "how do you do"—she walked out again, sliding the glass doors behind her.

"I like your family," Rosie said.

"I'm going to kill Raphi one of these days," Dvora grunted. "He's such a jerk."

I wanted to stay at Dvora's, listen to her records, watch her brother, watch her parents. But Rosie said she'd stayed away long enough—she had to get back. Raphi drove us home. Rosie asked to be dropped off first, and Raphi requested a goodbye kiss in return. Rosie leaned over and kissed his cheek.

"Cute chick," he commented, as he drove me to my place.

"Yeah," I said.

He stole a sideways glance at me, sly and sharp. "You agree, do you?"

"Yes."

"What did you say your name was?"

"Maya."

"You're different," he said. "You're not like Dvora's usual retard friends."

"Rosie's not a retard," I said.

"I didn't mean her—she's obviously in a league of her own."

A day or two later, the delinquents were caught breaking bottles in the locker room and were banned from the pool for good.

Towards the end of August, I wrote an obsequious letter to the principal of Eden Academy. *Dear Mr. Aigen, the dream of a lifetime would be fulfilled if* ... Mrs. Michaeli, who knew where the principal lived, delivered the letter by hand.

A few days later, an envelope with the school stamp arrived at our place, addressed to my mother. Inside was an application form and a letter. I would be accepted on condition that I pass a test. I'd have to answer questions about the holidays, write a composition in Hebrew, and demonstrate familiarity with biblical stories; I was allowed to bring an English-Hebrew dictionary and a Hebrew Bible. I began scribbling crib notes in the margins of my appropriated *Tanakh*. I still have those notes, I still have the heavy book with my pencilled annotations in the margins, thin and pale amidst the flowery print. *Passover: matzahs, oppressed by Egyptians. Hanukkah: candles, oppressed by Greeks.*

I arrived at the empty school on the Thursday before Labour Day weekend. Only the office showed signs of life: two secretaries were shuffling about, preparing for the school year. One of them was a woman with the widest smile I'd ever seen, like Tenniel's drawing of the Cheshire Cat, but kinder. She wore a pink sweater and matching button earrings, large and glossy, with gold trim. "Take all the time you need, sweetheart," she said, handing me the exam.

I wrote for hours: I was asked to expound on the Patriarchs, and since the examiners failed to remind me that there were only three, I included in my essay Noah, Joseph, Moses, Aaron, Solomon, Saul, Joshua, David, and anyone else who seemed important. Twice the secretary checked in and asked me with a worried squint if I was all right.

My performance on the exam was pitiful, and I knew it. My grasp of holidays was poor, and my Hebrew composition ("Why I Want to Attend Mei-Eden") was an extended wild guess, largely plagiarized from my Bible: *Let me go, I pray thee, and return unto my brethren which are in the school* ... I prepared myself for another round of begging and pleading; I wasn't ready to give up. But no one contacted us. I asked Mr. Michaeli to inquire, and he reported back, to my relief, that my name was on the roster for the coming school year.

I soon understood why my exam never resurfaced. It made no difference, as it turned out, what I knew and didn't know. You had to have Hebrew classes in a Hebrew school; beyond that, no one seemed to care much about them. The Hebrew teachers had resigned themselves to lesser status—the lucky ones had to endure forty minutes of being ignored by bored but somewhat subdued students; the unlucky ones were caught up in a storm of bad behaviour. The students walked the halls with an air of invulnerability and fraught nerves: the school was both battlefield and refuge, the teachers mock targets. The rules I'd fought against for seven years had already disintegrated here, and I surrendered happily to classroom tedium.

I was an outsider, but so was everyone else. Early in the year I asked the principal whether I could wear a navy blue dress to school. The mandatory tunic made me look like a deflated tent, and my white shirt was constantly bunching up under it.

"I don't want to start a trend," the principal grumbled.

"It's a plain dress. My mother made it," I said. "It's not my fault I'm so tall," I added plaintively. It hadn't taken me long to pick up the prevailing rhetorical style.

He gave in. I was the only girl who wore a dress, just as Rosie was the only one who wore a skirt and blouse. But we were all exceptions in some way. Naomi, whose father had died, never removed her winter coat; Joanie stayed away from school for days and weeks at a time; Karla's father flew into rages, during which he whipped his children with a belt—they had to wear long sleeves to hide the marks. A boy in ninth grade had food allergies and ate his lunch alone in the chemistry lab. Arlene had a hearing aid; Brian smoked in the boys' toilet. The school took us all in, as though we'd been washed ashore in a shipwreck. One doesn't expect conformity, or uniformity, from castaways.

In this new setting, my view of Rosie expanded. Rosie at her desk, Rosie staring at the blackboard, Rosie doodling in her notebook. In class I positioned myself next to her, but one row behind, and closer to the wall, so she'd be in my line of vision when I looked at the teacher.

I soon discovered that when it came to schoolwork Rosie was lethargic and scattered. Directed to prepare us for an inhospitable world, our teachers loaded us down with work. Eden students, especially the boys, took it as a given that they had to excel; those who were having difficulties felt ashamed and tried to keep their low grades a secret. Rosie didn't care either way. "It's pointless, when you really think about it," she said. I packed her books for her, I went home with her after school and showed her what needed to be done—not exactly the scenario of chivalrous rescue I'd conjured up in the privacy of my room but satisfying all the same. She nodded politely as I read *Julius Caesar* to her, but her glazed eyes betrayed her.

Infected by the culture of academic ambition, I also began to work hard. There were two problem areas, however. In History class, I sank into a stupor, impervious to any catastrophe, past or present. Back in fourth grade, when I had come up against the settlers and the Iroquois, Jacques Cartier and the fur trade, endless wars between England and France, and then the fur trade again, always the fur trade, whatever that was, I responded with obstinate apathy. This was not as bad as my mother's disarrayed chronicles from *there*, but as incomprehensible. The transition, in high school, to empires and revolutions didn't change anything, and during History class I mostly thought about what I'd be eating for lunch and whether I'd be seeing Rosie after school.

Biology, taught by Mr. Lurie, was problematic for different reasons. Even Eden, it turned out, had its drill sergeant. Over the years I'd perfected a number of return-to-sender tactics to ward off intimidation, but as soon as Mr. Lurie entered the classroom, I felt as forsaken as an old toy at the bottom of a lake. Mr. Lurie had comic-book features—furrowed brows, square chin, Superman hair—and his specialty was identifying the one imperilled place in the heart and squeezing there. My only defence was to fail so extravagantly that the hunt became embarrassing. And it worked: eventually my sad exams, not one question answered correctly, succeeded in silencing Mr. Lurie and he left me alone.

But I did well in my other classes. Chemistry was taught by Miss O'Connor; with her charismatic smile, rebel permissiveness, and exotic advocacy of this new thing, Women's Liberation, she won our hearts. She lived only a few blocks from Eden, and when I didn't understand the day's lesson, I walked to her flat after school for private tutoring. I'd sit at her kitchen table and struggle with covalent bonds while her shy, androgynous roommate—as we thought of her then—did her best to stay out of sight.

And finally, Math with Mrs. Adler. Recalling her, I want to invoke Prospero's Ariel, though Mrs. Adler was a frumpy, lumpy woman in unfashionable tweed dresses. Yet something about that elusive dexterity seems apt. There were rumours that she'd lost her children in the war, but I didn't believe it; she was too hardy, too circumspect and good-natured to have been *there*. She promised to dance a jig if anyone scored ten on the weekly test. It was easy to get nine out of ten if you studied, but the last question was for mathematicians only, and we relied on Ephraim, the class brain, to solve it. He did, every now and then, and in her ill-fitting tweed dress and flat, heavy shoes Mrs. Adler would twirl and stamp her feet as we cheered her on.

With everyone back from vacation, I was afraid of losing sight of Rosie, but I need not have worried. Rosie kept me by her side as she managed the endless demands on her judgment, attention, generosity. *Rosie, I don't know what to do, Mrs. Shapira said I— Rosie, I don't know what to do, I lost I told I accidentally I forgot.* Also: *Oh, Rosie let me do your hair, can you come skiing with us, this sweater doesn't fit me, it would look great on you—*

But not everyone wanted Rosie in the same way. I was her closest friend, comically glued to her from morning to night. After me came Dvora and Sheila; Rosie confided in them, and if she needed something I couldn't give her—the weather forecast, foolscap paper—she asked them. In the third sphere of intimacy, to their annoyance, were Rosie's boyfriends, whether from Eden or other schools. I was going to say that everyone else was consigned to the next circle, but I think the line between the boyfriends and the rest was blurred.

Rosie had no enemies. If a spiteful rumour reached her, she would approach her traducers and say piteously, with a tremor in her voice: "Are you angry about something?" and then, "Please come to my party. You'll meet my parents, we'll have fun, I promise." It was impossible after that to persist.

During the summer I'd been too busy with Hebrew to write at any length in my diary, but now my preoccupation with Rosie found expression in a magnum opus of bedtime ramblings. And if while doing my homework I didn't understand some concept—the difference between *l'imparfait* and *le passé composé*, for example— my frustration transferred itself to erotic desire and I'd lapse into one of my rescue fantasies. Rosie was in a car wreck, unharmed but trapped, and with preternatural strength I pulled her to safety. She called me late at night, distressed because she'd fought with

Avi, and I rushed over to offer solace ... I'd become unbearably aroused, and I had to relieve the insistent pulsing with the pressure of my scarf (a more efficient system never occurred to me).

The Saturday-night parties were filled to capacity now, and standing/crouching/cross-legged bodies spilled over into the kitchen, hallway, and front room. The boys who wanted Rosie to themselves sulked or glared as she danced with their rivals. They tried not showing up but never stayed away for long, because staying away didn't work: they neither forgot her nor succeeded in manipulating her to seek them out.

Sometimes Rosie disappeared into her bedroom with a disgruntled suitor, to "have a talk." One night, after everyone had left, I learned, to my—to my what? What's the word I want?—I learned that "have a talk" was a euphemism for sex. It was as if I'd come across a quivering kitten in a storm, cowering in a place I couldn't reach.

Haight Ashbury's Summer of Love had come and gone, leaving in its wake a glorification of promiscuity. We were, the media told us, in the midst of a sexual revolution; communes and youth clinics were springing up everywhere, and men in their twenties and thirties had only to grow their hair and sport Rasputin beards if they wanted to have sex with fourteen-year-olds and not feel bad about it.

But none of these developments reached Eden, and though the free-love mythology must have provided some degree of camouflage, it wasn't what led Rosie, in the middle of a party at her parents' house, to have sex in her bedroom while the rest of us played charades.

There had been other clues that a more complicated state of affairs lurked beneath Rosie's easy benevolence. Even her attachment to nursery rhymes was suspect. She couldn't fall asleep without her Mother Goose album crackling through the small speakers of her record player. *Cobbler, cobbler mend my shoe, Have it done by half past two ...* Everyone knew about her Mother Goose record; Rosie herself laughed at her dependency. But at the same time she was a miniature adult, and the nursery rhymes were pieces of an unattainable world that mocked her in the slippery darkness, like a puppet show turned sinister in a bad dream.

The loneliness of the Mother Goose ritual reached me as I lay on the teetering sofa bed in the living room, listening, or trying not to listen, to the trained voice on the record. *Ride a cock horse to Banbury Cross—Jack and Jill went up the hill—Cock-a-doodle-doo, my dame has lost her shoe …*

But when it came to the conferral of her body, I really was too inexperienced to see things for what they were. It wasn't only me— no one at the party was astute enough to recognize the signs: the way Rosie came out of her bedroom and headed straight for the bathroom with an air of sudden, fatalistic solitude; the boyfriend's confused departure; maybe even some faint, unfamiliar odour. Rosie must have set conditions, she must have told the guy he had to be discreet. But the Michaelis couldn't have been oblivious. I have to assume they were aware of what was happening and said nothing.

I'd thought, before her confession, that her sexual encounters were limited to a few poetic gestures: hands on thighs, maybe even breasts. But one Saturday evening, after the guests had gone, she said, "Things didn't go too well with Kris today. He got all mad … he said I was thinking about other things during sex, not about him."

"Sex? What do you mean?"

"It's no big deal," Rosie assured me.

"You mean you do it?"

She nodded, and her face was blank, unreadable.

"Just with Kris?"

"No, that's the problem … they want me to themselves."

"But you're only fourteen," I said.

"Fourteen isn't that young. My father was performing with orchestras at fourteen."

"But …" I was hazy about sex; I didn't really know what it was all about, didn't want to know. It seemed ridiculous, basically—a strange rite, strange enough to give a person the willies. Reading the nasty, demeaning seduction scene in chapter two of *The Group* (which the Atwater Library refused to carry—"Trash," the head librarian sniffed, but Esther lent me her copy) had only confirmed my suspicions.

"It doesn't mean anything," Rosie said. She draped her arm around my shoulder, and the warmth of her body surrounded me like a swirling genie. "I wish it did, but it doesn't. Maybe there's something wrong with me. Oh, Maya, I'm so glad we met." I didn't dare move. Bone of my bone, flesh of my flesh.

"What if you get pregnant?" I asked, thinking back to the letters she'd shown me. They seemed menacing now; decoded missives from the enemy. There were clues in the letters that I'd missed at the time: *When I felt you shivering …*

"I make them put on a safe."

"A safe? What's that?"

"A rubbery sort of cover they put on their thingie."

"Really!" I imagined a little cap and wondered how it stayed on. Maybe you tied it with string. "How did you find out about that?"

"I saw it in that *Head and Hands* booklet. But I think I already knew—maybe Jeff told me."

"But do you like it?"

"I don't mind. It's not a big deal," she repeated.

"Your parents …" I began, not knowing exactly what I wanted to say.

"Aren't they great!" It was a non sequitur. Rosie wasn't saying that her parents were great because they let her do what she wanted. They were invoked because they were there, always—like deities who've renounced their power so they could live among humans.

"Who was the first?" I asked.

"Jeff. But it was my idea. I mean, I knew he really wanted to, and I'm the one who said he could."

"I'm never going to have kids. I'm never going to have to do sex with anyone."

"You're so funny, Maya. Don't be scared, it's okay after the first few seconds."

"How do the safes stay on?" I asked. I didn't know exactly what men looked like naked, but from what I'd seen in art books, there wasn't much to it: Michelangelo's Adam, for example, appeared to have something the size of a small whistle, or the head of a robin, resting on his thigh. Rosie unwrapped a discarded tissue to show me a condom, and though I tried not to show it, I was appalled— it seemed all those artists were exercising poetic licence, so to speak—and who could blame them?

"I will never, ever do it," I said. "Why do you let them?"

Rosie shrugged and smiled. "It means a lot to them." Leaning forward, she kissed me good night, her lips landing briefly on mine. Then she slid from her chair to the floor and pretended to die. I knelt down, placed my hand on her forehead. "My poor Rosie, can you be saved, or will algebra be the end of you?" And she whispered weakly, "Save someone else."

After that night, Rosie kissed me always: when we met and parted, at school, at bus stops, at her house when we said good night. She would raise her hands to my shoulders, stand on her tiptoes, and pull me towards her. A consolation prize that achieved its purpose: I was consoled.

I was woken at eight-thirty this morning by a call from the depart- ment's academic coordinator; she had a question about a form I need to fill in. My mother phoned at a more reasonable hour with questions about the new luggage regulations, though she won't be leaving for her winter condo in Florida until next month. I promised to explain it all again tonight, when I go over for my weekly visit *chez elle*, but she said she needed to know immediately, she was packing. "Liquids and sharp objects are allowed in checked-in luggage," I told her, as I've been doing for months. It's not that she forgets or doesn't believe me; what worries her is that the rules may have changed since our last conversation. Then I said, "I'm writing about Rosie Michaeli." Yes, she said, she remembered her well—*the girl you you loved so much*—My mother is full of surprises, always.

Lately—I thought this only happens in dotage—I feel the distant past moving closer as it becomes chronologically more remote. At times I can retrieve not only the narrative thread of the past but the contours of tone and colour and sound. I think this regeneration of memory is a craving for solace, because those times are prelapsarian—we had not yet sinned, not yet fucked up, not yet done all the things that will make us cover our faces with shame. A form of prayer, one could say.

Time to walk Sailor and pick up groceries. I buy most of my food at three neighbourhood stores. That way, Sailor can see me through the window while I shop, and I can see him. I avoid the muzak-plagued, phosphorescent-lit supermarkets; the same hypersensitivity keeps me away from malls. I'm not bothered by warehouses, though, and every few months I drive to Costco and load my car with crates of dog food, detergent, and whatever else I can squeeze into my Mazda. I stock these essentials in the unoccupied, or temporarily occupied, apartment below me. Another advantage to keeping that flat empty.

1970

I met Patrick, or rather, I spied on him, on a Sunday morning in April.

Sunday, let me explain, was no ordinary day in the Levitsky household. On Sundays, my mother disinfected the flat. She allowed me to dust our peat-brown, urethane-coated, delusion-of-wood furniture, but that only took ten minutes; she insisted on tackling the rest of the housecleaning on her own. With her pail and sponges and ladders, Fanya was as innocently indomitable as Charlie Chaplin.

Groggily, while Bubby fried me an egg, I watched the Sunday offensive on unsuspecting germs. My mother, perched on the middle rung of the stepladder, reached up as if about to be carried away by a chariot swinging low and swished a soapy cloth back and forth several hundred times along the ceiling. "You missed a spot," I shouted at her.

When I was through with breakfast, I sprayed and wiped imaginary dust from various bits of furniture, but as soon as my mother turned on the vacuum cleaner, I escaped to my bedroom and shut the door against the deafening whine. My mother was engaged in an ongoing battle with the suction mechanism, which never seemed to work—*even a hair it doesn't pick up*—and this meant the industrial noise would persist, on and off, all morning. I gathered my schoolwork and library books and made my way to Rosie's.

Rosie's bedroom. White rays of sunlight slant in through the window and dust motes dance inside the beams. It's the time of year when springtime showers revert overnight to ice, and all morning trucks have been scattering salt pellets on the streets. A mud and salt smell lingers in the air, the smell of winter dissolving. Rosie and I are eating plums and reading, while on CHOM-FM Joni Mitchell serenades us with songs about blue roses and men from mountains. I'm fourteen, Rosie is fifteen.

Rosie was more watchful now that she was older, more attuned to detail; there was a searching quality about her, characterized by a slight furrowing of her brow, an almost startled look in her eyes. Possibly only I noticed the change, or maybe her parents had as well and for this reason had planned a surprise birthday party for her in December. Rosie's birthdays usually passed without fanfare. There was a cake for dessert instead of the usual canned peaches, but there were no candles on the cake, no one sang "Happy Birthday"—the Michaelis all agreed that the nearly tuneless tune was musically offensive—and the unwrapped gift, a new record, wasn't very meaningful, because Mr. Michaeli bought records all year-round. "We're not really into holidays," Rosie explained. "A day is just a day."

Rosie was expecting, therefore, only the usual Saturday-night party on the week of her fifteenth birthday. My job was to keep her at my place while the balloons and streamers went up. When I brought her back, the windows were dark and Rosie panicked. Her father must have had a relapse, she said—we had to hurry to the hospital. The door opened, the lights came on, and everyone shouted, "Surprise!"

There were piles of presents. I remember a Mother Goose cereal bowl, a sexy nightgown, an anti-war T-shirt (*Nixon, don't make the same mistake your father did, withdraw before it's too late*), chocolates, candles, incense, and a red-and-white life preserver from Avi— either a private joke or a nostalgic nod towards the summer, when he'd watched Rosie from his lifeguard's perch. Convinced that it would do her good to break away from the Michaeli tradition of bare walls, I gave Rosie two Toulouse-Lautrec posters for her bedroom. The gift that attracted most attention, and which oddly paralleled Avi's, was a diamond and ruby ring from his adversary, Jeff. Jeff's father was a jeweller, but even so, it was a charged gesture, and one that ended unhappily. When the party was over and only Jeff remained, Rosie told him she couldn't accept the ring. He threatened suicide, Mr. Michaeli laughed at him, and I was dispatched to give solace as he wept in the bathroom. "Maybe you should go away for a while," I suggested. He was older than Rosie and would soon be graduating. "Yes, yes," he sobbed. "I'll go to Morocco. I have a friend who's already there." He was sitting on the edge of the bathtub, and like someone groping in the dark he reached out for my belt. "Please," he whispered.

"No way," I said, removing his hand.

Jeff didn't mind. "I know, I know," he sighed. "I just wanted to save the little that's left of my masculine pride."

Rosie's party satisfied my birthday-celebration needs, and when I turned fourteen I chose to mark the occasion Michaeli-style. Bubby baked a two-layer chocolate cake, and my mother, dressed in a silver satin dress that made her look like a stuffed toy elephant from the Far East, ceremoniously presented me with a four-speed record player and three records. The records had been enthusiastically recommended, she assured me, by the salesclerk at Sam the Record Man. We plugged in the record player, slid one of the records on the turntable, and the three of us listened to Creedence Clearwater Revival; Bubby seemed quite taken by "I Put a Spell on You" and bobbed her head to the beat.

The following day, the Michaelis gave me an illustrated edition of *War and Peace*, and that's what I was reading in Rosie's room that Sunday. Rosie lay sideways on her bed, leafing through teen magazines and an assortment of comic books: *Archie*, *Supergirl*, *Casper the Friendly Ghost*. Dvora, whose collection was the envy of many, had been forced by her mother to tidy up her room, and the next day Raphi had dropped by with a bagful of comic-book treasures. I sat on the floor with my new book, sucking on the pits of plums until their sugary insides leaked out, my back against the bed. Rosie had a habit of wriggling her feet as she read, and every now and then her toes brushed my upper back.

"Is he good?" Rosie asked me, referring to Tolstoy.

"Yes. I like reading about desperate people. I'd like Archie comics if Archie was struggling with heroin addiction."

Rosie smiled. "Is everyone desperate in *War and Peace?*"

"Pretty much. Desperate or foolish. I can relate to the desperate characters and I get to feel superior to the foolish ones."

"Listen to this. 'Dear Dianne, My boyfriend's hair reaches down to his shoulders. I'm afraid to ask him over because I know my dad will make fun of him. We're very serious and have been discussing marriage. What should I do?'"

I said, "Dear Dianne, I feel very guilty because a boy liked me and I didn't like him back, and I should have told him right away but I didn't, because I liked his records and chocolates. What should I do?"

"Don't feel bad about Earl," Rosie said. "I think it's working out with him and Naomi."

Things had come to an abrupt end with Earl. I'd finally refused, one Saturday night, to dance with him. Rosie came over to me and pleaded on his behalf. "Maya, please talk to Earl. He's really upset."

I had tried to be a good friend at least to lanky, hollow-cheeked Earl. He had so much already: a bunk bed, an extended family, an American mother with a Brooklyn accent, a father who was born in Winnipeg, a shelf of ping-pong trophies. Why did he need more? And why me, of all people? In all the hours spent listening to music and eating Black Magic chocolates in his clubhouse basement, we had not succeeded in moving beyond his craving and my resistance. He wanted my female body, but his desire only made me protective of that body, and it was Earl's shyness, though he may have cursed it when he was alone in his bunk bed, that made it possible for me to hang out with him as long as I did.

I took Earl to Rosie's room, shut the door. He sat on the bed and I sat next to him. "Earl," I said, "You have to stop calling me."

"You've met someone?" he asked suspiciously.

"No, of course not. It's me, can't you see? Look how long we've known each other—and we've never even kissed."

"Can we kiss now?"

"Okay."

But when I felt his restless tongue against my mouth I drew away. "I can't, Earl, I'm sorry. It has nothing to do with you. I'm never going to have a boyfriend."

"You're just trying to get rid of me."

He stormed out of the room, and a few minutes later left the party with Naomi, who spent her free time browsing through bridal magazines.

That was three weeks ago. Earl hadn't spoken to me since.

"I think—" But before I'd finished my sentence, the doorbell rang.

"That's Patrick," Rosie said. "He usually comes on Friday, but he had to switch. He's really funny."

I never visited Rosie on Fridays. Friday was her dating night, and also the day I was held food prisoner at the Levitsky Institute for the Work Deprived. The food tournament got off to an early start. At seven in the morning Bubby entered the kitchen and shut the door, dismissing me with a firm wave of the hand. By the time I came home from school my mother had joined Bubby. The kitchen remained off-limits until six o'clock, when I was called in for a multi-course meal, complete with tapered white candles, a bottle of oxidized red wine the three of us pretended to sip, and musical accompaniment in the form of an obscure melody hummed with vague urgency by Bubby.

In order to give either herself or my mother a break, Bubby would not allow my mother to leave the table once we were seated. The serving of this meal proceeded at a leisurely pace, and between courses my mother lifted my feet onto her lap so she could massage them. I felt ridiculously spoiled.

"Funny in what way?" I asked Rosie.

"Oh, it's how he says things. He hates piano, and he's always arguing with Daddy. Want to hear?"

We peeked out as Patrick made his way to the music room. Straggly chestnut-brown hair, Nelson Algren sweater, wire-rimmed glasses, hunched shoulders—Patrick seemed to be aiming for as low a profile as he could manage, but he radiated a dark, intense energy that was impossible to ignore.

Rosie and I slid to the floor and tried to hold back our giggles. From the doorway we could hear without being seen.

"So, Patrick, here we are again," said Mr. Michaeli.

"Yes," Patrick sighed. A heavy, histrionic sigh, part parody, part resignation.

"So, let's hear the Bach."

Patrick played a short piece. When he was through, Mr. Michaeli said, "Good, good, the fingers are definitely on the right keys. So what is the problem?"

Patrick sighed again. "You don't like it."

"And why?"

"Not in conformity with your concept of aesthetics?"

"Yes, correct. So maybe today we will conform more and give consideration to bringing out feeling?"

"How am I supposed to bring out feeling from a box of mechanical hammers hitting a bunch of steel strings?" Patrick protested. It was a stand-up comic's act: pointing out some essential, absurd injustice with ironic exasperation. But his was an introverted version of a comedian's routine, and seemed almost involuntary.

"Ah, yes—maybe it's the piano. That reminds me of a joke I now forgot."

"I wouldn't mind moving on to a new piece."

"Absolutely," Mr. Michaeli said. "Enough Bach. *Adios*, Bach. We are tired of you. Here we have some Liszt."

"I'm not up to Liszt."

"So, who do we play next?"

"I didn't say I didn't want to play Bach," Patrick said. "You could let me demolish another Bach prelude."

"If only you will try, you will not demolish."

"I told you, I don't have an aptitude for this."

"You are soon sixteen, no?"

"In two weeks."

"Maybe the time has come to tell your mother?"

There was a long pause. "All right," Patrick said. "I will."

"I don't believe it!" Rosie whispered.

"Good," Mr. Michaeli said. "We are ready at last to be free. Go home, and come back any time, we can sit and discuss philosophies, and I will pretend I read those books."

"I'm sorry I've been such a bad student."

"Au contraire, mon ami. From you I've learned some interesting ideas. And a good ear you definitely have."

There was a sound of shuffling as Patrick packed his music books.

"Now they fight over money," Rosie told me. "Let's go watch. Maybe if we're there, it won't be so bad."

I braced myself for a scene. Mr. Michaeli recoiled from money with even more ferocity than Bubby Miriam on laundry detail. If anyone tried to break through his repugnance, he'd respond with a look of shocked fury, almost of hatred. When his students handed him their crumpled five-dollar bills, he gave them in return toys that had cost three times as much. His salary from Eden was spent as quickly as possible on strange, bumpy fruit from a small, poorly lit Caribbean store on Victoria Street; on stamps sold by an impoverished man who lived in a basement apartment downtown and who kept himself alive by slowly relinquishing his stamp collection, salvaged from the war; and on dinner at The Brown Derby, which recovered for its customers their beloved dishes: schnitzel, borscht, kishke, chopped liver. I was often invited to these urgent sprees. "Order everything! Everything the heart desires!" he'd tell us, though he himself only drank coffee. Obediently, charitably, we stuffed ourselves. What was left after the first round of spending went to Europe, to someone Mr. Michaeli knew there.

Occasionally, I, too, was the victim of his devastating gifts— usually a record he thought I'd like. My forced "thank you" exhausted me, and I wished there were some way to give him something in return. Rosie was the only one who remained untroubled by her father's manic saintliness. She laughed at him, sang under her breath, *One for my master, one for my dame, and one for the little boy who lives down the lane.* "I can't bear all this generosity," I told her one time. "Don't feel bad," she said. "He can't help himself."

The two of us strolled casually into the music room. Patrick, bizarrely, didn't seem to see us. It wasn't shyness; it was deliberate technique. Patrick, I would soon find out, had trained his vision over the years, had by now achieved impressive selectivity.

He took out his wallet and Mr. Michaeli stepped back, raised his arms.

But I could see that this was the only part of the lesson Patrick enjoyed. Handing over money was the one safe procedure in Patrick's vexed life. There was no room here for error, humiliation. Unlike Mr. Michaeli, who gave so he could retreat, Patrick wanted only justice, a moment of glorious simplicity.

"No, no, keep for this week the money. We made no progress today, my young friend. Buy for yourself a book on theories in aesthetics, yes? Now you are free as a bird."

Someone had to lose out. Patrick's body tensed with predicament. He placed the money on the piano and ran down the hallway and out the door, forgetting everything: his music, his gloves, his cute black beret.

Rosie and I looked at each other and burst out laughing. We knew at once what we were going to do: if Patrick really wasn't coming back, we'd track him down at his place. He had no hope at all of getting away.

We waited to see whether Patrick would yield either to his mother's wishes or his own morose compulsion and resume his piano lessons. When three weeks had passed and he hadn't called, we decided to go ahead with our plan, and early in May we set out to return to Patrick the items he had, like Cinderella, left behind.

It was a chilly day, and the anemic sky seemed determined to sap the colour from everything beneath it. As we waited for the bus, icy gusts of wind swept down on us, and we shivered under our thin spring coats.

"Alpine rescue vehicle!" I cried out when the bus crawled towards us at last.

"I think he's rich," Rosie said as we slid into a double seat. "He goes to a private boys' school."

"Poor him," I said. Lindsay Anderson's *If* had recently been detonated on impressionable audiences, and I had visions of evil prefects, long echoing corridors, rows of demoralized boys in suits and ties.

Patrick lived in Beaconsfield, wherever that was. The trip took over two hours, and when the last of three buses drove away, we found ourselves in alien territory—not exactly the country, but unlike any city street we'd ever seen. On one side of the paved road, stately houses had been erected between tracts of forest as if sent by some distant monarch to impose order on the wilderness; on the other side, a silvery lake stretched out to the horizon like the sea. It had only recently thawed, and a shadowy indigo hue skimmed the water like mist.

"Wow, I didn't know Montreal had something like this," Rosie said, casting her eyes on the *terra incognita* of the upper classes.

"We don't get around enough, Rosie," I said. I consulted our map, and we set off in search of 4 Hillside Road. I wondered why there were no sidewalks; maybe it was because the population was so sparse, or maybe everyone who lived here travelled by car.

Patrick's house was immense, but it was only partly visible through the elaborate tree and shrub garden surrounding it. I imagined women in crinoline dresses and men in white suits sipping tea under the willow trees; Lily Briscoe at her easel. A shoulder-high garden wall made way for double-swing black iron gates with ornamental gratings. One of the gates was ajar.

Rosie gasped. "Wow, it's a mansion. I feel like Julie Andrews in *The Sound of Music*."

"Or *Mary Poppins*," I said.

"What should we do?"

I shrugged. "Go up to the door and ring the bell?"

"I bet a butler will answer. I didn't think he was this rich."

"How did he find your father?" I asked.

"Oh, you know, one person tells someone else … or maybe Patrick's mother knew about my father in Europe, before the war …"

We proceeded through the gate and up the path. The house appeared to be quite old, though it may have been the twined ivy clinging to the rough-hewn grey blocks and the architectural style—arch-happy neo-Romanesque—that gave it an antique look. There was something lonely and expectant about the long rows of window-eyes and copper-green shingles; like the self-sacrificing statue in *The Happy Prince*, I thought.

"I'm nervous," Rosie said. "Maybe we should have called before we came."

I rang the bell. "Think of it as an adventure."

There was no response at first, and we were trying to decide whether to ring again when a woman's voice called out: "Just a second!" The door opened and there stood Patrick's mother—and my one-time psychiatrist.

I need to backtrack for a moment.

When I was small, my mother was chronically frantic about my health. I'd been rushed to the hospital several times: I was prone to chest colds, and since from her gallery seat, life was a tragic opera, my mother's diagnosis was always drastic. The phantom ailment was asthma, and when the doctors insisted that there was nothing wrong with me, she got all huffy—*like the rest of the so-called doctors who who can die first*—She repeated her macabre accusations on the bus, pulling me closer to her as if I were her accomplice. It was an intimate ritual, and gave me as much pleasure as the cool, gentle touch of the stethoscope against my skin.

Eventually the asthma fell out of favour. Instead, when I was eleven, my mother decided that I had a bone deformity. I was soaking in the bath when she first noticed my affliction. She asked me to stand up, looked me up and down, and tears streamed from her eyes: my arms, my legs, my shoulders—none of it was quite right. Over the next few weeks we trekked from waiting room to waiting room; no one could persuade my mother that my bones were properly aligned. This was a year or two before our national health plan came into effect, but I don't think anyone charged my mother—the last thing they wanted was another phone call from her. I didn't mind these outings. I enjoyed the predictable cycle of hope and dismissal that shaped my mother's pursuit of physicians, and since her various phobias kept us mostly at home, any excursion was a treat.

We were rescued, finally, by Dr. Frankel. It was early autumn, and wet leaves lay scattered on the sidewalk like discarded party decorations. I bent down to collect two or three of the prettiest ones—all crimson or all gold, without spots or perforations.

Dr. Frankel's office was located not in a medical building or a side extension of his home but behind a restaurant in the East End. To reach it, we had to turn onto a narrow lane that ran along the windowless back walls of stores. Facing these brick walls, on the other side of the lane, were struggling backyards separated by simple wooden fences. I was intrigued by the little fenced yards, with their sprinkling of dandelions, neat rows of garbage pails, a tricycle or two; I felt certain they were portals to a warm, orderly but eventful world to which I had no access, could barely even imagine.

Dr. Frankel's door was embedded in one of the brick walls. A hand-written note instructed visitors to walk in and have a seat: the doctor would be back shortly.

We entered and found ourselves in a room with a coat stand, five folding chairs, a pile of neglected magazines on a stool, and a mystifying tangle of wire coat hangers on the floor. I could see at once that there was something wrong with this setup—anyone could see. Doctors' offices were supposed to have carpets and smell of disinfectant; a receptionist handed you forms to fill in; there were other patients ahead of you.

All the same, we sat down as instructed. Looking through the dust-coated magazines I found one with the promising title, *True Confessions*, and soon I was deeply absorbed in the pornographic tale of a girl with a psychotic father. The father, a religious fanatic of some sort, catches his daughter swimming naked in a pond with a boy, and not only that, but on a Sunday morning, when she should have been in church. Enraged, he forces her to walk naked through the town, while he goads her with a switch made of prickly branches. Before long, the girl runs away and marries Rialto, a man with a thin moustache and perverse tastes who wants to show her off to his friends ... This bizarre narrative was interrupted by Dr. Frankel's entrance.

Although it was a warm day, Dr. Frankel wore an ancient capelike coat, and since I was well trained by then, I knew that he, too, had been *there*, and that his coat had come with him from Europe. He removed the coat, draped it gently over the coat stand, and held out his hand. "Good day, Mrs. Levitsky. Good day, Mrs. Levitsky's daughter."

We followed him to his office. "Please to sit down, Mrs. Levitsky and Mrs. Levitsky's daughter," he said. His hair was spotted with dandruff, his knuckles were hairy, his ears were hairy. His white doctor's jacket lay crumpled in a heap on his desk. With his large hairy hands he clutched the white fabric and shook it into shape.

He slid his arms into the sleeves of the jacket.

"Please to step out, Mrs. Levitsky, and I will examine your daughter."

When the door was shut he nodded and asked me to touch my toes. "Very good," he said. "Would you like a candy?"

He handed me a lemon lollipop and called my mother back inside.

—well doctor well well—

"Bad news, Mrs. Levitsky. *Very* bad news. Your daughter has a definite bone deformity, as you so well observed. Incurable, I am regretting to say."

—Yossi Yossi—

Dr. Frankel handed her a tissue, leaned forward, and said confidentially, "Listen, if we don't tell to anyone, no one will know. It will be our little secret."

Instantly my mother cheered up.

—yes thank you yes yes—

As we walked back to the street, my mother congratulated herself on finding, after so many wrong turns and dead ends, a true doctor, and not only a doctor, but a fine human being as well.

—here is what you what you call a gentleman—

To celebrate, we bought chocolate ice cream at the three-booth greasy spoon on the other side of Dr. Frankel's office. Our waitress spoke only French, and my mother licked an imaginary cone and repeated *chocolate, chocolate,* which she assumed was a universal term. My mother was resourceful, if nothing else.

At home, my mother gave Bubby, who listened or did not listen, heard or did not hear, understood or did not understand, her version of our deliverance.

—such a gentleman such a gentleman—

My mother decided, after this happy result, that my body didn't require further medical attention. Instead, under the influence of her card-playing friends, she became preoccupied with my mental health.

Fanya was devoted to cards, and every Wednesday night several of her friends invaded our flat, eager to gamble and dispense advice. Sitting in the kitchen, I had a clear view of the living room, where the card table was set up. Since my mother and her friends were too poor to risk the loss of a few dollars, they gambled with sunflower seeds. The seeds, along with Mrs. Blustein's bare feet (she suffered from "heat attacks") and

Mrs. Kaplan's kerchief, tied peasant-style under her chin (in case of lice), gave the scene a rural charm. With a box of soda crackers by my side and my legs resting on two chairs, I watched these social gatherings and wrote down slivers of conversation, which I transcribed into imperfect haikus. *Ai these varicose / the lettuce wrap in a cloth / on Tuesdays is best.*

Other entertainments included my mother's transformation into Greta Garbo. Eyelashes sticky, breasts heaving up and down under a dress that drew its inspiration from a wedding cake, my mother was not usually demure. When confronted with a hand of cards, however, she fell silent: not a word, not a syllable. Instead, her eyebrows and the corners of her mouth expressed the intensity of her insights, the wry amusement aroused by her opponents' benighted moves. When it came to gin rummy, Fanya Levitsky was nobody's fool.

It was during one of these visits that my mother's defeated friends suddenly latched on to me. Whoever heard of a child locking herself in the bathroom in order to sing Harry Belafonte songs at the top of her lungs? And what about my troubles at school—my poor grades, my detentions? Why not schedule a consultation with Dr. Vera Moore? She completely cured the Rothman boy. Of course, she had a waiting list, but in some cases (the women looked at one another knowingly), she took patients right away.

My mother nodded thoughtfully. Yes, they certainly had a point, these friends of hers.

My sanity became the new topic of conversation. Was I suffering from a Freudian complex, a trauma, maybe even a split personality?

—what can I do with my education stopped in the middle—

After a few days of deliberation, my mother phoned Dr. Moore, and three days later, at seven in the evening, we set out for the medical building on Decelles Street. Dr. Moore had extended her office hours for us, just as my mother's friends had predicted.

The building on Decelles was by now a familiar destination; we were well acquainted with the large round elevator buttons, the silent hallways, the oracular names on the frosted-glass door panels: Goldstein, Greenberg, de Vries. But we'd never seen anything like Vera Moore's waiting room, in this building or anywhere else. You wanted to be early, if you were going to wait in a room like this one: chairs upholstered in velvet, framed paintings, a Persian carpet, a rolltop desk equipped with paper and pastels. I settled into one of the chairs and gazed at a watercolour of imaginary creatures resting in a cool, blue forest. Half-eagle, half-lion. Half-lizard, half-butterfly.

Following our success with Dr. Frankel, I associated medical brilliance with starker settings, but maybe it was the peculiarity of the room that boded well. I began to feel drowsy; I wanted to curl up on the carpet and shut my eyes.

Dr. Moore opened her office door and said, "Maya?"

I hurried towards her, leaving my mother alone in the velvet armchair, her stiff black alligator purse balanced precariously on her lap. I felt important as I entered the secret office. I imagined that I belonged to an indeterminate species, here to be observed and properly classified—maybe I, too, was a hybrid: part girl, part something else. I think I almost believed that Vera Moore had supernatural powers. Not spectacular powers, maybe, but minor ones, like being able to guess the contents of your fridge, or what page you were at in the book you were reading.

It may have been Dr. Moore's presence rather than her profession that made her seem clairvoyant. She was majestic, and her voice was soft and certain, as if she harboured many unspoken thoughts, clever and amusing thoughts that would require intricate elucidation. Yet at the same time there seemed to be a towering shadow by her side, casting its gloom on her alone. You couldn't see the shadow, but you could see its effect on Dr. Moore: it slowed her down, gave an odd pliancy to her face.

"Would you like to sit here?" she asked me. She placed her fragile, veined hand on a rotating globe chair upholstered in orange corduroy—like a little house, if you were Thumbelina and lived in a walnut shell. They used to be common, those chairs, though I never see them any more.

"Okay," I said, arranging myself inside the corduroy cocoon. Dr. Moore sat facing me. Between us, on a low table, she'd arranged several polished stones and mineral samples, as well as a wooden egg made of intersecting geometrical pieces. You were supposed to figure out how to take the egg apart and then put it back together. I couldn't be bothered with that sort of puzzle, but I liked the smooth polished wood, and I reached out for it.

"So, why are you here?" Dr. Moore asked, gazing straight at me. Her clear blue eyes made me think of Heidi—snowy Alps under blue skies, wheelchairs, miracles. Dr. Moore had naturally frizzy hair which she'd gathered into a bun; the loose strands were held in place by marbled combs, the kind you saw in drugstores. Her hair resisted both the bun and the combs, and lone filaments escaped in all directions. Try conditioner, I thought.

"My mother brought me."

"Do you know why?"

I swivelled my chair gently from side to side. "She likes doctors."

"Oh?"

"She likes them, but she also doesn't like them."

"She has mixed feelings?"

"Yes. She wants them to help us, but when they don't find anything, she hates them. She says they're just waiting to see who will die first."

"Really!"

"Everything's multiplied for my mother," I explained. "You might see one rock here, on the table." I pointed to the mineral samples. "My mother will see a million rocks. And believe me, she'll have something to say about each one."

Dr. Moore smiled, and I noticed that she had dimples, though they were partly lost inside the soft, unhappy brackets of her smile.

"And you, Maya? Do you listen when she goes on and on?"

I shook my head and said triumphantly, "That's the whole point."

"It's tiring for you?"

"Not really tiring. It's just … more like boring. The same thing, over and over. Over and over. 'Yossi, Yossi—Yossi—'" I mimicked my mother. "That's my father. She likes to say his name."

"Yes, she told me about him."

"She tells everyone."

"If you could change her, would you change what she says, or how much she says?"

I liked the question. "It's what she says. I don't mind that she talks a lot. Sometimes she's funny, and then it's okay."

"And when she's not funny?"

"Oh, who cares!" I rotated the chair, a full circle this time, and passed the wooden puzzle from hand to hand. Neither of us spoke for a few minutes. I liked Dr. Moore's unhurried pace, her equanimity. "She's just a fake," I said.

"She's putting on an act?"

"I can't explain. She doesn't do it on purpose."

"What about school?"

"I'm a problem student," I said proudly.

She smiled again. "Are you?"

"Yes. Apart from when I have Miss d'Arcy. She used to be a nun, I think. Now she teaches Geography. She's nice."

"And when teachers aren't nice, you refuse to be afraid."

"That's right! Why should I be afraid?"

"What about friends?"

"She has her friends. They play cards."

"I meant your friends."

"Oh. I don't have any real friends. Like that song, sometimes I feel like a motherless child."

"Maybe sometimes you *wish* you were a motherless child!" she said playfully.

"No, it's bad enough being fatherless."

"I think your mother said you just had a birthday?"

"Yes, two weeks ago. I turned twelve."

"And how did you celebrate?"

"Just the usual. Cake, candles, with one for good luck. My mother got me art postcards from the museum. I like art."

"Do you?"

"I like paintings that make you wonder what the story is. I like the watercolour in your waiting room."

"What's the story there?"

"Half one thing, half something else."

She nodded. "Well, Maya. I'll tell you what I think. Do you want to hear?"

"Oh, yes. Yes, I do."

"Here's what I think. I think your mother is presenting events in a very confusing way. That's how she copes. I don't know your mother, or how she thinks. I'm guessing that a part of her is living in the past, in the war. So you have two mothers. One is here, and one is *there*."

"Just my luck," I said, wondering how much Dr. Moore knew about *there*.

This time her smile was accompanied by a small, light laugh, and I joined in. She was easy to please.

"Maybe we can work on ways to make things easier for you."

"Okay."

"I'll talk to your mother."

I nodded, though I wasn't optimistic—and I was right: our first meeting with Vera Moore was also our last. In a separate conversation Dr. Moore offended my mother, and she became, in my mother's repertoire, Dr. Know-It-All or That Czech Woman.

And possibly in defiance of Dr. Know-It-All, my mother decided that I was a paragon of mental health after all. When her

card-playing friends came to our house that Wednesday, she
summoned me for display.

—*mamaleh come here come I want to show you to my friends*—

I stood at the entrance to the living room and Bubby lurked
behind me with a towel. I took the towel from her and, impersonating Lawrence of Arabia, draped it on my head. My mother burst
out laughing.

—*you see you see what a flower I have*—

And now, two years later, here I was, on Dr. Know-It-All's
doorstep. Vera Moore was Patrick's mother.

It wasn't so unusual, in fact, that sort of interconnection.
Suspicions ran high among our parents: even in Canada, who
could you trust, really? Only someone who had passed the test of
multiple customers, someone who *came recommended*. And so we
all ended up with the same optometrists and dry cleaners, the same
music teachers and psychiatrists.

For a second I didn't know why Patrick's mother seemed
familiar. Then I remembered Dr. Moore's penetrating blue eyes,
the sense she gave you that she knew interesting things which
would be difficult to explain, though she was willing to try. She
recognized me as well—my height and sprawling red hair gave me
away. She was puzzled by our appearance on her doorstep, but she
smiled with tentative cordiality. Maybe she thought we were
selling Girl Guide cookies. "Yes, can I help you?"

"I'm Rosie Michaeli—you know, the piano teacher's daughter.
And this is Maya. Is Patrick here?"

I could see Patrick's mother trying to hide her delight. Patrick had
visitors—and girls! "Please, come in," she said, furtively observing
us. "I'll let him know you're here." She shut both the outside door
and the vestibule door; she was eager to see the visit consummated.
Abraham and God's messengers. Lot and the two angels.

She lifted the receiver of a push-button phone and dialled.
Rosie and I exchanged glances, not only because Patrick had his
own line but because we'd never seen a push-button phone before.

"Patrick? You have guests ... yes, they've asked for you ... yes, I'm sure."

I'd never heard anyone address their child, or any family member, that way—with a kind of placid formality, a carefully rationed readiness to please, as if Patrick were a distinguished guest who'd come to dinner.

We hung our coats on wooden hangers. From the end of the hallway, hands in pockets, Patrick slouched towards us.

"Oh, hi," he said. "Would you like to come up?"

He was struggling. The problem, I gathered, was that he believed in camaraderie in principle, but the principle was at odds with his personality.

"We'd love to," Rosie answered.

Blindly, as if walking through a cave or tunnel, Patrick led us past gleaming surfaces, sandstone sculptures, an indoor fountain, humid clay pots of cyclamen on blue-and-orange ceramic tiles. *This is the house that Vera built*: a house made of marble and polished wood, satin and silk, a house designed for creature comforts. Yet somehow it all fell flat. Dr. Moore had courageously chosen the furniture, the tiles, the plants, but the end result was someone else's set—a set that was as recalcitrant in its way as the Michaeli home, and as disjointed.

We followed Patrick to the kitchen, where, to our confusion, he walked into a pantry. There was an unpainted wooden door inside, camouflaged by shelves of assorted jars and tin boxes. Patrick opened the door and disappeared up a narrow, unlit stairwell. Once upon a time, these must have been the back stairs to the maids' quarters. Rosie and I held on to the walls as we climbed up after him. "What is this, the secret lair of the Marquis de Sade?" I asked.

"Oh, is it too dark for you?"

"No, no, we love not being able to see two inches ahead of us."

"Maya's a riot," Rosie said, protective of both me and Patrick.

"Sorry. Here ..." He pushed open a door at the top of the staircase and a shaft of light filtered down on us. Like his mother, who

had shut both entrance doors to prevent us from escaping, Patrick
needed two barricades to prevent people from entering.

We stepped into the kitchen of an attic apartment. There was
no foyer or hallway, and the rooms opened onto one another like
cars in a train: kitchen, bedroom, living room—not ahead of us,
but to our right.

The kitchen was in a farcical state of disarray. The floor was
strewn with several strata of empty takeout containers, muddy
pizza flyers, alleyway bottles, discarded cigarette packs. There were
only two items of furniture in the room other than the fridge: a
glass-topped table and an exceptionally ugly high-backed chrome
and vinyl chair, its yellowish brown padding tacked into place by
rows of metal studs. Tall mounds of coagulated coins rose from the
table like hills in an architect's table model; no doubt they'd come
into being by way of the big bang, or little clink, of the male
pocket-emptying ritual.

"I see you're really into housekeeping," I said. "But then, you
don't have Bubby Miriam to tidy up."

Rosie smiled. She understood that I was deliberately trespassing,
understood that the preliminary platitudes which served as safety
nets for most people made Patrick nervous. The only solution was
to charge through intimacy as if through some cosmic black hole
and emerge on the other side. A foreboding of what might come
to pass was replaced by the fiction that everything had already
taken place.

"Is it that bad?" He looked around dubiously.

"You know, I don't think I've ever seen a chair this ugly," I said.
"You could have nightmares about a chair like this."

Patrick gazed at the chair as though he were noticing it for the
first time.

"Where did you find it?" I asked.

"The builders left it behind. Some builders came to change the
windows or something ... I don't see what's wrong with it."

"Liar," I said, and Patrick laughed. A voiceless, breathy sort of chugging sound, but unmistakably a laugh.

Forging a path through the trash on the floor, I entered Patrick's bedroom. A piece of black fabric, cut at a slant and reverting to threads along the sides, had been fastened with thumbtacks to the window frame, and there was also, I realized, a dog with long fleecy ears on the bed, partly concealed by the rumpled blankets. The dog peered at us with expressive eyes.

The bedroom was in the same state as the kitchen. The bed didn't have a headboard, and I noticed a dark patch on the wall where Patrick presumably leaned his head while reading. The desk looked like a rummage-sale table à la Miss Havisham: under a coating of dust lay a ship in a bottle, the Eiffel Tower in a snow globe, a pair of Buddy Holly glasses, a broken radio, a backgammon set, a model airplane, and I can't remember what else. The only articles apparently in commission were a harmonica and a bottle of painkillers. The bottle had been tucked inside the airplane, on the pilot's seat.

"Codeine ..." I examined the pills. "I take codeine for migraines. Sort of migraines—I don't know exactly what they are. Is that why you have them?"

"No—those are from when I fell off my bike and bashed my knee."

"How did you fall?" Rosie asked.

"A car backed into me."

"How awful!"

"Yes, very awful," Patrick echoed satirically, detaching himself from everything—the accident, the pain, Rosie's commiseration.

"I see you have two pillows," I said. "You have girls up here?"

"No, no ... well, once ..."

"Once, you had a girlfriend, or once, someone came here?"

"Once, someone came here. She got locked out of her apartment ..."

"Who was she?"

"Comrade Cynthia," he said. "She hates me now."

"Comrade Cynthia! What are you, some sort of communist?"

"Yeah, I'm a Party member." His tone was skeptical, though whether he was being skeptical about himself or the Party, or both, I couldn't tell.

"Why does Comrade Cynthia hate you?" I asked.

"Oh, it's a long, humiliating story."

"And what about this harmonica, do you play?"

"Not really ... but Woofie likes the sound, he sings along. One of the few things he still does, other than eat and sleep. Isn't that right, Woofie?" And without warning, he stepped into another persona. He stroked Woofie, murmured endearments without a hint of inhibition. Then it was over, and he was flung back like the rebel angels into the thorny human world. He rose from the bed and suggested we move to the living room.

Patrick's living room was an extension not of the unholy mess but of the soulful cuddle with Woofie. Here, in who knew what surge of duty and hope, he'd assembled a sofa with wooden armrests, two matching armchairs, a braided rug, bookcases, a stereo system, and, near the window, three thriving floor plants with enormous jungle leaves. These gestures, like the cuddle, modified but did not entirely negate the general atmosphere of edgy, fatalistic solitude.

"Who chose this furniture?" I asked.

"I guess I did."

"That's kind of heartbreaking," I said.

"Very heartbreaking. What can I get you to drink? Coffee— something stronger? Vodka?"

Rosie and I burst into childish laughter, which made Rosie snort accidentally, which made us laugh even harder. I wasn't allowed to drink coffee at home, and our Friday-night bottle of wine usually lasted several weeks. There was a prehistoric bottle of whisky under the sink at Rosie's; we once poured a little into a glass, tasted a drop, and yelped hilariously as we spit it out.

"What is it?" Patrick asked.

"I'll have what you're having," I said.

"Are you sure? I'm having vodka. I could make you a screw-driver."

"What's that?"

"Vodka and orange juice."

"Why do drinks have such weird names?" I asked him.

"Do they?"

"Any sort of juice or cola for me, please," Rosie said.

"What was so funny? Why were you laughing just now?"

"We were remembering when we tried some whisky. We don't usually drink," I said. "We're too young."

"You don't have to. I mean … if you don't want to."

"Patrick! Don't drive us crazy."

Rosie handed him the plastic bag we'd brought with us. "By the way, you left your stuff at Daddy's."

"In case you're wondering why we're here," I added.

"Oh … thanks." He dropped the bag carelessly on the floor and left in search of drinks. He returned a few minutes later with a bottle of vodka, a jug of vodka and orange juice, a carton of pear juice, and three somewhat greasy glasses.

Patrick sat on the sofa, and Rosie and I settled into the armchairs. He poured pear juice into one glass, the vodka and orange juice mix into another. "'I had a little nut tree, nothing would it bear,'" Rosie sang softly. "'But a silver nutmeg and a golden pear.'"

Patrick downed his vodka, which he was drinking straight, in one shot.

"That was fast," I said.

My strategy of trashing small talk was working, as was the vodka: Patrick smiled and a measure of strain moved away, improving his appearance. His smile was unexpectedly sweet, a smile left over from childhood, trusting and happy. "Sorry about the mess. I'm not used to guests," he said.

"Why?" I asked. "Why don't you have more friends?"

"I don't like situations I can't control."

"'I who abandon what I can't control, first the people I know, eventually my own soul.'" I quoted. I swirled my vodka and orange juice; I was finding it difficult to overlook the greasy residue on the rim.

"Well, you have nothing to fear from us!" Rosie assured him.

"Yes, we're very ordinary," I said. "How about some music?"

"Sure." Patrick sprang to his feet, glad to have a task. "Anything in particular?"

"You choose."

He dropped a Santana album into place, and Rosie curled up in a fetal position and shut her eyes, lost in the music. Patrick was the first person I'd come across who was completely immune to Rosie; he was immune to everyone. She accepted his self-imposed quarantine, but I didn't. I wanted to nudge a few nuggets of sociability out of him. There was something about Patrick that made it seem worth the trouble: a talent for humanity, for humour—all that trapped brilliance. You felt it would come bounding out if you could only tap into it somehow, if you could free him from whatever it was that was binding him to his Promethean rock.

"I see you read a lot," I said, scanning the crammed bookshelves.

"Oh no, I hardly read anything."

"You're just saying that. You're just saying that so no one can accuse you of anything."

Patrick grinned. "No, no, I really don't read much. I hardly read at all."

I picked up a paperback from the side table. "*The Harrad Experiment.* I've seen this somewhere. Is it good?"

"I didn't finish it."

"Why?"

"I got bored."

"Then I won't borrow it."

"No, no, take it—that's just my opinion."

"If you hated it, why would I like it?"

"Good point."

Close to my feet, on the braided rug, a newspaper was folded to the story of the Kent State shootings. Ordinary students gunned down, just like that. "Sick, sick, sick," I fumed. "What is wrong with that country?"

"As opposed to which country, exactly?" Patrick asked, hoping for a political debate.

But I only shrugged. "If you think about everything, you might as well kill yourself … Hey, I almost forgot. I know your mother. You won't believe this—I saw her once. As a patient, I mean—when I was twelve. My mother decided I needed a shrink. But we never went back, after that one visit. She's Czech, isn't she?"

"Yes."

"Is Czechoslovakia still around?" I wondered.

"What?!"

"Well, you know how countries keep changing."

Patrick was amused. "Yes, remarkable as it may seem, Czechoslovakia is still around."

"Well, you never know."

"That's right," he nodded. "You never do know. Here today, gone tomorrow."

Rosie, who had been half-listening to our conversation, roused herself from the Santana spell. "Was your mother also in the camps?" she asked.

"I guess."

"Which one?"

"I don't know. She never talks about it."

"Poor her! Was that where she met your father?"

"My father isn't even Jewish. He doesn't live with us."

"Oh! That's too bad … Where does he live?"

"Who knows? Japan, India, Australia … he could be anywhere. He travels around."

"On business?" I asked.

"On a spiritual quest," Patrick said, carefully modulating his tone so it covered all bases—scorn, tolerance, indifference.

"How come you live up here?" I asked.

"I don't know, I just do."

"When did you start?"

"I guess I was eight or nine."

"Eight or nine—what were you, Quasimodo or something?"

"I just wanted to live here. I asked Mr. Davies—he's the cook—to help me carry the bed up. I was already spending a lot of time here, playing ..."

"Playing! Human after all—what did you play?"

"Oh, the usual, you know. Let's see, I had a train set." He leaned his head back on the sofa; he was on his third shot of vodka. "And cars, and make-believe."

"Make-believe! That's so adorable, Patrick."

"I used to pretend I was a teacher," Rosie said. "My stuffed animals were the pupils. Then I was a nurse. Not too original!"

"I imagined I was Harry Belafonte's missing daughter," I said. "You know, the one he deserted in Kingston Town. I thought she was his daughter, for some reason, and I imagined I was her, and he was going to come get me. Or else Tintin would, or else Nancy Drew. Your turn, Patrick."

"Me? Oh, I don't know, it's a blur."

"How can your childhood be a blur already? It was only last year practically. Have you been dropping acid every day or what?"

"No, it's just—I don't think about it. I never think about it. But ... I liked to pretend I was Robinson Crusoe or Long John Silver."

"Long John Silver! Wasn't he the evil pirate? Weren't you supposed to identify with the boy?"

"The boy was a wimp."

Rosie and I laughed, and I remembered what she'd told me about Patrick's school. "Do you go to a scary high school?" I asked.

"Scary? I'm at St. George's. We just sit around and moan about our existential crises. I'm not getting an education," he added, switching to the comically aggrieved mode that served as a substitute for trust.

"I thought you were in one of those fascist boys' schools ..."

The hypodermic pulse of Santana's guitar seemed to tilt the prints on the walls—Henri Rousseau's lunar sleeping gypsy, the oddly suspended nude in Gauguin's *The Seed of the Areoi*, a stupid Malevich (two squares on white from his why-bother period)— and I felt as if I really had been drinking. I examined Patrick. He hid behind his uncombed hair, his round glasses, his irritable resignation, but he had a faintly flushed complexion that made him look healthy despite his underground, or rather garret, style. He'd inherited his mother's intelligent, deep-set eyes, her high forehead.

"Did you say you had a cook?" I asked.

"My mother has a cook."

"He lives here?"

"Yeah, in the basement."

"How come? How come you have a cook? Does your mother have parties and things?"

"No, he cooks for her. She's into gourmet food." He didn't want to talk about Mr. Davies.

"Cool."

"What was she like, my mother? When you saw her?" Patrick asked with sudden intensity, as if taking advantage of a rare opportunity, as if he'd been wondering for years.

"She was okay—I liked her. I didn't think she could help me, though, so I didn't mind, really, when my mother said we weren't going back. My mother's a basket case."

"Why did she take you to a psychiatrist in the first place?" Rosie asked.

"Oh, who knows? She's completely crazy herself. '*Mamaleh mamaleh* my heart my soul my life—'" I mimicked, my voice tremulous with agitation and despair.

Patrick made several attempts to restrain himself, but he lost the battle, and his body shook uncontrollably as he laughed his soundless, breathy laugh. I was all too familiar with the phenomenon of laughter that has a mind of its own. I'd experienced several attacks myself—most recently during an amateur production of *Mother Courage*. On one memorable occasion a fit came over me in Mr. Lurie's class. The fearsome Mr. Lurie was, for the first time ever, at a loss. He stood uncertainly behind the front desk, his stern facade disintegrating into self-consciousness and sexual discomfort. "Perhaps you had better leave the room and take a drink of water, Miss Levitsky," he said, but the words lacked his usual authority.

Despite the one-time bonus of seeing Mr. Lurie transformed into Dr. Jekyll, I dreaded these outbursts, and I hoped Patrick would be able to tell that Rosie and I didn't mind.

"Her mother's a darling, really," said Rosie.

"Darling! I'll do my mother and you judge whether she's a darling."

I had no difficulty reproducing my mother's unique blend of melodrama, railing, and general lunacy. I jumped up and began flying across the room, flailing my arms and commenting haphazardly on the plants, the view from the window, the house, the absent cook, Patrick's mother: "'That Czech woman her her I know the type, with her money, from me everything they took, at the hotel, the hotel with the teapots—'" I was as unstoppable as she was.

I was successful, at least, in driving away Patrick's laughter; he was now staring at me in horror. "My God, how do you manage?"

"Well, it would be worse for you," I told him. "I say whatever I want."

"What's the hotel thing about?" Rosie asked.

"Who knows? I think she was working at some hotel, and then something went wrong. She had to pretend to be a puppet or something, or someone else did—oh, who cares! Now I'll do

Rosie's father." I glanced at Rosie to see whether she had any objections. She extended her hand in a be-my-guest gesture.

She was right, of course, to trust me: I knew that Mr. Michaeli was not as hardy as my mother. Nor did I want to recreate his eclipsed view of the world, his shadow being. I meant to aim my parody—if you could call it that—only at his unnerving gifts.

"Here," I said. "Take this, here." I placed a few books on Patrick's lap. "And this, and this. Take this, here, and take also this." Spurred by the urgings of Santana, I began to accelerate, hunting more and more frenetically for objects to pile onto Patrick's lap, and when there was no longer room on his lap, then next to him on the sofa. I gathered ashtrays, pens, magazines, paper clips, the cumbersome German-English dictionary with *Der Spiegel* inserted inside, I emptied my pockets, poured out the contents of my fringed shoulder bag, and threw the shoulder bag itself at him, and Rosie smiled and Patrick said, "Okay, okay, I get the point," but he was enjoying himself, and then there was nothing left to impose on him, so I pulled off my shoes and socks and added them to the heap and removed my wide leather belt and my jeans and blue plaid lumber jacket and finally my underwear until I was standing in the room as naked as a Woodstock bather and I stopped and giggled. Patrick gazed at me complacently, his clever, deep-set eyes absorbing with amusement five feet, eleven inches of white freckled skin.

There was a knock on the door to the apartment, followed by Dr. Moore's brave, hesitant voice. "Patrick?"

Patrick sighed and made his way to the kitchen while I got back into my clothes. Through the closed door he said, "Yes?" The antagonism in his voice startled us.

"Would you like some snacks? I brought up a small tray."

Patrick seemed to sag, somehow, as he opened the door. His mother remained on the stairs, and though I couldn't see her from where I was standing, I could see Patrick. He stared at his mother with what looked like hatred. "We don't need anything," he said, and his hostility was all the more potent for being contained—like bad guys in old movies who spoke between their teeth. Seething anger: you don't know its limits because the limits are kept hidden.

Dr. Moore did her best to sidestep him. "Well, then, if you change your mind, I'll leave the tray here."

"We really don't want anything."

Dr. Moore laughed uneasily and we heard her footsteps fading away on the stairs.

I don't think Rosie had ever witnessed anything quite like this, and she was on the verge of tears. I said, "That was mean."

But now I'd gone too far. Patrick's face darkened and he turned on me. "You don't say," he replied, straight out of the Ice Age, or maybe the Cold War.

"Did something happen between you?" Rosie's voice had turned mournful. She could have been wandering through the stormy heath, she could have been asking, *Is man no more than this?*

"How do you mean?" It was Rosie's turn to be shoved to the corner of the ring.

She nodded sadly. Even she knew that at times there was nothing to be done.

"'Li-la-li,'" I sang. Simon and Garfunkel's "The Boxer" had come out the previous year, and I couldn't get enough of it. "'Li-la-li li li li li li, li-la-li.'" Rosie joined in, and we sang the entire song together. If anyone had ever harboured the memory of each blow that had struck him, it was Patrick.

"We can't really stay to eat anyhow," Rosie said. "I have to go home. But please come to my party."

"I don't like parties." The fight was over. Patrick had flopped back on the sofa as listlessly as a dying hero in the last act of a tragedy. He rubbed his eyes beneath his glasses.

"You'd like my party. I have one every Saturday night, you can come any time."

"You wouldn't have to talk to anyone," I assured him. "I'd guard you."

"I'm really not into parties … Sorry you didn't like the vodka." He'd noticed my untouched drink. Rosie had politely finished her pear juice, but I'd set my own glass aside.

"No, I'm sorry. I'm just being neurotic. I wasted your vodka—unless you drink it."

"I've had more than enough," Patrick said, staggering a little as he rose. "I'd offer you a lift—"

"We'll be okay. Will you?"

"Sorry, I shouldn't have had so much to drink. Social situations make me tense."

The tray of delicacies—brie, French bread, chocolate mousse in three fluted dessert glasses—was sitting on the floor at the top of the stairs. I knelt down and wrapped two slices of bread and a chunk of cheese in a napkin, slid them into my shoulder bag; this way I'd be able to thank Dr. Moore for the food if we saw her on the way out. I handed Rosie one of the dessert glasses, and the two of us wolfed down the mousse. It was my first chocolate mousse experience, and the start of a lifelong, exacting addiction.

But we didn't run into Dr. Moore on the way to the front door. As we pulled our coats out of the closet, Rosie asked Patrick, "Do you have any brothers or sisters?"

"I have a brother," he replied. "He doesn't live here any more. He's in California."

"How nice! What's his name?"

"Tony."

"You don't have very Jewish names," I said.

"We're only barely Jewish."

"I wish I had a brother!" Rosie cried out, and she threw her arms around Patrick and held him tightly, as if he were in danger of falling off a cliff and only she could save him.

Patrick didn't know what to do with himself. Then he smiled his sweet, childhood smile. But he didn't come to Rosie's party. He wasn't ready to step out of his Robinson Crusoe seclusion, and two years passed before we saw him again.

Ah, it's a stormy day today, a blizzard is raging, and Sailor, who has forgotten that he's a St. Bernard, refuses to go out for his walk. He's afraid of wind in general; wind combined with snow he considers simply an insult. I've trained him to use a grated litter box in the backroom instead.

Trained is not the right word. I simply told him what to do. Sailor understands everything I tell him. I need only say, with explanatory gestures, "Sailor, you can lie on the wool blanket, but not on the linen," and he'll never go near linen again. I can even say, "This blanket is fine, but not that one." He was mistreated by his first owners, and I think he developed this penchant for instant obedience in order to survive, poor thing. At least he's happy now. I admit that I spoil him, and for every blanket I ask him not to lie on, he has several requests of his own. "Your wish is my command," I rumble at him, and he wags his tail.

Blizzard or no blizzard, Sororité won't be deserted tonight. I was dragged to Sororité one time in the middle of a snowstorm, and I discovered that we're a hardy species, we bar addicts. The person dragging me was Carmen, a woman from Texas who was staying in the empty flat for a few weeks. She was a chef, and good company—lively, droll, her voice strong and fearless as she commented, amused and amusing, on everything around her. She had a rice pudding recipe that was immeasurably better than the one I'd been content with until then, and I went into a rice pudding craze when she was here. I still use her recipe, though it's not quite the same as when she made it. It was Carmen who persuaded me to brave bad weather one stormy Friday night, and when against all odds and surmounting challenges worthy of Shackleton we made it to Sororité, we found the place packed.

Occasionally I toy with the idea of severing the Sororité umbilical cord. Occasionally I ask myself why I go. For the past eight months—since Tyen left—I haven't met anyone I particularly wanted to invite home. Though, let's face it, it's been years since I met anyone I particularly wanted to invite home. I invited them anyhow; I invited them, then hoped they'd leave. That semicolon after "anyhow" is probably the most conveniently nebulous bit of punctuation I've ever used—a semicolon that serves to sweep over the colossal wreck of my own monument to boundlessness.

I blame my house. It has a life of its own and refuses to accommodate guests. Tyen was a rare exception.

1971

The army rolled into our city during the October Crisis of 1970; the media managed to frighten outsiders, but we were amused by the sight of goofy-looking soldiers in tanks as we made our way to school. Joshua and Peter, who were in the grade above us at Eden, were arrested at a French bookstore when an altercation broke out between police and two angry customers, and they spent the night in jail. They were released the next day, and an account of their adventure provided a full day's entertainment. Reassured by her card-playing friends that she had nothing to fear—"What can you do, there are always a few troublemakers"—even Fanya refrained from issuing doomsday forecasts.

Kidnapping was one thing, but when the troublemakers strangled their hostage, they lost whatever public sympathy they'd had. Three months later the sad, brief drama had been replaced by the drama of political debate and brutal weather. We were in the clutches of a deep freeze.

Temperatures fell and remained locked in the penal zone, day after miserable day. Cars turned to metal ice in the middle of the road and had to be abandoned where they stood because there weren't enough tow tucks to rescue them all. Hell really was freezing over, the dreaded Mr. Lurie joked dryly. Extreme weather seemed to cheer him up.

In January, in the midst of this meteorological assault, I turned fifteen. I blew out a lone candle on a cinnamon cake, and Bubby handed me the colour-blended wool scarf she'd been knitting all week. To spare my mother a polar expedition, I bought myself the gift I would have asked for: A Treasury of Art Masterpieces.

Each morning I defiantly prepared for battle by layering my clothes: undershirt, T-shirt, vest, jeans, school dress, sweater, scarf, winter headband, hat, hooded coat, gloves under mitts. I felt like a mummy in a horror movie as I lumbered to school—three blocks to the bus stop, the long wait for the bus, then another two blocks to the steaming foyer of Eden. The school reeked of something— no one could figure out what it was. Old bananas, milk gone bad, some small, trapped animal decomposing? The vents were being checked out, but so far the vent-men hadn't found anything. I opened my locker, peeled off my clothes, and waited for my extremities to thaw out.

It was on one of these arctic mornings, as I was warming up, that the high school secretary asked me to deliver a file to the elementary side. My height, and possibly the fact that I was an outsider who had made a valiant effort to get into Eden, made me a prime candidate for small errands.

The corridors of the elementary school always resurrected, for an electrifying second or two, my first time there—Mr. Lewis, Rosie's locker, the towers of books in the supply closet. Welcome to the Promised Land.

At first I was drawn merely by curiosity to the noise coming from one of the classrooms. I peeked in through the little square window at the top of the door and saw Mr. Michaeli. He was standing behind the desk, grinning helplessly and shielding his face with his arm.

But the grin was not a grin; it was a grimace, a mask. And the helplessness was not helplessness but a cadaverous frieze. It was as though he had lost all human traits, even the human trait of surrender, and what remained was someone else's indistinct memory of who he had been.

He was under attack by the children. They threw spitballs and pieces of chalk and paper airplanes at him, they shouted, they pretended to cry. He'd been teaching a song in a minor key, and as they sang they sobbed, wiped their eyes, lay their heads on each other's shoulders and wailed. *By the waters of Babylon, there we sat and wept ...*

I opened the door. Instant silence—amazing how these children can stop and go, like mechanical toys. Mr. Michaeli came towards me with a smile. He had reinhabited his body, more or less, but I found myself unable to detach his approaching figure from the cowering apparition I'd seen through the window. "Maya, hello, hello."

"I was on my way to the office," I said, stumbling on the words.

"Yes, yes, down the hall, on the left."

The children stared at me with wide-eyed innocence from their desks. It was impossible to leave, impossible to stay.

In the washroom, in one of the stalls, the familiar onslaught, a headache of Martian proportions. Once again I was in the worm museum, running down the halls with my mother, seeking an exit, the small worms wriggling under glass globes. I wasn't hallucinating; I knew where I was. The images, however, seemed all too real—like a film you're forced to watch, like something out of *A Clockwork Orange*. The nausea and pain were definitely real, and I moaned.

"Maya?"

I must have been there for a while, because Rosie had come searching for me. She crawled under the door, joined me in the stall.

"I'm sick," I said.

"Daddy told me you looked pale."

"Where is he?"

"In the teachers' room."

"The kids were throwing things at him—" I began, though I'd told myself I wouldn't say anything. But the words tumbled out, toads instead of diamonds.

"Oh, that! Don't worry about that, Maya. He knows what kids are like!"

How did she do it? How did she come by her faultless choreography? Practice, I had to suppose. All those hours, doing the Bachanova … I was the opposite, tripping and slipping. And I couldn't find a way to get untangled.

"I feel really sick," I said.

"I can get you an aspirin from the office."

"It won't help. I need to go home."

"You don't have to worry about Daddy," Rosie said. "He wouldn't want that."

"I don't care, I don't care," I said. "Just get me my coat and stuff, please. I need to go home."

Rosie brought me my things and saw me to the door. It was as if the shadow of an enormous liquorice wing, low and ferocious, had crept over me. Why were buses so sadistically slow in coming, in a city as cold as ours? Decades of incompetent administration, as everyone knew but did nothing about, and we were the ones who suffered. Rush hour was over, which meant nearly an hour at the stop. By the time the bus came, my fingers and toes had undergone the miserable transition from aching to numb, and the heat inside the bus failed to penetrate. I ran the last three blocks to our house, fumbled with the key, and burst inside, limping and crying. Bubby phoned my mother at work, and in her usual tempestuous way my mother rushed home in a taxi. I was already in bed by then.

That very week Mr. Halpern had taught us about 'ir miklat, the city of refuge, where murderers were held for their own safety until they were forgiven or tried. If they killed someone by accident, they had to stay in the 'ir miklat forever—or at least until a High Priest died. That's what I would do: I would stay in my bed forever, safe from the avenging mob. My bed was narrow and not long enough, but Bubby ironed our heavy cotton sheets and remade the beds every five days, and the smooth, sturdy linen that swaddled my naked body was, like all sensuous pleasures, reassuring, consoling.

My mother assumed at first that I was having one of my worm museum episodes. But this was different. The museum had dissolved in the frigid air as I'd waited for the bus, and my headache and nausea had vanished with it. What remained was an absence that seemed narcotic, and all I could imagine wanting, ever, was to sleep.

"Tell everyone I'm not going back to school," I instructed her.

Rosie phoned, Dvora phoned, the principal of the school phoned. My mother was forced to overcome her fear of the ominous rings and take the calls herself. "Say I'm sleeping," I murmured. My thoughts collided like ocean debris swept to shore by the waves—the remains of a shipwreck or a plane crash. The debris would be useful if you were stranded on a desert island. But I had everything I needed, apart from, possibly, a compass.

Who was I before I met Rosie? Who was I now? Though such pseudo-ontological queries were standard currency at the time—a fashion fed by Hermann Hesse's esoteric quests and Castaneda's far-out encounters with the all-knowing Mexican shaman, Don Juan—my view of myself had never been problematic. I was Maya: tall, pale, and freckled, feet as long as a man's, arms that forgot to stop growing, breasts that forgot to start growing.

Now the variables had shifted. Something new and threatening hovered at the edges, always at the edges. I was tired.

I wanted my father—I longed for him. I was used to thinking of my father in terms of my mother's requiem, recited not as a plea to the gods but as a reminder of their malevolence. Now, for the first time, I put in a claim. It was possible, after all, to uproot my father from Fanya's personal narrative; I'd lost him too. And though I didn't know what he looked like, I had an image in my mind so particular that I wondered whether it had travelled in some paranormal way from my mother's brain to mine.

The story of my parents' courtship was the only one of my mother's stock pieces that had a beginning, middle, and end, and the only one I enjoyed hearing. My parents had run into each other on the ship that was carrying them to Canada, or, more accurately, my mother had run into Josef, my ailing father. His lungs had been damaged in the war by the deadly fumes of a chemical plant—*some they kept alive to do work*—my mother veered for a few minutes into *there* before returning to the ecstatic reunion. She recognized my father at once; he was sitting on a folding chair with a blanket over his shoulders, and she flung herself on him.

They'd grown up in the same neighbourhood, had gone to the same school, and eventually performed together in a cabaret. Though Josef was three years older than my mother, she knew him well, was in fact in love with him, as were, she boasted, all the girls. It wasn't only him—his entire family was revered. Josef's house was famous for music, theatrics, prophecies. His mother, Miriam, was said to have second sight; his father could play musical pieces backward on his violin and extract coins from ears. They were jolly and generous. Just as some families were cursed, theirs was blessed; everything they touched turned to gold, my mother said, and every one of them was gifted: Josef, his four sisters, even the mysterious Aunt Hilda, who lived with them and was rumoured to be a novelist writing under a pen name.

It was Josef, though, who made my mother's heart stop, and she mooned over him day and night, trying to come up with schemes to make him notice her. And then her prayers were answered: she was chosen to perform in a skit with my father, and rehearsals were to take place at his house. She had found a way into that favoured circle. It was a coveted place, and she was coddled by them all— they brought out the best in you, my mother explained, made you feel deserving. In the skit my father played a dictator and my mother was a peasant; the story had something to do with water from a well and included a kiss. My mother dreamed about that kiss for weeks.

The show, according to my mother, was a great success, and had war not broken out, she and Josef might have married far sooner, for my father, she was certain, had looked forward to that kiss with as much secret longing as she had. And on the night of the cabaret, Miriam had taught her a magic incantation—time and again, during the war, that incantation had saved her life. My mother wanted to teach me the magic chant, but at this point her story buckled under the weight of unmanageable events, and

signifier collided with signified in a spectacular disintegration of
meaning.

The plot recovered with the reappearance of Josef on the deck
of a ship that was taking both my parents to Canada. Here he was,
Josef Levitsky himself, sitting on a folding chair, staring out to sea,
a blanket around his shoulders. A shadow of what he'd been, the
life drained out of him, but alive nevertheless. And still young,
after all; only thirty-two. He'd spent nine years working at a resort
in Sweden—*nine years we wasted not knowing we both were living*—
until the owners decided to relocate to Canada and suggested my
father come with them.

My mother rarely mentioned her post-war years in Europe,
though I gathered she worked as a dressmaker and waited for
missing relatives to show up. At some point Mrs. Blustein came
into her life, initially as a customer, and encouraged my mother to
join her in applying for a Canadian immigration visa. She was
Irma Zimmer back then; her cousins had moved to Montreal years
earlier, and they wrote long letters that made her envious. They
described toilet seats covered in pink fur, long hot showers,
carpets, time-saving kitchen appliances, television … the list went
on and on. It wasn't only a question of comfort: Canada was safer,
it didn't matter if you were Jewish or Zulu, and there would be
more eligible men to choose from. And who knew when Canada
would change its mind about taking in immigrants, and revert to
its wartime policy? My mother and Irma received their visas in
time to board the very ship that was taking my father and his
Swedish friends to Halifax.

For several days my mother stalked my father with reminiscences and, fortunately for me, my father lived long enough to
humour my mother, whose ecstatic agenda included marriage and
a child. She managed to find a rabbi among the travellers. At first
he protested: no, no, he wasn't a rabbi, he believed in nothing, he
hated God. The passengers insisted: everyone remembers you, you
can't hide.

Sullenly, the man followed them to my father's cabin. My father sat on the bed in the tiny cabin and my mother stood beside him, beaming. Ten witnesses had somehow squeezed in as well, or at least peeked in through the doorway. A Hungarian who was a stickler for proper procedure handed my mother a kerchief and a skullcap, for her and for my father. My mother tossed the head coverings back with a laugh, and quickly, to avoid an argument, the rabbi muttered a few words. My father repeated them—and there! My parents were married. A bottle of wine appeared, toasts were made.

Six days later a virus, or maybe food poisoning, struck the ship. The passengers, who had barely recovered from a turbulent storm the previous week, lay in their beds groaning. My father knew this was the end for him and, according to my mother, didn't much care. He'd asked himself why he'd bothered holding on, for as far as he knew, his entire family—parents, sisters, grandparents, cousins, uncles, aunts—had been killed. "It's my time," he told my mother. "I can leave at last. I'm no use anyway."

My mother begged him to take a more optimistic view. Her efforts were futile; in the early hours of the morning, my father died. The rabbi was summoned again. This time he was adamant. Locked himself in his cabin, refused to come out. The Hungarian would have to do: he'd studied to be a rabbi and would have been ordained if not for the war. The required prayers were chanted, and my father, hidden inside sheets, was sent sliding down to the depths of the ocean. His body, weighted down with a heavy object, sank at once. His body, which was neither tall nor short, only devoid of life. *Those are pearls that were his eyes.*

On the third day of my bed-in, nightmares worse than any worm museum struck me like a Passover plague. In the nightmares I was aware that I was dreaming, and because I was dreaming I knew that anything could happen—inanimate objects could speak, the floor could crumble under my feet, a door could open onto a brick wall. Terrifying events lurked ahead, and then the things I was afraid of began to happen—sometimes in wild succession—and I would try desperately to wake up, I would try to locate my body in my bed, in my room, so I could wake, but I couldn't do it, and with every failed effort the terror increased. When I managed, somehow, to emerge from sleep, I couldn't shake off the fear. I kept the lights on, and the radio, I tried to read novels to take my mind off my fear and so I wouldn't fall asleep, but sleep tugged at me; it was as if I'd been drugged, and my eyes grew heavier with every word. As soon as I shut them, the nightmares returned.

My mother's catastrophe meter went haywire. Luckily she had to work, and I had long breaks from her fidgety attentions. When she was away, Bubby took over, brought me meals on a borrowed trolley, straightened my blankets. Then my mother would come home, brimming with new ideas about what might be wrong with me. Possibly I was exhibiting the first stages of anemia, or maybe it was the Generation Gap that had turned me against society. I tried to stay awake as she expounded on her theories, but my nightmares reached out for me like the Hydra, and my mother's voice became another horrifically transformed fragment of the real world.

I'd been in this purgatorial state for a week when Sheila showed up. She didn't bother to call—she simply rang the doorbell and let herself in.

In a single, elegant motion Sheila sank down cross-legged on the carpet next to my bed, retrieved cigarette paper and marijuana from a leather pouch, and began rolling a joint. She was aiming for decadent chic, with her wine-red crushed-velvet skirt, dancer's leotard, and long hair that fell down her face as if she'd just woken up and who knew where or with whom. But her oval face and refined features were more reminiscent of a da Vinci saint than a turned-on, tuned-in dropout.

Sheila took a drag from the joint, and we both peered at the thin, spiralling smoke that promised so much.

"Want?" she offered.

"No, thanks," I said, falling back onto the pillow and pulling the blanket up to my chin. "You know I don't like to get high."

"Remind me why?"

"It's all I need," I said. "Have you met my mother?"

She turned on the radio. Joe Cocker was getting by with a little help from his friends, and from a new arrangement. He started off on his throaty own, and then suddenly there they all were: the organs and guitar and backup singers.

"I saw Joe Cocker," Sheila said. "I was really close to the stage— I could actually see him. It made you realize, Woodstock, how easy it would be to brainwash the masses. Everyone was zonked."

"I'm trying to stay awake," I said. "If I drift off, shake me, okay? I'm having these crazy nightmares. Promise to shake me awake."

"Okay."

"How are you?" I asked her.

"Everyone thinks happiness is so important," she said, shutting her eyes. "People think joy and happiness are important."

My mother knocked on the door, entered with a tray. Kasha and bowties, canned green beans, fried potatoes.

"Thanks, man," Sheila said, and my mother glanced at her hopefully.

—*such a smell here*—she began but thought better of it and retreated. There were rare moments when my mother had tact.

"Another case," Sheila said. "We're surrounded by the living dead. One foot in hell, one foot here. My own parents give me the creeps."

"I always meant to ask you, Sheila," I said. "That leotard—what happens when you have to go to the bathroom?"

"Yeah, it's not too practical."

"You know, I never knew, until last summer, that men had so much hair down there—just like women. I was shocked. I thought women had the hair, men had the floppy appendage."

"How could you not know?"

"How would I? You can't tell from a sculpture, and you don't really get a lot of male nudes in paintings. It's hard to paint a nude guy, for some reason—maybe because you can't hide anything. It's either you see it or you have to cover it."

"Well, how did you find out?" she asked, taking a long drag. "Since obviously not by getting laid."

"I saw *Women in Love*," I said. "Alan Bates running through the forest. I was totally shocked. I still can't believe it."

"Well, congratulations. Now you have information you'll never need, as far as I can tell. What's with you and Rosie, by the way? Are you mad at her?"

"No, of course not."

"She said you wouldn't come to the phone when she called. I thought maybe you had a fight."

"I'm just not in the mood to talk to anyone."

"She's a mess too, you know. She's living in a dream."

"It's a nice dream ... " I said.

"God, you sound wistful. I never heard anyone actually sound wistful. Well, dreams are fine as long as you know where you really are. Does Rosie know? I doubt it."

"She knows. She just doesn't always let on."

"I guess you know her better than I do."

"Sometimes I'm sure I know her, and then suddenly I think I don't know her at all. It's scary, when that happens. When things suddenly change even though they're standing perfectly still."

"Is that what brought this on? Realizing we know fuck all?"

"No, nothing like that ... I wish my father hadn't died."

"Yeah, that's the pits."

"And on the darker side," the radio DJ cooed. Radio announcers had stopped being perky and upbeat. Now they had to sound semiconscious. "Let's have some 'Sympathy for the Devil.'"

"Altamont, what a bummer," Sheila said, shaking her head. "Evil is never good. Evil is evil, good is good." She stretched out on her back and held up a tiny pasta bowtie. "Kasha—dry, absolutely tasteless, with the texture of animal feed. They only ate this back in the shtetl because it was so fucking cheap. And now we're stuck with it!"

"It's not so bad with fried onions," I said, and Sheila came as close as she ever did to laughing—a soft chuckle accompanied by a wary smile.

"Fried onions, the solution to everything. It's the first thing I do," she said, "no matter what I'm cooking—fry an onion."

"I wish I could cook. My mother won't let me. She won't let me do anything—I'm not even allowed to change a light bulb."

"Yeah, well—she lost everything, she wants to make up for it by giving you everything."

"It just makes me feel guilty."

"I wish I had that problem. I wish I had something to feel guilty about. I'm like a slave at home. Listen, Maya, you're going to have to come back sooner or later. You can't lock yourself up here forever."

"Are you going to university?" I asked.

"Why not? Nothing else to do. And you?"

"I'm not going anywhere."

"Well, you don't want to stay in your mother's house forever. Think about it. Think, Maya!"

"What will you study?" I wasn't sure she'd hear me; my voice was so low I could barely hear it myself.

"Education. I want to be a teacher. Long vacations—and, you know, everyone looking up to you, believing whatever you tell them. You're the boss."

"I'm tired. Even chewing is an effort!"

"You can't always get what you want. You're living like a nun here, man. No dope, no sex, what a downer. You should read Rollo May."

"Remember I washed your underwear at camp?"

"God, don't remind me! I was so hung up! The effects of growing up in the Middle Ages. You were the exact opposite. So open and free. Though maybe now we've changed places, is that possible?" She stubbed out her joint, dropped what was left of it into her little pouch, and began picking at the kasha and potatoes. "Aren't you eating?" she asked.

"I'll eat later," I said. "You can have mine, if you're hungry. You're way too thin … What's happening at school?"

"Oh, nothing. Dvora moping over that Carlos guy. Alan said the Dust Bowl was when all the dishes got dusty. The usual."

"I'm not going back to school."

"You have to graduate, you have to go to university. You dig art, why not go into art history? You could work at a museum, or you could teach like me. Spread your wings."

"No, I can't do it."

"Why? You're smart, you're together. So what's the problem?"

"I don't know."

"Listen," Sheila said. "I could show you a couple of things. Do you want me to?"

"Show me what?"

"You know, sex."

"Oh! That's okay, Sheila. Thanks, though. You're very nice to me. I'm just not … I'm not … what's the word? I'm not …"

"Brave?"

"Yes, that's it. I'm not brave enough. I'm going to stay here for now. Sheila?"

"Mmm."

"I've been having such nightmares. I can't get rid of them."

"You mean like Nazis chasing you? I get those all the time."

"No, no, nothing like that. No, it's more like objects start talking—or animals, or babies—and then anything can happen and I can't wake up. I know I'm dreaming, and I try to wake up, I try everything I can think of, but I can't, I'm trapped in the dream. I never knew fear was so hard to take. I don't think I even knew what fear was, really."

"How did your mother survive, do you know? My mother was with her parents and some other people, they all had to strip and dig a big hole and then get inside and be buried alive. And her mother just said to her, run. And so she ran. They shot at her, but they didn't get her, they missed, and she saw a wagon on the road and she climbed under the sacks of barley or whatever. Insane, man. What are the odds? I wouldn't be here if not for a crazy wagon and whoever gave her clothes and a place to hide. They put her in a convent, actually. My father got a job in a work camp, and he was good at it, so they kept him alive. What I don't get is how anyone stayed alive in those conditions. Wouldn't you die of typhoid or whatever right away?"

"Oh, who cares," I said, barely listening.

Sheila shrugged. "Taboo subject. Too gruesome, or something."

"I really don't care," I repeated.

"Fuck this suffering," Sheila said complacently. "Karla's father— he really should be committed. Have you seen the marks on her arms? He completely lost his mind over there. On the other hand, look at Mrs. Adler, dancing when Ephraim gets all the answers right."

"Mrs. Adler …" I said absently, as if I were very old and hadn't seen or thought of her for years. She was determined to be happy, determined to enjoy life. All the pieces of her life were in place, held together by logic and popularity.

"Was Mrs. Adler *there*?" I asked sleepily.

"Yeah, and she came out normal. Normal and happy."

"Normal and happy …"

"I can't wait to get away. Why should I take it all on myself? I have my own life to worry about."

"I'm falling asleep," I muttered. "Don't let me sleep."

With Sheila in the room and the radio playing "Let It Be," I slipped away, and when I woke up, sweating and terrified, Sheila was gone and the radio had been turned off. My mother, whose built-in radar monitored my levels of consciousness, scuffled into the room with a tray of cookies and a glass of milk.

The next day, in what can only have been a gesture of either true love or true desperation, my mother decided to contact Dr. Know-It-All. The answering service informed her that Dr. Moore was out of town.

My mother was skeptical: Dr. Moore was no doubt making up stories to avoid going out in the cold—all very well for some people. Remembering that I'd been to her house, my mother asked me for the address. She sat down at the kitchen table with the telephone book in front of her and ran her finger down the list of Moores. Halfway down she found not Vera's number, which was unlisted, but Patrick's.

The door to my room was open when she phoned, and I heard my mother's end of the conversation—*yes yes Maya's mother who is this*—

I assumed she was talking to Patrick. I got up to pee and brush my teeth, then returned to bed. I hadn't washed in days, but I felt clean; Bubby was now changing my sheets every morning, and twice a day my mother rubbed my back and legs with a warm, wet towel, as if I really were bedridden. I shut my eyes and forgot about Patrick and his mother.

I was half-awakened from sleep by the sound of Anthony's voice. I was sure I was dreaming; so far it was a good dream, but a good dream could skid into nightmare in a matter of seconds. Anthony was asking my mother, "How are we today, Mrs. L.?"

I opened my eyes and leaned forward so I could peer into the foyer. There he was, standing in the dim light in his socks, wearing jeans and a dark-blue pullover, his black coat slung over his arm. I grabbed a pair of pyjamas from my bureau and slipped them on.

My mother as usual eclipsed any surprise I might have felt. She lifted her arms as if facing a volcanic eruption and sank backward into the small, flimsy seat attached to the telephone table. Fanya had acquired this perilous piece of furniture by collecting several hundred supermarket stamps, and I was sure the chair would one day break away from the table and my mother would come crashing down to the floor.

—*it's the child the child*—

Anthony was unimpressed. "Take it easy," he said.

*—the child the child—*my mother began to wail—*we all we all saw with our own eyes—*

In response either to the claustrophobia my mother generally elicited in people around her, or to an intuition that I was watching him, Anthony turned around. He saw me staring at him through the half-open door, and without further ado he abandoned my mother, came into my bedroom, and shut the door behind him. He looked older—not only by three years, but as if he'd moved into another stage of life altogether. He was more sedate yet also more scattered, more efficient and energetic yet wearier—as weary as me.

He dropped his coat on the desk, and without a word lay down beside me, placed his arm around my waist, and shut his eyes.

Anthony! It was not my father but rather a surrogate brother who had appeared out of nowhere. His body was snug against mine, and his socks warmed my ankles. I remembered the postcard he'd sent me from New York, and I wondered what it would be like to be intimately acquainted with Bleecker Street, the Chelsea Hotel, Spanish Harlem …

I, too, dozed off. When I woke, a long time later, he was gone. I hadn't dreamed it—Anthony had come to visit. That's what you were supposed to do, visit the sick. Anthony understood what was happening to me because he was in the same predicament, exactly the same. We'd crashed into the present, and seeing it up close, stripped and exposed, we no longer had any inclination to focus on what lay ahead, couldn't focus on it. But Anthony hadn't solved the problem by becoming a recluse; he'd gone off in search of greener pastures. With his arm around me, I had slept peacefully for a change, a deep sleep, free of nightmares.

I'm slow, always slow, always a few steps behind everyone else. That was the way I was then and that's the way I am still. It took me a few minutes to piece it all together: Anthony was Tony, the brother Patrick had mentioned. At Bakunin, he'd been Antonio,

Anton, Antoine, even Antonius, but never Tony—like me, he must have been hoping for a breach. Now it turned out that we were all linked, like the dancers at the end of *The Seventh Seal*; everyone knew everyone. Patrick had mentioned that his brother was living in California—he must have moved from New York to California, and now he was back in Montreal for a visit. Or maybe he'd returned for good.

As soon as I made the connection, I spotted, as if in confirmation, a bulky white envelope leaning against my radio. It was a letter, addressed to Tony Moore, 4 Hillside Road, Beaconsfield. The envelope was made of textured paper, soft as fabric, and the handwriting was tall and spidery. Under overlapping postmarks, the faded stamps—a sea-dragon, a grey and gold goddess launching rays of light—seemed to transmit a foreign loneliness. The return address was barely legible, but I was able to make out the first and last lines: *Gerald Moore, Japan.*

Anthony had left me a coded message. That's what Anthony did—he used codes. I'd thought when we were at Bakunin that he was being evasive, but I was wrong: he was trying to say more this way, not less.

The letter inside the envelope took up several sheets of pale blue airmail paper, folded in four and covered with the same spidery handwriting. I padded to the kitchen, dug out a box of soda crackers from the cupboard, and returned to my room. Sitting cross-legged on the bed, I began to read.

Here's the letter, which I've kept inside my diary all these years. It's remarkably well preserved. Well, maybe it's not that remarkable: in terms of document conservation, even a hundred years in dry, anaerobic conditions is not a long time. Only in small-scale human terms is it nearly impossible to reconcile the stark numbers with our own inept tallying.

March 17, 1968

Dear Tony, my firstborn son, it's two in the afternoon here and your birthday. I had such a longing to talk to you but don't have your latest number or, in fact, any number for you. There's so much I want to tell you, not my usual rambling, but more in the way of biography or autobiography or what have you, and even if you don't want to read it now or ever, at least I want you to have the option, and also to tell you where you can find more information. I'm in a small room here, on a mat on the floor, paper-thin walls, or rather bamboo thin, and I can hear the woman who runs this place cleaning up. There are chickens in the courtyard, though it's not really rustic; the noise and hullabaloo outside feel urban, the smells are urban. It's another universe here, and since I barely speak a word of Japanese, I'm as good as deaf and mute.

I'm waiting for word from the monastery, and if they take me, I may not have another chance to write. I don't know what the arrangements are there, what one can and cannot do there. I feel so far from being where I long to be, though even thinking in terms of a goal is probably all wrong ... but I promised I wouldn't ramble and I won't. What I want to do is tell you some things that I woke up this morning wanting to tell you—maybe because suddenly you seem old enough, or maybe it's that "lonely impulse" Yeats describes—do you remember our Sunday nights, reading poetry by the hearth? One of the memories I cling to. The Yeats poem was a favourite, wasn't it? Do you remember? "An Irish Airman Foresees his Death" ... There is something about telling, just telling, that seems almost like soaring through enemy fire.

What I'm trying to say is that the impulse may be thoroughly self-centred, a way of shedding something or other before I enter the monastery—if I do go in; a way of trying to move on, or move somewhere, or learn not to move—or whatever it is I need to learn and unlearn. If the impulse is self-centred, forgive me. I feel I've lost touch with who you are to such a degree that I can't gauge these things properly, and maybe that was never my talent. Certainly I have much to atone for as a father, as I well know. For that, I don't deserve forgiveness, though forgiveness is something I now know has to do with oneself, not others, both the doing and the requesting. Anything else is just manipulation. I'm rambling again ... my worst trait, or one of them, anyhow.

In any case, I would like to tell you about Vera, and also about how we met and how you came to be. If you don't want to know about it or be dragged into it, here is your chance to stop, throw the letter in the fire, or put it away for another day. Above all I need to say at the outset that this is in no way any kind of justification or even explanation. Why things fell apart, you know as well as I and better, looking at us with your child's all-knowing eyes. But where it all began—that's what I want to tell you. You have already heard some things about how it happened that we met and married, the usual answers one gives to a child. We left out all save the quaint, picturesque details, or rather details that could be made to sound quaint and picturesque—Vera was delayed in London, we met in Hyde Park, etc.

Here then is what actually happened. The memory has done the opposite of fade; it gets more vivid with time. Isn't that odd? Like a backward spring, propelling me into the past and giving me more of it each time I visit.

It was a year after the war—that you know. June 2, 1946, to be precise. London was still in ruins, though also in the throes of reconstruction—not just the buildings, but everything—peace, the future. It's hard to describe the atmosphere of that year. Horror and grief swept up and discarded, as if it were a duty to dispose of them, which of course it was. To be replaced by work and hope.

My brother Anthony, whose name we gave you (perhaps wrongly), fell in Dieppe in August of 1942. Of course he was the talented one; a brilliant painter with a great future ahead of him ... and I can't blame my mother or anyone else for resenting that I was the one who was spared and now I was the one who was going to inherit the family fortune—and I didn't give a damn about any of it. Instead, for reasons that were obscure even to me, I was studying for the ministry before the war broke out, despite my conviction that the story of God and the subsequent addendum of a Son were fiction. I suppose you'll find this incomprehensible, but I thought even so that I could somehow do some good. Or maybe it was all some adolescent romantic urge to escape from the madding crowd that to this day has a hold over me.

I left my studies as soon as the war came. How could I ever have thought that an atheist would really fit in? I must have been mad. I started off as a Conscientious Objector—volunteered to do any job that didn't involve carrying a weapon. I wasn't a fanatic like some of the others, who refused to participate in any way at all. After Anthony was killed, I would have fought, in fact, but I was needed where I was. Mostly I helped to clear up after the bombings. Thousands of bodies had to be buried, thousands of homeless people had to be sheltered and fed. It was Russian roulette, every minute of every day and night; you never knew where the next hit would be, and towards the end, with the diabolical V2s, there wasn't even the five- or ten-second warning.

Your grandparents stayed out in their big house in Hertfordshire, though one wing was being used for some military purpose or other. They were involved in art evacuation and all sorts of other wartime projects. After Anthony was killed, they went on, stoically, but they needed me more than ever, supposedly to help out in the family business, though really for moral support, and I made up my mind to yield as soon as the war was over. I would become a part of the family antiques firm, in spite of my deep aversion to that whole scene. Auctions made me sick, everything about them. And I had no talent for it, no gift at all. I couldn't tell one saucer from another, one century from another. I never told you or anyone else about my aversion to your grandparents' occupation, mostly because I didn't think Vera would understand, and we had enough chasms over which to shout at each other, and you know if there's anything Vera loves besides her sons, it's beautiful things. I only thank my stars that when we first met, I was a well-brought up English boy and didn't breathe a word against my parents or what they did, and by the time we were close enough for me to tell her ... but I'm jumping ahead.

Back to the fateful day. I was sitting on a bench in Hyde Park with a sandwich I wasn't eating—it just lay on my lap, wrapped in paper. I didn't want to eat in front of the woman who was sitting on the bench opposite me because she looked hungry and food was still very scarce, and anyhow it seemed rude. Of course I couldn't go up to her, a total stranger, and offer her half my lunch.

So I sat there with the sandwich on my lap. I'd stayed on volunteering, with your grandparents' blessing, of course, and I'd been at it all week, clearing debris sixteen hours a day, but I'd changed back into civilian clothes. I was headed for Hertfordshire for a weekend leave, and I dreaded going, as usual, so was taking my time, gathering emotional energy for the journey. The woman—Vera—was wearing white gloves and her hands were folded on her lap. I'd never seen anyone sitting so motionlessly, as though she were posing for a painting, or had turned into one.

I tried not to stare. She was haunted and haunting then, and the attraction I felt was like a sort of rope hauling me towards her—towing me, that's what it felt like. There is no real explanation for these things. Somehow I found the courage to cough and then smile at her, and she didn't smile back, but she nodded and that was encouragement enough for me. I asked her whether she was a visitor—she had a small suitcase with her, so it seemed all right to ask.

She nodded again and said, "I was supposed to leave today for Canada. The ship has been delayed, they do not know for how long."

She spoke excellent English, though with a European accent—she's almost lost it entirely now. I introduced myself and she said, "I'm Vera Elias, from Prague." I said something daft about the weather, and I wanted the earth to swallow me up in shame, but at the same time I just couldn't let go. I really was worried about her. So I asked, "Have you got a place to stay?"

She said, "I have an address of someone ... I have not yet contacted." She stared at me with those blue eyes of hers, and both of us knew that I was going to offer her a place to stay and that she would accept. Because there was absolutely nothing available that summer. It was impossible to find a room anywhere; there were still thousands of homeless people. It turned out later that the address she had was of the cousin of a maid who had worked for her friends in Prague. At best she would have shared some attic bed.

I said, "I have a flat where you could stay, if you like. I was on my way to my parents' house in the country, so you'll have the place to yourself. I can check in on you in the morning." And then I asked her if she'd like to share my sandwich. "It's beef," I said, because it occurred to me that she might be Jewish.

She removed her gloves and accepted half my sandwich, but her hands began to tremble so uncontrollably that I had to take it back. She was perfectly composed otherwise; only her hands shook. I could tell it wasn't that she was ill—it was nerves. I'd seen that sort of thing often enough after a bombing, trying to give tea to people who had lost their homes and possibly half their families, and their hands shaking so they couldn't lift the cup.

She said calmly, "I'm sorry, it must be the journey, it's tired me out," and that helped a little, but I was at a loss. "Let's walk," she suggested, "and I'll eat while walking." On the second try she dropped the sandwich on the ground. She laughed. That's your mother for you, isn't it? She laughed at herself and picked it up. Though everything was still being rationed, I didn't want her to eat bread that had fallen on the ground. She seemed amused at

my concern, but she separated the two pieces of bread and managed to eat
the part that hadn't touched the grass, and the rest she scattered for the birds.

We walked and she told me that with the help of the father of an old
schoolmate of hers she'd succeeded in getting a student visa for Canada and
now she was going there to complete her medical studies, which had been
interrupted by the war. I started telling her about myself, but I saw that she
wasn't interested, or couldn't concentrate, so I stopped.

We went to my service flat in Fitzrovia and when we got there she asked
me not to go to Hertfordshire. She said she wanted me to sleep with her
because she didn't like sleeping alone. I assumed she meant sleep on the sofa,
but that's not what she had in mind … Forgive me for writing about this. I
don't know how to leave it out. I wondered what I'd done to deserve this
angel landing in my life from out of nowhere. And then she decided to tell
me about her experiences during the war. I think it was because she thought
she would never see me again and she wanted to discard as many of her
experiences as she could relate in a single night, record them in another
brain, my brain, and then leave them behind forever, like an exorcism.
That's what I think. There may have been other reasons … some sense of
duty, some historic urge. Or a deeper need—who knows? I felt it was
because she trusted me. She didn't love me or desire me, she thought it was
only some chance encounter, and she knew I was safe.

As it turned out, we spent the whole of my leave together. After I'd heard
her story I was afraid to touch her, but the last thing she wanted was to be
cast out because of her experiences, to be pitied or set apart, and I understood that. I owe your mother so much—beginning with the vistas of freedom
that she opened to me. Mostly, I was just overwhelmed—first with joy, then
grief and horror. I confess I knew very little about the atrocities. There were
rumours all the time, and an abysmal waxworks exhibit based on those
rumours, with a free amusement corner for children, which I kept hoping
someone would have the decency to shut down. The stories in the newspaper

about what the Nazis were up to were often just as sensationalistic, and that created a screen, because you didn't know what was true and what wasn't. Everything is hidden in war, everything is censored, secret, even information about the bombs falling on your head. A month before the war ended, some newsreels came out, but I didn't join the queues to see them either. I suppose I'd had enough of dead bodies, and I couldn't help wondering whether the people in those queues were motivated by the same sort of prurience that drew visitors to the waxworks. It took me weeks, really, to assimilate every-thing Vera told me, and I began taking an interest after she left. I felt there wasn't enough awareness, and I wrote an article, but no one would publish it. It was "in poor taste", its sources were "questionable", it was time "to put all that behind and move on".

Then Vera left for Canada. She wouldn't let me see her off. It never occurred to me that she might be pregnant, even though she wouldn't let me take any precautions—she seemed convinced it wasn't necessary. When she found out that she was expecting, she remembered the address in London, and she wrote to me there and told me. I don't know what she had in mind; I have never asked her what she was thinking. Maybe she barely knew herself. Of course, I was beside myself with happiness, that she was willing to take me, to marry me, because I was heartbroken, really heartbroken, when she left.

The thing is, my dear boy, and this is what my letter is really about, I wrote everything down, after she left. I think I got most of it, because there are things you hear that you can't forget even if you want to. She doesn't know that I did this, though I think she hated me simply because I knew, and my presence reminded her, when the plan had been to forget. I put a dent in that plan, do you see? So telling her would have made it even worse. I suppose I was misled by her one-time outpouring, thinking it was because of who I was, not knowing it was an aberration and that what she trusted was that I would vanish along with her story. And in due course I did. I have vanished.

Now, Tony, this is very important. I've hidden the notebook in the bottom drawer of my filing cabinet. It's brown, leather-bound, with our family name embossed on the front. The key to the cabinet is in the jade cigarette case next to the paints in the basement. I don't know why I hid the key, maybe to protect you. But if you want to read about your mother's past, though, that's where the key is. It's a choice you must make for yourself.

I'll just tell you this one thing, before you decide. Vera was married before the war and had a baby. Her husband and the baby were both shot together the day they were arrested, because her husband protested. That was how they got people to be quiet and do exactly as they were told ... shoot on the spot anyone who spoke out, or a child who was crying, or a mother who was hysterical or even someone who was sitting quietly, just to keep everyone terrified. So that's what happened. Her husband was holding the baby and they were shot together.

The rest, everything that happened to her after that, or at least what she managed to tell me, you can read in the notebook.

That night, when she sat on the bed and in her soft voice began her story, there had been a power failure and I lit candles, and there were such eerie shadows in the room. Ambulances passed every so often from the hospital nearby, and it was as if her words were setting off the sirens. I had to leave the room a few times. I pretended I was going for a glass of water, though really I needed to vomit, but I came back and listened to more, and then more, because I loved her, and when you love someone, you can bear anything. I told her I loved her, but she didn't seem to hear me. All she said was that she would not allow her past to shape her future. I think if you read what I wrote, you'll understand her better, because no matter what Vera did after the war it was heroic, and no matter how much I suffered it was nothing, absolutely nothing, compared to what she's been through.

I never told you any of this—how could I? It would have meant betraying Vera, and anyhow you might have misunderstood about the way we ended up marrying, because I loved you from the second I heard you existed or were about to exist, and Vera did too—she loved you and loves you both. That's what I want you to know.

I have a headache coming on—yes, I was up too late and there was too much carousing but soon all that will be over, I trust. So I'm going to stop here and mail this before I regret writing it. I hope this is not the wrong thing to do.

Your loving father, Gerald.

After I read the letter, I showered and dressed, put on my mummy outfit, and went outside for a walk. My mother and Bubby were asleep and didn't hear me leave. It was as cold as ever, but I didn't mind—I'd manage not to freeze. I filled my lungs with glacial night air until I was dizzy, then climbed one of the high mounds of snow that lined the curbs. I lay on the snowy hill and looked up at the empty sky, its stars obliterated by city lights.

Yes, I decided, I would be brave. I'd sign out of the monastery, I'd return to real life.

The next day, a mahogany sleigh bed arrived at our place. My mother was at work when the delivery men rang the bell, and I was sure they'd made a mistake—my mother never purchased anything without a great deal of pre-publicity. But they showed me the receipt, and there it was: our address for shipping, the Moore address for billing. Anthony had bought me a double bed.

I let the two men in. I didn't own a bathrobe, and when the doorbell had rung, I'd grabbed my winter coat. "Where do you want it?" the men asked. I was clutching the coat around me so it wouldn't slide open; my bare feet and tangled hair completed the Hogarthian scene. In only three weeks I'd lost the ease one normally has with strangers, and I found myself stuttering as I directed them to my bedroom. The delivery men looked frightened—they must have thought I was a mad shut-in—and they fled before I had time to find change for a tip.

Bubby and I stood at the entrance to my room and gaped. In spite of my modest efforts—clippings on the wall, an Egyptian runner draped over the lampshade—my bedroom was condemned to suburbia manqué, while the antique sleigh bed would not have been out of place in one of the lost rooms of Wuthering Heights. I never dreamed I'd own anything half as beautiful as this.

"Try it," I said to Bubby. Gingerly, she uncrumpled her body on the striped silver-and-blue mattress. Her splayed feet, knobby inside soft cloth slippers, slid sideways like small burrowing animals. I stretched out next to her and held her hand, which was as round and smooth as a child's.

"Well, Bubby," I said, "here we are."

1972

The hospital waiting room, with its inhospitable cadmium yellow chairs. Rosie is sitting on one of the chairs, her bare legs folded sideways, an open bag of peanuts from the food machine on her lap.

It's autumn, the beginning of our final year in high school, and something has come over me. Even my handwriting, in diaries dating from this time, is ragged and jagged, as if pushing against a barrier, yielding gloomily, pushing again. Malfunctioning staplers, knots in shoelaces, transparent tape that twists before you have a chance to use it—every small thing sets me off. An insane perfectionism makes my life intolerable. If the peas my mother serves me are oversalted, I stomp out of the kitchen. Fanya's ludicrous response—running after me and begging forgiveness, when what I deserve is to be ignored, at best—only adds fuel to my aggravation. If it were possible, I'd be turning my mother into more of a wreck than she already is, but luckily it's not possible.

It all reached an intolerable pitch this morning. When I arrived at school, already in a state because the bus had taken forever to come, because it was overcrowded, because why, why, *why* couldn't this stupid city run more buses at rush hour, because sines and cosines were *idiotic*, designed to bring misery to millions, were only ever meant to be studied by *mathematicians*—when I charged into school, I found everyone in a heightened state of excitement as they broadcast the news: a shipment of frogs had arrived at the lab for dissection. Mr. Lurie must have mentioned the dissection while I was immersed in *Under the Volcano*—he no longer bothered regulating my behaviour, as long as I sat in the corner and didn't disturb anyone. Or else I'd been skipping class altogether so I could catch matinées at our downtown repertory cinema.

Dvora spotted me and came over. She held her stomach and groaned, "I. Feel. Sick." The staccato syntax meant that she was more than usually upset, but it wasn't the prospect of dissecting frogs that was making her sick. She'd been in a staccato mood for several weeks now, partly because she was hopelessly failing all her subjects, but mostly because she'd been dumped by Carlos, her drug-pushing boyfriend. She wanted to run off to San Francisco with flowers in her hair, and on weekends she switched to hippie attire that was meant to convey a belligerent, anti-establishment impulse. The effect was more genial than radical; the wide print headbands suited her sweet, round face, and under tie-dyed T-shirts her braless breasts seemed to be issuing a gentle invitation.

Animals and the way we treat them—this is what I'm ranting about, here in the hospital waiting room. Rosie's also been skipping school, though not in order to watch movies downtown. Her father is sick, and she's installed herself semi-permanently at St. Mary's Hospital.

"How can people not care about animals?" I fumed.

Rosie lowered her head. "I know ... but I like steak. I'm very selfish."

There were shadows under her eyes. "Go home and get some sleep, Rosie," I said. "I'll stay until you come back. Take your time, I don't have anything else to do."

"You're so nice to me, Maya."

"I'm a bitch these days," I said. "I'm just a jangle of nerves."

"No, no—and you're right about the animals," she said. Then she stood on her toes and kissed me goodbye. A mystic kiss to ensure that the gods looked upon me kindly. "I'm just going to shower. I'll be back soon!" she promised.

I dug into my ever-dependable shoulder bag and retrieved a package of soda crackers and *Under the Volcano*, which seemed never to end. You read page after depressing page, and it was still the Day of the Dead in Quauhnahuac, the Consul was still drunk, Yvonne was still drifting. I set the book aside and peeked into Mr. Michaeli's room, but he was asleep. At long last, Rosie returned. Patrick was walking morosely behind her, like a stalker under arrest.

"Look who I met in the elevator!" Rosie announced happily, as if we were all there for a wedding. "He's here to visit Daddy."

"I have a book for Mr. Michaeli that I promised to give him two years ago," Patrick said.

He hadn't changed—but I had. He'd been Vera Moore's son when I last saw him; now he was Anthony's brother. And not a very good brother, as far as I could tell.

Patrick sensed my critical eye, and the expanse it opened up between us relaxed him. He switched to courteous mode and asked, "How's it going?"

"I'll go see whether Daddy's awake," Rosie said.

Though there was no one else in the waiting area, Patrick slumped into a chair on the other side of the room, as far away as possible from other life forms.

"I know your brother," I told him. "He was my counsellor at camp."

"Really?" Patrick managed to modulate his voice so it hovered halfway between neutral comment and, just in case, disparagement. I remembered the strategy; he had used it when he'd referred to his father's spiritual quest. I'd never met a more distrustful person.

"Is he back in California?" A year had passed since Anthony had slept in my bed; I'd not seen or heard from him since. I was hoping he'd call me or send me a postcard from wherever he was—New York, California, or maybe Paris or London. But he seemed to have forgotten all about me. I missed him.

"I guess so."

"I wish Anthony was my brother," I sighed. "I've always wanted sisters and brothers. I used to wish I had a twin sister."

"A twin!" Patrick shuddered.

"We had twins at Camp Bakunin. For some reason, they never even talked to each other. I couldn't understand it. One of them went off to live by herself in a separate bunk house."

"How surprising."

"What's Anthony's life like down there? Does he like it?"

"I wouldn't know. We don't talk much either."

"How come? How come you don't talk?"

"Not much in common, I guess."

"You guess, you guess—don't you know anything?"

Rosie returned before he could respond. She sat down next to me and her navy skirt climbed upward. The skirt from another planet, with a will of its own. A skirmish ensued as Rosie tugged it down, human versus apparel.

"I'm sorry, Patrick," she said. "Daddy's too tired to see anyone. And you came all this way. He appreciates it, really—and I do too."

Patrick rose from his chair. "Guess I'll get going," he said.

"Can I come over?" I asked. I wanted to see the house again, I wanted to see Dr. Moore. They were all more shadowy now, the Moores, and at the same time more exposed. I knew things that possibly Patrick himself didn't know. I wondered whether the key was still in the jade cigarette box.

"Why?" Patrick asked, genuinely puzzled.

"So gracious," I said.

"Yeah, sure, if you want."

I tried to persuade Rosie to join us, but she wasn't ready to desert her post. "I have to stay with Daddy," she said. "Have fun!"

There was limited parking at St. Mary's, and Patrick had left his car, a white Mercedes, a long way from the hospital. It was a cold October day, and I was shivering by the time I let myself in on the passenger side.

"Are you cold?" Patrick asked, inserting a key in the ignition. "I can turn on the heat."

"Aren't you cold?"

"I don't get cold," he said.

"Lucky you. Remember the cold spell last year?"

"Was there a cold spell?"

"Why do you do that?" I snapped. "Why do you duck like that?"

"I'm insecure?"

"Oh, forget it! There's no point trying to talk to you."

"I like winter," he said, suddenly in a good mood. It was the driving—I could tell he liked navigating his vehicle, like a Hardy character perched aloft a village cart, pulling at the reins.

Dr. Moore didn't come to the door when we entered her house, but we passed Mr. Davies, the cook, in the kitchen, patting dough into a baking dish. He was tall and gaunt, with thinning hair and vampire eyebrows. I couldn't decide whether he was strange and forbidding or merely felt out of place.

Patrick and Mr. Davies ignored each other, but I said, "Hi there, Mr. Davies." He looked up from his food preparations, nodded briefly.

Patrick didn't seem to notice this small exchange. He dodged into the pantry and began climbing up the Dickensian staircase.

"Isn't there any other way of getting to your part of the house?" I grumbled.

"I can get you a flashlight."

"No, it's okay. I'll just risk breaking my neck. Where did your mother find Mr. Davies? He's kind of weird."

Patrick didn't answer. He opened the door to his loft and said, "Do you want coffee, or tea—or anything?"

"Maybe later. I wouldn't mind some music. I'm so pissed off!" I added, the words rushing out of me.

"Why is that?" he asked, but his good mood had vanished and his voice was unfriendly.

"You're not really interested," I said. I selected a few novels and settled in one of the living-room chairs. Patrick drank vodka and leafed through the latest issue of *Logos*, our local underground newsweekly, printed in various hard-to-read colour combinations: pink on orange, orange on lime green.

But I was too jittery to read. I set aside my book and interrupted him. "What's Anthony doing? Does he have a job?"

"Yeah," Patrick yawned. "He works for a magazine. He writes about money."

"Money?"

"Economics."

"Why economics?"

"I have no idea."

"How does he know about that sort of thing?"

"Just picked it up, I guess. It's not that complicated."

"Is he a Marxist too?"

"I wouldn't know. The magazine he writes for certainly isn't."

"Do you have any photographs of yourselves as kids?" I asked, suddenly craving that entry into their lives. Photos of Anthony and Patrick as little boys, of their parents, their grandparents—a feast of revelations.

"I don't know where they are."

"Can't you ask your mother?"

"I'd really rather not," he said wearily; it was a kind of deep, all-consuming weariness, and it reminded me of my own breakdown the previous winter, when I couldn't pull myself out of bed, out of nightmares.

The phone rang and Patrick said, "That's my mother. She wants to play chess." He picked up the receiver. "I can't right now, I'm busy—"

"No, no, go ahead!" I swung my arm emphatically, then caught myself. If I turned into my mother, I'd have no choice but to join a convent.

Patrick told his mother he'd be there in a few minutes. "No, no, it's no one. I mean … yes, Maya is here. No, she says it's okay. We're coming down." He hung up.

As we made our way downstairs, Patrick abandoned me, abandoned everyone. His unapproachable distress was almost frightening; it was like coming across a suffering animal, large and harmless—a giraffe with a broken leg or a beached whale—and no one there to help.

Dr. Moore was waiting in a room that made me think of the word *rectory*, whatever that was: tall leaded-glass windows, a fire in the fireplace, walls lined with book cabinets, a small ladder for reaching the higher shelves. Patrick's mother was sitting at a chess table close to the fire. "Hello, Maya," she said politely. I couldn't tell whether she was glad to see me this time round; her hopes for that first visit, long ago, had not been realized. But at least I was back, at least I'd not entirely lost touch with Patrick.

"Hi. So nice here—I love fireplaces."

"Help yourself to a milkshake and fruit pie—homemade by Mr. Davies." She laughed dryly, as if embarrassed but also mocking her embarrassment, and indicated a corner table, where two milkshakes in fountain glasses, a sliced pie, and a bowl of glistening cherries were arranged on a wooden tray with raised sides. "Or would you prefer tea—or coffee?"

"No, this is fine, thank you. Cute tray." What interested me was the bowl of cherries. It's easy to forget now what a luxury imported fruit was, once upon a time. Suddenly I was Neil Klugman in *Goodbye, Columbus*, discovering in the Patimkin basement a fridge brimming with fruit. Like him, I wanted to stuff handfuls of cherries into my pockets. I was thinking of Bubby and my mother as well as myself. They would set the bowl at the centre of our kitchen table and marvel.

"We can play chess later," Dr. Moore offered. "I had no idea you were here. Or perhaps I'll leave you two to play."

"That's okay, I don't play chess—I'm too dumb. I don't mind, really. I'll just sit on the window-seat and watch."

"Why don't you take the cherries with you," Dr. Moore said. "I'll ask Mr. Davies to bring some more." I was transparent; my greed was transparent. It seemed to me that if I had any strength of character, I'd refuse, but I accepted. On the cushioned window-seat I could gorge myself freely.

And they really were delicious, those cherries. The window, with its latticed diamond panes, looked out on a copse of autumn-splashed trees; inside, Patrick and his mother moved chess pieces in silence. I dropped the cherry pits into my shirt pocket and picked up a copy of *The Rubaiyat of Omar Khayyam* that was lying next to me on the cushioned seat. It was a beautiful edition, with illuminated Persian artwork on every page. *A flask of wine, a book of verse, and thou* ... Maybe the plump, wide-belted, gold-turbaned man sitting under the palm tree was right. Live for today.

Dr. Moore broke the silence. "For Kant, the 'I' was a set of *a priori* conditions. But according to Fichte, that 'I' in Kant's division of 'I' and 'the world' is a tyrannical formalism."

Just like that! She must be resuming some previous discussion, I thought. But Patrick ignored her. He said nothing, and of course I said nothing.

She wasn't discouraged. She must have told herself that luring her son out of his shell, breaking through his resistance, would be good for him. Best to forge ahead.

"Because it posits itself independently of the world."

Patrick's long, slender fingers enclosed a knight.

I could see that his mother was not merely jousting for fun: Dr. Moore really was trying to make sense of the world. I tried to imagine my mother discussing Kant with me. I wondered whether in a calm state (a circumstance I could barely envision) Fanya would be able to enjoy, say, Jane Austen. In her own way, my mother was as clever as Vera Moore.

"But Hegel would say that Fichte is getting Kant wrong. Kant at least acknowledges the problem that exists between 'I' and 'the world.' Hegel describes this formalism as the morbid beautiful soul, pure in itself, but unreal and empty."

"Very interesting," Patrick said apathetically.

Dr. Moore ignored the rebuff. Apart from her blueprint for Patrick, she was hungry for conversation. "And Hegel's solution—the 'I' swallows the world, and the world is the objectification of spirit."

Patrick made a small, restrained sound, something between a grunt and a chortle. His mother looked up at him, tried to conceal her excitement. "Why are you laughing?"

"Nothing. It's a good solution."

"How? How so?" She was pleading with him now, and the scene made me think, for some reason, of Ghirlandaio's *Adoration of the Shepherds*—the ox and donkey peering curiously over the sarcophagus; a shepherd, apparently the artist himself, pointing with his index finger at the baby with the shower-cap halo and cheerful raised knee. Dr. Moore, in the present version, would be the fair-haired, slightly pouting Mary, and the chess pieces were the parade of people in the distance, coming to see what was what.

But Patrick only said, "Check."

"Ingenious," she said, nodding her approval.

"Very ingenious."

"Now I think you have got me in a trap."

Without antagonism, pleased with himself, Patrick said, "Maybe."

And his mother's cool, tangential voice also grew more intimate. "Yes, it looks bad for me. I think now I have no escape."

"Maybe," he repeated.

"If I move my rook?"

"I'm not saying."

Three moves later Patrick won the game.

"Very impressive," Dr. Moore said with satisfaction, as if she'd been the one who came up with the clever move.

Patrick, enthusiastic against his better judgment, showed her how she could have saved her king.

But tactlessly she destroyed the unguarded moment. "So, through chess you feel more validated, I think?"

Now Patrick wasn't only angry—he was disgusted with himself for having let go. "Very validated," he said, his voice like a clenched fist. "In the *Fichtean* sense."

"I was wondering ... " I interrupted.

"Oh, Maya, you were so quiet I forgot you were here. You see how I lose to my son!"

"I was wondering, could you tell me what this dream I had means?"

"You see me as the dream interpreter?"

"Aren't you?"

"Well, what's the dream?" She leaned on the arm of her chair and gazed at me attentively. With her blue eyes and aquiline nose and her regal posture, she could have been posing for a court portrait.

"I'm in this small movie theatre, I'm the only one there, and this movie comes on—there's this operating table, except it's very long, it goes on and on. First what you see on it are instruments and vague sorts of bits that could be parts of the insides of creatures. Then you see a dead bird that's been gutted out, then a mammal, and a bigger mammal. Each one is higher on the evolutionary scale. And then right at the end there's a fox on the table, and its insides are spilled out, and then I see myself, I'm on the table, and I've been gutted out too. Only I have blonde hair instead of red. And then the title of the movie comes on and it's called The Fox."

"Like the short story by Lawrence?"

"I guess. Only I haven't read that story. All I read was Sons and Lovers. So, do you know what the dream means?"

"Well, how did you feel watching the movie?"

"Curious. It isn't scary. Whoever gutted these creatures hasn't hurt them, they were already dead."

"I think you wish to have courage. You don't want to be gutless. You don't mind being foxy. And you want to have fun, like in the television commercial, 'Is it true blondes have more fun?' That's my guess, but it's only a guess. Really I'd have to know more about you."

"Thanks," I said. It was hard to tell with Dr. Moore, but I had the distinct feeling that she didn't like me. "You know, Anthony was my counsellor—did he tell you?"

"Your counsellor at that camp?"

"Yeah, he was really good. Everyone loved him."

"Oh?" Dr. Moore's smile was partly diffident, partly pleased, the smile of an adult opening a birthday gift. Then I saw that she was trembling slightly. I was shocked, and thought I'd misperceived some small movement, but no, her entire body was trembling. I remembered Gerald's letter and felt abashed.

"He was great. We adored him." But I added, stupidly, "He made us laugh," and ruined everything. Her smile faded into covert disappointment, an acknowledgment of Anthony's failings, or maybe his unhappiness, which she'd known about all along. Not her son the beloved but her son the clown. Like Patrick, she shut down, and the trembling ceased.

Patrick had had enough. He got up and left the room.

I waved idiotically to Dr. Moore and followed him. "'Gimme shelter,'" I sang under my breath as we returned to Patrick's lair.

I sat on Patrick's ugly kitchen chair, shut my eyes, breathed in deeply, exhaled. For the first time in weeks, I wasn't about to blow a fuse or go to war with a jammed zipper. The monkey was on Patrick's back. It had been there all along, of course, but I only saw it now, and somehow it made mine superfluous. I had witnessed a scene as unruly and peculiar as any in my own home. With a gift of this magnitude, I no longer had any urge to lash out.

There were two knocks on the door, followed by the sound of footsteps quickly retreating, clomp clomp clomp, down the stairs. The knocks were Mr. Davies's signal that food had been set out in the kitchen. "Why is he running away?" I asked.

"He doesn't want anyone to expect him to talk."

"I guess your mom doesn't like to cook?"

"She's into food. He makes things like partridges for her."

Mr. Davies had left a vegetarian lasagne and a mushroom pie downstairs on the kitchen table—both culinary masterpieces, as anyone could see. Yet as far as Patrick was concerned, they might have been scraps left for stray animals. He heaped a mid-sized serving of each dish onto a plate and, still standing, ate so rapidly and blindly that he seemed to be neither chewing nor swallowing. It was as if he had shut himself down again, had cancelled the very act of eating. I'd never seen anything like it. Even Bubby, with her deliberate efficiency, was a *gourmande* next to Patrick. "Well, see you upstairs," he said, when he'd finished. He dropped his plate in the sink and left me alone with my meal.

I, on the other hand, was in food heaven. Mr. Davies was brilliant, no doubt about it. I stuffed myself until I was bursting at the seams, then made my way back upstairs.

Patrick was kneeling on the living-room rug, setting a lit match to the bowl of a gold water pipe. The pipe was too pretty, I felt, to be taken seriously—it looked more like a trinket or a toy. *Go ask Alice* ... if a caterpillar in a children's book could puff on something like this, so could I. But as soon as I tasted the bitter smoke I pushed the thin tube away, grimacing. It was too late. A procession of dream images floated before me: my mother bouncing and pouncing like a deranged human strapped to a flying machine, Vera Moore slyly quoting bits of Hegel as she plunged her fork into Mr. Davies's partridges, Mr. Michaeli wilting under paper airplanes. Rosie in a white sari, pretending to be dead on a bed of Archie comics.

"You should be nicer to your mother," I said. "Though who am I to talk?"

"I'm very nice to her," Patrick replied, as if amused to find himself wrongfully accused. The opium had driven away his anger, and suddenly he reminded me of Anthony. Anthony did the same thing—spoke elliptically, humorously—the only difference was the aggression. Patrick had it, Anthony didn't.

"Did you know your father wrote about your mother's past in a notebook?"

Patrick seemed to be half-asleep: his legs were stretched out in front of him on the carpet, and he was leaning against the sofa cushions, his head tilted back, his eyes shut. "Yes," he said. "The famous notebook."

"Did you read it?"

"No, and I never will. I'm phobic about things like that."

"Yeah, me too," I said, and at that moment I felt close to Patrick, and I wanted to squeeze his hand, but he would have pulled away, and that realization pushed the moment aside.

I don't know how long I stayed there, sprawled in the armchair, staring into space. When it was time to go, I offered to take the bus home.

"No, no," Patrick said, pulling himself up. "I'll drive you."

"Are you hallucinating?" I asked.

He gave a stoned laugh. "It takes more than this."

The next day I returned to St. Mary's with a contrite heart. My unwinding was now in its last stages and like a spinning top rocking unsteadily to a halt, I felt slightly off-balance as I slowed down.

"I'm starving," Rosie said, as soon as she saw me.

"So am I. And I finished all my soda crackers on the bus. Sorry!"

"Wait here—I'll see what I can find at the cafeteria."

There were several other visitors in the waiting room, all of them silent and glum and in a state of contained tension, as if their clothes were scratchy and the air was too dry. I began to feel suffocated by their presence, so I strolled down the hallway, checked in on Mr. Michaeli.

He had a private room—I suppose the bed situation in hospitals was not as dire forty years ago. He appeared to be sleeping, but the heavy door creaked as I pulled it back, and he opened his eyes. His lips curved into his familiar disconcerting smile, tenuous and dismissive. "Ah, Maya! How are you, our good friend, Maya? Every time I see you, I forget how tall you are and how long is your hair. I knew once a girl with such red hair as yours. We called her Lita. She's dead, unfortunately."

"What exactly is wrong with you?" I asked him.

"What's wrong, what's wrong, who knows! The doctors like to invent problems. Everywhere they look, they see a problem. Kidney, problem. Heart, problem. Stomach, problem."

"My father's lungs were damaged in the war."

"So far, they have not found a lung problem. Maybe if we give them another week."

"You're the opposite of a hypochondriac."

"That means?"

"Someone who thinks something's always wrong with them. Like in that play by Molière."

"Ah, Molière. When I was a boy, my father took me to Molière. And now here I am speaking to you in a hospital in Canada about Molière. And my father is dead. In German we saw it, or maybe in Yiddish. Yiddish theatre was big business. Let me tell you, Jews love plays. Too bad we ended up attending the worst play in history."

"Who cares," I said, and instantly—for the first time—I regretted the heartless dismissal, but the words were out and they hung in the air like glass birds.

"I agree. Some things are too far from the mind to understand."

I walked to the window and looked down. Tiny toy people, tiny toy cars.

"Maya, come here. This is not your problem. And your mother, I saw her on a date. She is—how did my little Rosie say—courted? By a very nice man. They were in a restaurant holding hands."

"My mother!"

"And for who you think she wears that perfume? For you?"

"I can't believe it."

"We all saw, and my Rosie said, wouldn't Maya be surprised. And I say, better not tell, it could be a secret. But now out of the bag I spill the beans."

I tried to picture it—my mother and a suitor, at a restaurant, holding hands. What most startled me was that my mother could keep something to herself. I had not thought her capable of even the smallest subterfuge, this woman who recounted to anyone who would listen her close calls with reckless drivers and rancid butter. Not to mention the ongoing forays into a disjointed alternate universe.

And of course, beyond that, what man would choose to spend time with a woman most people crossed the street to avoid?

"What's he like?" I asked.

"They were speaking Yiddish. Maybe in Yiddish your mother is more herself. He was dressed well, in a suit and tie. His shoes were shiny. I would say he is a quiet man."

A quiet man! Well, he'd have to be, wouldn't he?

A nurse peeped in, nodded cryptically, disappeared.

All at once, in a surge of irritation and disgust, Mr. Michaeli said, "My wife and daughter don't want to let me go. Already in the Red Cross I was ready to die, but my wife insists for her sake I live. Why this fear? Death, you know, is nothing. But Gitte believes in getting back. Showing them you won. So here I am, waiting for my gold medal."

"They love you," I said.

But his outburst had exhausted him. "Yes, yes," he said, his voice retreating. "Love we definitely have." He shut his eyes; he wanted me to leave.

It seems we have countless ways of knowing—we surmise; we half-know; we know and don't know—and everything between. With dismaying clarity, Mr. Michaeli had spelled it out for me: Rosie's project was to offer compensation for her father's suffering by means of her talent for happiness, while Mr. Michaeli's project was to satisfy Rosie and Mrs. Michaeli by staying alive.

"I'll wait outside," I whispered. I wasn't sure whether he could still hear me.

I returned to the waiting room and considered the news of my mother's secret courtship. In fact, it made sense: for the past few months she'd been taking off several times a week, just before dinner. If before Mr. Michaeli's revelation I thought about these excursions with anything other than relief, I must have supposed that my mother's circle of card-players was expanding.

She had also made herself some new outfits recently: a sequined black dress, a white jacket with a purple collar. Her soft cherubic knees were now in view; her lipstick was palest pink. Wandering into her room one evening I had come across a paperback entitled, remarkably, *How to Massage Your Man*. All the same, it hadn't crossed my mind that in the real world there might be a man for her to massage. I was accustomed to thinking of my mother as sole inhabitant of a microcosm that no one could alter, and that, there-fore, no one could enter.

I felt betrayed, until it occurred to me that an entire area of discourse was in fact consistently absent from my mother's fractured soliloquies. The taboo subject wasn't sex; on the contrary, when free love was celebrated as a revolutionary concept I thought both its proponents and its critics were strangely obses-sive.

Rather, it was the future that, apart from generalized presenti-ments of disaster, was missing from our lives. I'd never heard my mother mention prospects or plans; we avoided discussing even the week ahead, never mind the broader outlines of hope and desire. I once showed my poor mother a photograph of mirrors reflecting each other to infinity. I was fascinated by the photo: we humans were truly amateurs, incapable even of grasping a concept as basic as endlessness. But Fanya covered her eyes and backed away—*don't don't show me already I am dizzy*—

It was not, therefore, a polite Russian man my mother was hiding; it was what he might be planning for the two of them.

I leaned my head against the wall and stared at the barren fluorescent lights. *Titorelli ... Titorelli ...* I was a frequent patron of the Verdi, a repertory cinema on St. Laurent Street that ignored the censorship board's eighteen-and-over age restrictions. I enjoyed it all: the good, the bad, and the sexist. David Hemmings's libidinous camera and gestalt investigations in *Blowup*; Rita Tushingham wide-eyed and overwhelmed in *The Knack*; circus burlesque and hat fetishes in Fellini's *Juliet of the Spirits*. Other movies educated me: the focus on cunnilingus in some obscure Swedish film was particularly illuminating. And if I had trouble falling asleep at night, I had only to think of Romy Schneider displaying her webbed fingers to Josef K and asking, *Has she any physical defect?* or recall the mad, lascivious laughter of the wild girls who reached out through bamboo bars and cried out, Titorelli, Titorelli ... and I'd drift off.

I drifted off now in the waiting room chair, and in Proustian pre-sleep I reconstructed the words *tinker tailor soldier sailor* according to shape and size and colour. I had a confused notion that when I graduated I'd find a job diving underwater in search of people who had lost their vision by drowning. I'd bring them to shore and teach them Braille.

By the time Rosie returned from the cafeteria I was wide awake. She handed me a container of rice pudding and a plastic spoon.

"Ooh, yummy," I said. "Thanks, Rosie."

"How did it go at Patrick's?" she asked.

"It was crazy. Patrick played chess with his mother and they talked about *Hegel!*"

And the word, for teenaged-girl reasons, made us collapse into helpless giggles.

1973

I've come to the last diary, the one that seems to glow like kryptonite, the one that marks off a before and an after. This is where they make their appearance, the demons who rise from the underworld to clutch at our ankles.

It's silver, in fact, this notebook, not kryptonite green; I remember how pleased I was with the colour when I bought it, just before we graduated—how fitting it seemed, for soon I'd be starting a new life, and who knew what splendour it would bring?

You think you can change things when you're young, that you control the plot, and if something goes wrong, that you can step over it and move on. If your raft capsizes, you can swim to shore, even make a sport of it.

I did swim into this afterlife, this aftermath, but it strikes me, now and then, that I may have headed in the wrong direction.

We wrote our last matriculation exam on a Friday morning in late June. I could hardly believe as I put down my pencil that I was free, absolutely free, for the rest of my life, to do as I pleased.

I had picked up a velvety blue-green corduroy shirt, and I wore it everywhere. My mother had sewn two embroidered bands onto the ends of my bell-bottom jeans, and I'd found a perfect pair of leather sandals with braided straps for only three dollars. I had a hat too—a funny, floppy felt hat, and Janis Joplin sunglasses. Janis herself had died, along with other music celebrities, and we were at the tail end of the hippie era, but the defiant, pacifist spirit and flower-strewn iconography were still a part of the landscape.

What I wanted now was a celebration. "I'll die if I don't go somewhere," I said for the third time that afternoon. Rosie and I were sitting at my kitchen table, nibbling on Bubby's fruit salad. Rosie didn't like the grapefruit, I didn't like the sliced banana, so we traded. "Where can we go?" I whined. "There must be somewhere."

Rosie was also at sea: that morning, her parents had left for Paris with a small group of post-war immigrants from Europe. Mr. Michaeli had resisted at first, but his wife was suddenly animated—even the colour of her eyes seemed to change from dull grey to soft blue. As far as I could tell, Mr. Michaeli felt it would be inexcusable to hold her back; he had commented more than once that she hadn't known what she was going into when she married him. As for his health, a new drug had worked wonders, and his doctor said he could travel if he didn't overstrain himself.

The wonderful coincidence—Rosie available just as I was hankering to get away—proved that it was meant to be.

"We need someone rich," I said. "Someone who can drive us and pay all our expenses."

"Patrick!" we exclaimed in unison. Rosie wasn't entirely serious, but I immediately began looking for his number.

Though Patrick and I had not stayed in touch, and I hadn't heard from Anthony, I often thought of the Moores in their various hideaways around the globe: monastery, attic, mansion, LA.

I dialled Patrick's number. "This isn't Giovanni's Gardening Supplies," he said glumly.

"Patrick? Is that you? It's Maya."

"Oh, hi," he said. He seemed pleased to hear from me. "I keep getting calls for this gardening supplies store. They printed my number on some flyer or something."

"How are you?" I asked. "Rosie's here, she says hi."

"I'm the same," he said with his signature sigh.

"Listen, can we come over? We want to ask you something."

"Yeah, sure. You want a lift?"

He remembered my address and said he'd be there soon. Rosie and I sat by the front window, on the lookout for a white Mercedes. "Where should we ask him to take us?" I wondered, drumming my fingers impatiently on the sill.

"Ottawa?"

"Ottawa! I was thinking of something a little more exciting, Rosie—like the Rockies, maybe. A road trip, right across Canada—that would be cool. Like *The Electric Kool-Aid Acid Test*, except we wouldn't be as obnoxious as those guys. Or stoned out of our skulls."

"Let's get stoned!" Rosie cheered, and we belted out an unrestrained, partly improvised rendition of "Rainy Day Women #12 & 35." We moved on to "Lucy in the Sky with Diamonds" and were in the midst of making loud, silly sniffing noises along with reluctantly aging Lather when Patrick's car screeched to a stop in front of the house. We sprinted downstairs and toppled onto the leather seats. Patrick was half-baffled, half-relieved by our giddiness. He'd grown a beard since we last saw him, a friendly, curly beard with surprising threads of gold.

"Cute beard," I said. "Makes you look like Che Guevara."

"I just got bored shaving. What did you want to ask?"

We told him what we had in mind.

"The Rockies ..." he said doubtfully. "That seems like a long way off. I mean, what if we get on each other's nerves? We'll be stuck. But ... well, I'm not sure it's still around, but we used to have a country house up north. You could go there, if it hasn't been vandalized. Or sold. I'll have to ask my mother."

Rosie, who was sitting in front, touched Patrick's shoulder in gratitude. He drew away with an unmistakable flinch. Rosie wasn't offended. She turned around and said, "It is kind of far. What if I have to come home suddenly? What if Daddy has to come back? I wouldn't want to be way out in Alberta!"

Patrick's body relaxed, though whether because Rosie had withdrawn her hand or the plan, I wasn't sure.

We asked him what he was doing with himself these days. He told us he'd missed the application deadline for Cégep, and for the past year he'd been working, rather pointlessly, at a sleazy magazine store downtown.

"Better than studying for matrics," I said. "Thank God that nightmare's over."

The matriculation exams, in those days, were the only ones that counted for graduation, and I knew I'd have to pass them all. I'd discovered that I didn't need Biology to graduate; I only needed one science credit and, with the help of Miss O'Connor's after-school tutoring, I'd been initiated into the esoterica of chemical inclinations.

That left History, which I'd managed to ignore for four years. I had no choice but to cram, and I spent several nights making lists of calamities, for history in the end was nothing but a series of disasters strung together by treaties and agreements. War and more war; there was always someone with an army, ready to fight. My extracurricular reading helped a little. I knew from Lenny Bruce that Hoover was president of the United States during the Depression, and from Hemingway that the Spanish Civil War had Franco on one side and the Republicans, who hid in caves, on the other. Exams were easy back then, and I managed to pull through. *The first city in history to be atom-bombed was a) Hiroshima b) Tokyo c) Munich d) Nanking.* Now I wanted to rid myself of the super-fluous information I'd been forced to house, exhaustingly, in my brain.

We found Dr. Moore executing an effortless backstroke in a kidney-shaped swimming pool. Rosie and I hadn't noticed the pool before; it was concealed by a high wall of cedar hedges and wasn't visible from Patrick's side of the house. The expression on Dr. Moore's face as she glided through the water—all worldly woes forgot—was one I hadn't seen before. As soon as she noticed us, she swam towards the edge of the pool. She looked like a pink sea plant with her long-sleeved, water-darkened pink leotard and matching cap of jiggling flowers and protruding dots.

"Hello," she said with casual courtesy. She lifted herself out of the pool and wrapped a towel around her waist. "Are you both well?"

Before we could answer, Patrick interjected, "Do we still have that country house?" He never addressed his mother by name. He never addressed anyone by name.

"The cottage in the Laurentians?"

"Yeah. Is it in one piece or has it gone to wrack and ruin?"

"The house is intact as far as I know. Were you thinking of going up there?"

"It's us—we're the ones who asked," I explained. "Me and Rosie."

"Ah. So you would like to go into retreat." I saw that she wanted to be invited; or rather that she wished it were all different, that she was part of a large, happy family. I almost asked her to come along, but Patrick would have killed me. And I don't think she would have accepted the invitation; she knew we wanted to be on our own—that was the whole point. "I can understand that," she said evenly, and her controlled, forlorn voice made me think of one of those shipwrecked sailors you read about, who hang on to sanity by repeating the Latin names of trees.

We discussed the practicalities of opening the house, and it became evident that Patrick would have to come along. He didn't mind being roped in—he was bored with his job and feeling restless. For the first time in our lives there was nothing to hold us back, and we decided to leave the following day. Patrick said he wouldn't be missed at the magazine store; the owner, Sam, was insane and wouldn't even notice.

Rain fell intermittently on the morning of our departure, but I wanted to wait for Patrick downstairs. My mother and Bubby came with me; they huddled under two umbrellas and tried to persuade me to join them. Instead, I lifted my face to the fine drizzle. Soon I'd be playing house with Rosie; the two of us would recline on a rug in front of the fire, go for long walks in the forest. In this sylvan setting, Rosie would realize that what she really wanted was me, and on a leafy bed I'd finally do with her all the things I'd been dreaming about for four years …

I was expanding on these *Girl's Own* adventures when Patrick's Mercedes appeared like a ship against the horizon, ready to take me on board. My mother sniffed and wiped her eyes as I bounced into the car with my knapsack. But she relied on Patrick, who clearly had resources, and I promised to phone from the corner store every day.

Rosie was waiting inside the doorway of her house, with her new guitar—a gift from Avi—by her side, and her arms crossed in front of her as if she were cold or stranded. She was wearing jeans and a black, close-fitting sleeveless top I hadn't seen before. I knew all her clothes, and I wondered whether the top belonged to her mother.

"I'm so glad you're here! What a night—all the rooms creaked, I had to keep the lights on, and I don't think I slept at all. I'm sure there were ghosts."

"You should have called me," I moaned.

"Well, I kept thinking I'd get brave, but it only got worse. I'm never spending a night alone again. Let me get my stuff."

Rosie's stuff turned out to be two enormous, battered suitcases with rusty metal clasps. Her parents had taken to Paris only what they could fit into a small shoulder bag—a change of underwear, T-shirts, their toothbrushes. This eccentric adherence to the bare necessities was in keeping with their usual low-key style, but maybe there were other reasons this time, maybe the old suitcases reminded them of their relocation, or dislocation. They were embarking on a different kind of trip now, a return not exactly in triumph but at least with pleasure in mind.

"The trunk's full," Patrick said. "We'll have to try the back seat." Then, totally out of character, he blurted out, "What do you have in there?"

"Just things we might need. You know. Pillows, sheets, kitchen stuff."

"The house has all that, and my mother gave me sheets. Whatever's missing, I can buy."

We unclasped the suitcases and I helped Rosie remove dishes, cutlery, pots, linen, scissors, rope. "What about games?" she asked hesitantly, pulling out a tattered Monopoly box held together by a rubber band.

"I'm pretty sure we have Monopoly," Patrick said.

Under her black top, Rosie's breasts announced themselves modestly to the world, and in a rare moment of forgetfulness, Patrick stared at the curved outlines as she repacked. He caught himself with a start.

"I love your top," I said slyly. "It suits you. Very femme fatale."

"I don't know about that! I figured now that school's over I'd look kind of weird wearing white shirts, so Mummy bought me some things."

"Patrick, what do you think?"

"About what?"

"Doesn't that top suit Rosie?"

To my delight, Patrick blushed. "Okay. Yes. I think we're all set."

Now that we'd removed the household items, Rosie found she didn't need either suitcase. She stuffed her things in a plastic bag and headed for the car. I asked her to sit in front so I'd have room for my legs.

We were about to set off when she exclaimed, "Wait! Is there a stereo there?"

"I'm not sure it works. But I brought a radio."

"Hold on." She ran back in and returned with her portable record player and the Mother Goose record. "It helps me fall asleep," she said, a little sheepishly.

"Mother Goose?" Patrick was amused, and I think charmed, by Rosie's open admission.

I stretched out on the back seat with two pillows under my head and Rosie's guitar next to me on the car floor. Even when he was home from the hospital, Mr. Michaeli was no longer up to accompanying Rosie on the piano, and she'd stopped singing arias. The

Saturday-night parties weren't the same without Rosie's perform-
ances, so Avi bought her the guitar and taught her a few chords.
Visionary narratives came to life as she sang; her voice echoed
subway wall prophecies, rang out from a lonely tower. We were the
ones who wanted to travel with her—but no one had touched
Rosie, neither her body nor her mind, not really.

Before long we were on the highway that followed old native trails
through the great mountain forests of the Laurentians. The only
sign of human presence in this primeval landscape was a shorn
strip, forged for skiers, slicing down one of the hills. Patrick had to
explain what it was.

"Looks sinister," Rosie said.

Patrick chuckled. "Yeah, who knows what those ski runs could
be up to."

Marcel, the man who'd been taking care of Vera's cottage all
these years, ran a gas station and convenience store at the turnoff
from the highway. He was sitting on a stool behind the counter of
his store, his eyes fixed on a portable television. I was afraid that
when he rose from the stool, the ribbons of yellow flypaper
hanging from the low ceiling would stick to his hair, but he deftly
avoided them as he jumped up and came towards us.

He was slim, white-haired, and wore denim overalls; I wondered
how he felt about the appropriation of his ordinary work clothes by
urban youth. He knew who we were and had been expecting us,
but a proprietary wariness made him grumpy. "You have to turn on
the water," he warned us.

Patrick assured him, in impressively fluent French, that we'd be
fine.

Marcel reverted to French too. He offered us a good price on
firewood and said he'd bring it over later if we liked.

"Parfait," Patrick said. I'd never seen him make this sort of
effort—he was trying to be affable, and it really was a struggle.

Rosie had wandered over to a long, narrow warehouse with a flat roof and corrugated metal siding, just behind the store. The words Marché aux Puces had been painted in fire engine red on the siding. I thought at first that the wavy letters were meant to be decorative, then I saw that the lettering was merely following the furrowed metal.

"I've never been to a flea market," Rosie said. We tried to peek through the windows, but they were dark and dusty, and all we could see was a reflection of ourselves looking in. "Pouvoir regarder?" she asked Marcel, struggling to remember one or two of the hundreds of French classes that had led, apparently, to not very much.

"Fermé."

"Quand … ouvre?"

Marcel took pity on her and switched to English. "That's the affair of my brother-in-law. Ask to him."

While Patrick filled up, I strolled into the miniature store. Four bruised pears, a rusty iceberg lettuce, Kraft cheese slices, chocolate bars, a few tins of soup and baked beans, all looking as if they'd been salvaged from a train wreck. With the ten-dollar bill my mother gave me I bought as much as I could.

As we drove away, Patrick shook his head. "Imagine living in the same small town all your life. The same people day in, day out. How can you not go mad?"

"I'd like it," Rosie said. "I'd like knowing everyone around me. You could see their lives change."

"Yes. The new tires on their car. The postcard from their grand-child in Seattle."

"'There is a place in London town,'" Rosie sang. "'My railroad boy goes and sits down. He takes a strange girl on his knee. And he tells to her what he won't tell me.'"

"Man," Patrick said as we pulled into the unpaved driveway.

I'd expected a simple wood cabin, but Vera Moore's cottage, like her city house, was made of stone and had an Old World look. The prominent pitched roof covered the rectangular walls like an orange-pink lid, and its two dormer windows glinted with hooded eyes in the sun. The screened-in porch, built in a very different style, seemed to have been added on for fun, like an impish architectural afterthought.

The area immediately surrounding the house had been cleared, and a patchy lawn sloped downward from the back porch to the lake. The clearing extended on both sides to the edges of a spruce and white birch forest. The slender birch trees were wrapped in brown and white and black-tipped veils of bark. They cast a siren's spell on me, and I walked over, tugged at the curled end of a papery strip. Parchment for a pillow-book.

"I can't believe this place is still here," Patrick said. He was leaning against the hood of his car as if he hadn't yet decided whether to stay. "I was sure it would be a hollow, burnt-out shell."

"But your mother told us it was in good condition," I reminded him.

"She's easy to dupe."

Rosie had strayed meanwhile to the back lawn. "Look at the lake!" she called out. "Our own private beach—there's even a dock! God, I could stay here forever."

But Patrick ran his hand through his hair and groaned.

"Headache coming on?" I asked.

"No. It's the country. Too much nature." He drew a cigarette out of his shirt pocket and lit it. "I don't like the country."

"Now you tell us," I said. "Were you here a lot as a kid?"

"Oh yes, oh yes, we came every summer. God, what a nightmare."

"Why?"

"No one wanted to be here, but my mother thought it would be good for us. She forced us to go swimming and sailing and canoeing ... I don't like canoes," he added emphatically.

"Did she enjoy it at least?"

"No. We were all miserable. I was miserable because I hate water, which tends to be cold, and nature, which tends to be unpleasant. My mother was miserable because she's allergic to just about everything that grows here. And my father was miserable because he was always miserable."

"Your father was here?"

"Yeah, it was before he left."

"What about Anthony?"

"Tony? I don't know. It was hard to know what was going on in his mind. He went into town a lot, hung out at the local pool joint."

I tried to picture Patrick in a bathing suit. On my bedroom wall I had a print of Piero della Francesca's *Baptism of Christ*, which I'd found in a library discard. It was a glorious scene: the River Jordan in a Tuscan landscape, three seductive angels quietly watching as John and Christ succumb to erotic holiness, a convert stripping in the background. The bearded Christ looks atypically casual as the transparent water encircles his white ankles, while the convert, pulling off his shirt, is caught in mid act, his head lost inside the fabric, his body lovely with readiness. I could see Patrick, white and naked, transplanted into this scene, but unlike Christ he was alone: everyone had left, and he stood unbaptized in the shallow water, exposed and chilly. Stoically he would endure the vertiginous sports, the shame, the mosquitoes.

"Poor Patrick," Rosie said. "We don't have to stay here. We can go to an inn or a hotel if you like. It's just as much fun."

"No, no. It's all in the past." He threw his half-finished cigarette on the ground and crushed it with his shoe.

"It won't be horrible this time round," Rosie promised. "It'll be fun. Can we go down to the water?"

"Sure."

I followed Rosie to the beach. If we squinted, we could make out three or four other clearings along the shoreline, but they were at the other end of the lake, and the houses were either hidden by shrubs or too small to be visible.

Tentatively I stepped onto the wobbly wharf and inhaled deeply, the way we do when we want to inhale a view. The shaded forest fringed the water like a tufted Afro, and the sky above it was a silk canopy of palest blue.

"I wouldn't walk on the dock," Patrick called out from above. "It needs fixing."

"It's fine!" I called back.

"I really wouldn't walk on that," he repeated, coming down to the beach. "I'll fix it tomorrow. I'll get some wood in town."

"Okay, okay," I said, stepping off. For a moment the three of us stood there, as still and silent as the lake.

"I feel like the first person on earth," Rosie said.

"Or the last," Patrick remarked. "I'm going inside."

Dr. Moore's cottage was a naked manifestation of her quest for family intimacy. Indoors, the layout was all open plan: kitchen, dining area, a study corner with a desk, sofas and a rocking chair around a granite fireplace. A picture-window ran the length of the back wall, and sunshine poured in, landing like a stage-light on the braided rugs and knotted floorboards. Everything was scrubbed clean. Dr. Moore must have instructed Marcel to prepare the house for us, and afraid of losing his cushy caretaker's job, he—or more likely his wife—had even washed the curtains.

"Far out!" Rosie said.

"How far out?" Patrick gibed annoyingly.

"Are the bedrooms upstairs?" I asked. A disquieting sensation had come over me. I felt we were trespassing on Dr. Moore's house, on her defenceless generosity. Her dreams of family vacations had fallen flat, leaving only this empty house, heavy with her lonely failure. It made you want to tread carefully, as at any burial ground.

"Yeah. I'll bring in the sheets and things."

We fetched the linen and carried it up the creaky stairs to the attic floor. The four bedrooms radiated symmetrically from a spacious vestibule. The vestibule was beautifully furnished with antique chests and bureaus, but the bedrooms themselves were small and poky, with steeply slanting ceilings and minimal floor space, as if to discourage reclusive tendencies.

"Who gets which room?" I asked.

Clutching a folded sheet to her chest, Rosie whirled around, her head thrown back, and for an odd second she reminded me of Sandy Dennis in *Who's Afraid of Virginia Woolf?*—vulnerable, fragile, and slightly mad. "Anything's fine with me," she said, and my vision readjusted itself. "They're all perfect."

Patrick seemed to have fallen into a semi-stupor. I tapped him on the shoulder. "I wouldn't mind the one with the brass bed. Is that okay?"

"Yeah, sure. That was my dad's room." The word *dad* surprised me, and I wondered whether Patrick was being drawn against his will into the house's—or his own—shunned past.

"You've deserted me!" Rosie called out from the room opposite mine. "Well, don't forget to write."

I sat on the edge of the big brass bed and stroked the polished casting; I had a fleeting urge to kiss it. A country smell clung to the wallpaper, a soporific brew of mushrooms and spruce and wet earth. I lay down, shut my eyes, and like the man in the song, I sank into a dream.

It wasn't until late afternoon that we realized we'd forgotten all about food. I spilled Marcel's derelict groceries on the table, and we stared at the grey lettuce, the bruised pears. Rosie and I had eaten the chocolate bars in the car.

"There should be a restaurant not too far from here," Patrick said.

"We can't go to a restaurant every time we're hungry," I said. "We have to stock up."

We decided to go to the nearest town to pick up groceries. As Patrick drove up the main street he said, "Man, this brings back memories. I'm not sure I'm up to it." His voice was stripped of its usual glib wrappings. "My father liked this place. He said it had a Byronic soul, whatever the fuck that means. Byronic," he repeated, shaking his head, but not derisively—sadly, if anything.

"You miss him," said Rosie.

"Yeah, I guess," he admitted, and I think we both wanted to reach out and embrace him, but of course we didn't.

The town's centre consisted of two streets lined with unassuming, well-maintained establishments: a few somnolent stores, a tall white church, a plant nursery, gravel parking lots, the supermarket, a pizzeria, a restaurant-bar, and a two-storey brick building with plaques that identified its inhabitants as notary, veterinarian, and, intriguingly, *Directeur de conscience*.

As we rolled into the supermarket parking lot, a small gang of teenagers who were hanging out next to a brick wall turned to gaze at us. Most of them were smoking cigarettes—out of profound boredom, it seemed to me.

Like trusting disciples, they approached us. Fifteen, sixteen, seventeen years old, decked out in leather wristbands, fringed vests, bangles, and bandanas. There was a fragile edge to their adopted style; they were pleased with themselves, but they also wanted others to be pleased with them.

A thin-faced, buck-toothed girl smiled at us. She had her arm around the waist of a handsome boy, his midriff smooth and tanned between hip-hugging jeans and a Led Zeppelin T-shirt. Patrick said, "Salut," and the boy touched the hood of the Mercedes as if it were holy. He began asking questions in French. I caught only a few words: *cylindres, suspension, vitesse*.

He was the leader—not because he was the handsomest but because of his courage. His eyes held a twinkling secret, his body was alert, reliable. And now his friends were goading him in

French to ask for a ride. He took up the challenge, swung his long hair as a pledge.

"Sure." Patrick tossed him the keys and the three of us headed for the supermarket. The morning rain had left muddy pools of water on the uneven ground, and Patrick stepped straight into the puddles as he walked.

"Patrick, you're getting your shoes soaking wet!" I said, steering him away from the water.

He peered down absently. "I didn't notice."

"What do you notice?" I asked.

"As little as possible."

The floor of the three-aisle supermarket was made of grey barn-wood and there were tinselly Christmas streamers hanging in loops from the ceiling beams. We filled our cart with apples and bananas, breakfast cereal, milk, juice, peanut butter, canned vegetables, pies in cardboard boxes, bread, cheese, eggs, soda crackers.

At the checkout counter, Rosie pulled a few magazines and comic books from the rack. She wanted to pay for them, but Patrick wouldn't let her. "I owe your father hundreds of dollars," he said.

The car came inching into the parking lot as we emerged from the store with our groceries. The entire gang had managed to squeeze in, and they shouted and waved at us through the open windows.

"Far fucking out," the guy with the bare midriff said in English, as he handed back the keys. "I'm Jean-Pierre, and this is Yves, Manon, Jules, Petit Oiseau, my cousin Glenn from Toronto, and my girlfriend, Jojo."

Patrick invited them to visit any time they liked and gave them directions to the cottage.

"Peace, man," Jean-Pierre said, and the others echoed, "Peace, man. Peace."

In the evening, Marcel came by with logs for the fireplace. It took Patrick a while to get a good fire going; he scrunched up sheets of newspaper, then went scavenging for small sticks. Finally, the flames caught, but Patrick couldn't find the fire-screen and tiny sparks flew out into the room. Rosie was afraid of the sparks and hid behind the sofa. When the fire settled down, she began strumming on her guitar, trying out chords for "Bridge Over Troubled Water." I found a pack of cards and Patrick taught us a new version of Hearts, harder and meaner than the one we knew. We played late into the night.

I woke up in a sea of sunshine. It was late morning, and daylight was pouring in through the dormer window and the half-open door. The little attic room had absorbed the heat, and I was drenched in sweat, but it was the sort of lazy warmth cats seek out. I checked in on Rosie. She was still asleep; she'd been so exhausted by her spooked night and our long first day that she'd gone to bed without her Mother Goose record. Just as well—what would Patrick have made of *Little Boy Blue come blow your horn* ringing through the house?

I remembered my promise to call home. Sunday was my mother's day off, and I knew she'd be sitting apprehensively by the phone, imagining road accidents, drownings, murder in the night. I'd wait for Rosie to wake up, in case she wanted to walk with me to Marcel's store.

I made myself coffee and sat with it on the stairs of the back porch. From this front-row seat I watched the lake's drama of converging colours, shadowy along the edge, then rippling shade by shade into light until the ripples reached the centre and flamed emerald gold. I wondered why I hadn't realized before that art was hard because you had to recreate not merely the scene but the way it soared into your soul and changed you.

Rosie was the last to get up; Patrick was on his second cup of coffee by then and I was on my third bowl of Shreddies. "I'm off to Marcel's to phone my mother," I told her. "Coming with me?"

"I'll drive you," Patrick offered.

"The whole idea is a walk in nature," I said. "Think Tintern Abbey."

Patrick gave a sleepy yawn. "I never did understand that poem."

Rosie and I set out on the country road, the siren forest on either side. For the first time since I'd known her, she hadn't braided her hair before leaving the house, and it tumbled down her arms as if exulting in its release.

"Everything is perfect," I said. "I wonder, will it last?"

"Yes, yes it will," Rosie replied. She wanted to wave a wand and make everything good, but in fact, in actual fact, she was as helpless as the rest of us. And that failure was a reply to my question, for it made me sad, and I reached out and stroked her hair.

Marcel's wife, a garrulous woman with a double chin and a booming voice, was running the store this morning. She asked us in Québécois French how everything was going. There was something specific she wanted to know, but we couldn't understand a word she was saying, so we stood there nodding stupidly and smiling. I left Rosie to handle the situation and called home from the public booth, hung up at the first ring, retrieved my dime, dialled again. Safeguarded by the secret code, my mother picked up the phone, and I held the receiver a few inches from my ear as she rehearsed her battles. Fanya in armour, a chubby knight on a chubby horse, wielding her sword.

Patrick had asked for a copy of *La Presse*; we bought chocolate bars with the change and munched on them as we turned back. A path trailing into the forest caught my eye. "Let's see where it goes," I suggested.

The sinewy path took us to three sun-bleached boulders on the edge of the lake—a popular lookout, judging from the empty cigarette boxes, discarded beer cans, and scrawled graffiti: initials inside hearts, the inevitable cartoon phallus. Millions of years on this planet, and males were still drawing phalluses on rocks. Rosie and I arranged ourselves on the slanted dips and panels of the grainy boulders. "I love being ordinary," Rosie said. "I love the idea of having an ordinary life."

We heard a sound behind us and turned. There were two men coming down the path, unpleasant men who made me think of roosters. Rosie and I jumped up with a squeal and rushed past them. The men clucked, blurted out something unintelligible, spread their arms in a show of interest. One of them touched my wrist and I slapped his arm with the only weapon at hand— Patrick's *La Presse*. Shrieking and laughing, we ran all the way to the road.

"How did they know we were there?" Rosie wondered.

"They probably have smell glands, like dogs."

A few minutes later a truck passed us and there were the two men, leaning out of the rolled-down windows. This time we heard what they had to say all too clearly: "Suck my cock!" With this intelligent communication they sped away, leaving a cloud of dust behind them.

"I think I would literally rather die than suck their cocks," I said.

"I would rather die ten times over."

"I would rather die ten times over and be tortured."

"I would rather die ten times over and be tortured and fall into a snake pit."

"With rats in it."

"And spiders."

"And killer bees."

Patrick was waiting for us in the driveway. To our astonishment, he was quivering from head to toe, as if in the grip of a fever. "Where were you?" he asked, his voice shaky. "I drove out to look for you and I couldn't find you anywhere."

"I'm sorry," Rosie said. "We were just resting on a rock near the lake. I'm sorry you were worried."

"I suddenly had a bad feeling," he said, still upset.

"We can take care of ourselves," I told him. "You're not responsible for us, Patrick. Relax!"

"Well, I was worried." It was a side of Patrick that was entirely new to us. A hair's breadth from the surface, he was harbouring all this.

"Want to come for a swim?" I asked.

"I'll pass," he said, back in form.

The lake had been frozen all winter and had not yet absorbed the summer heat to any discernable degree. We almost changed our minds about going in, but we held hands, counted to three, and ducked into the icy water with a howl. We splashed around while Patrick fixed the dock, then we stretched out on towels and read Rosie's magazines.

We were bored with hard-boiled eggs and canned peas, so Patrick drove into town to pick up some pizza. He returned with half the pizzeria, it looked like; luckily the freezer was large and we managed to store the extra boxes. After we ate, I took over the sofa and delved into *The Nazarene*, a novel by Sholom Asch that Esther, the ever-faithful librarian, had recommended—a hundred times better than Kazantzakis's *The Last Temptation of Christ*, she'd insisted, and I agreed. Patrick revived the fire, and Rosie rocked gently in the rocking chair, staring at the flames. On the radio Laura Nyro sang in her clear, aching voice about dying for her captain. The DJ promised a Laura Nyro evening; he was in that sort of mood, he confided in a low, languid, and possibly stoned voice. As night fell, an army of insects appeared on the picture-window. I recognized the moths, dragonflies, and beetles, but there were other creatures that looked like monster aliens in B-movies. "Insect carnival," I said, flattening my hand on the glass. But Rosie shuddered and turned to face the other way.

And then there was a loud knock on the door, followed by a gruff voice with a heavy, unplaceable accent. "Police! Police, open up!"

Rosie was terrified. She jumped from her chair and clutched my arm.

"Oh, Rosie. I'm sure it's nothing," I said. Then I remembered seeing a small stash of marijuana on one of the linen chests upstairs. "Uh-oh," I whispered. "Did you hide the grass, Patrick?"

But Patrick was calm. "It's only my brother," he told us.

He was right. It was you, Anthony, crashing into our lives, with the Angel of Death close on your heels.

You bellowed, "Police, maudit, open up, you goddamn hippie degenerates! Open up or I'll shoot the door down!"

Patrick muttered, "What's he doing here?" He unlocked the door and you walked into the house. You were wearing a suit and a green-and-black tartan tie, but the knapsack you'd slung diagonally over your shoulder was straight out of Desolation Row.

You said, "Ha, I knew it. Orgies, LSD—come on, empty your pockets, empty everything." And as you spoke, you yourself began emptying your pockets, pouring onto the counter handfuls of capsules, pills, white powder in little plastic bags, rectangular bars wrapped in tin foil.

You were completely wired. It was your Camp Bakunin repertoire, set to highest pitch. You hadn't changed all that much since I last saw you, but your face was pale, almost ashen.

"How ya doin', brother Pat?"

As if sensing that a buffer might be called for, Rosie glided over to you and introduced herself. "Hi, I'm Rosie. You must be Patrick's brother, the journalist."

"Rosie, Rosie." You took her hand and kissed it. "It's a pleasure to meet you."

Patrick asked, "What are you on? Do you want water, or something?"

"Good idea, my saintly brother." Then you spotted me. "My God, Joan of Arc—is it really you? Or maybe I'm just stoned and you're a figment of my imagination."

"No, I'm real," I said.

"My favourite person from our touchingly idealistic camp. How young we were."

"What are you on?" Patrick asked again.

"I'm on vacation, my good brother. Three weeks off, and my wife left me, how about that, so I thought I'd run up to see Mother Moore and my dear brother Pat."

A wife! It seemed impossible.

You wandered over to the window and peered past the insect invasion into the darkness. A pagan darkness, where lost souls wandered. In a lower, slower voice you said, "God, remember this fucking place? What a nightmare! Remember the canoe—Dad in the canoe in the middle of the night?"

"Not really," Patrick said, handing you a glass of water. The water was safe to drink but cloudy with sediment.

"Liar. You remember. Thank you, excellent." You stared at the misty water. "Water, water everywhere ... Want some truly fine acid? Abbie himself ... On second thought, I'd advise against it."

"How come you're wearing a suit?" I asked.

"Why am I wearing a suit? Because I had a business dinner this very evening, and I had to impress some extremely businesslike people, who were all wearing jeans and leather jackets, as it happens. Business chic."

Patrick made you coffee and set the mug next to the drugs. "Is that true, about Gloria?"

"Gloria, ah yes—Gloria, my wife. My former wife, I should say. My vanished wife. Gloria has joined a splinter group of a break-off group of an alternative group of the Black Panthers. We're no longer in touch. Or rather, she's not in touch with me. I've made numerous efforts to discover her exact whereabouts, but apparently it's a well-guarded secret."

"I'm sorry to hear that," Patrick said, and I was suddenly furious with him. He was covering himself as always, in case he regretted the emotion, in case someone took advantage of his vulnerability. But there were times when irony was unforgivable.

You didn't seem to notice. You said, "Yeah. It's too bad because you know what? I really loved that woman. Love. How's Woofie, by the way? I only had time for a quick hello."

"Did he recognize you?" Patrick asked, kinder now that the conversation had moved to Woofie.

"What an insulting question, though whether insulting to Woofie or to me, I'm not sure. He was delighted to see me, of course. How's his digestion these days?"

"Not too bad. We're keeping him on a strict diet. Why don't you sit down? You're making me nervous."

"Okay." You threw yourself on the sofa. "I'm usually like this," you said, turning to Rosie. "Ask Pat. Ask St. Joan. They know me at my worst. Is anyone here going out with anyone else?"

"No," Rosie said. "We're just friends."

"Yes, babes in the wood—literally. Well, you know what Oscar Wilde said about friendship between women and men. Or was it Chekhov?"

"Chekhov," Patrick said.

"That's right—*Uncle Vanya*. Patrick and I used to read plays together—did he tell you? But that was long ago ... Excuse me as I stagger to the toilet. I may need to throw up."

As soon as you'd disappeared into the washroom, Patrick said, "Sorry about this."

"Sorry about what? You don't deserve such a nice brother," I sniped.

"I didn't say he wasn't nice," Patrick replied evenly.

You returned, looking bewildered. You sat down on a dining-room chair, struggled to regain your equilibrium. "Has my brother been apologizing for me?"

"We're all glad you came," Rosie said. "You can unwind here. It's very peaceful. There's leftover pizza in the freezer, if you're hungry."

"That's very kind. But please don't bother about me. I rarely eat, isn't that true, brother Pat? I seem to remember there are four bedrooms in the Moore Resort, so if no one minds I'll just crash in one of them."

You left us, and we heard your footsteps on the creaky attic floor, followed by an eerie silence.

I felt restless; I wanted something. Oh, yes—I wanted to know more about your wife. People like you didn't get married any more, they just moved in together, hung out. "When did he get married?" I asked Patrick.

"I don't know. Around a year ago, I guess."

"Was there, you know, a wedding?"

"No. Or at least if there was, I wasn't invited. He got married in L.A."

"What's she like—Gloria?"

"She's beautiful."

"Beautiful! I've never heard you say that about anyone."

"Well, it stands out. I think she was a model."

"I'm tired," I said. "It's the country air, and that long walk. What about you, Rosie?"

"I feel wide awake! I think I'll stay up a while longer."

Inside a dream, Rosie's voice was calling me. "Maya?"

But sleep was reining me in, and I couldn't answer.

"Maya? I took something after everyone went to sleep—now I feel weird."

"What do you mean?" I mumbled. The words were drawn from a floating dictionary, page eleven fifty-nine.

"I took something from the counter. You know, all that stuff Tony brought."

I hauled myself to the surface, tried to sit up. "Well, how do you feel?"

"Energetic. I feel like swimming."

"No, don't go swimming. I'll come with you, we'll go for a walk."

With clumsy fingers I pulled on my jeans and shirt, grabbed my knapsack. Outside, a large albino animal squatted in the dark—it was Patrick's Mercedes; and behind it, fender touching fender, your funny yellow jeep. I knew Patrick kept a flashlight in his glove compartment, but he'd locked the car and I wasn't sure where the keys were.

I had better luck with your jeep, which you'd left unlocked. The light came on when I opened the door. There was a briefcase on the back seat, its lid up, and papers were spilling out of it in disarray. The glove compartment gave off a faint scent of perfume, and the tingling guilt of an intruder crept over me as I rummaged through ghostly female relics: makeup, hand lotion, blue-framed sunglasses. No flashlight.

"I guess we won't need one," I said. It was a cloudless, moonlit night, and little quartz stones glimmered on the road. "But the mosquitoes are going to eat us alive. Let me get you a sweater." I went inside and found someone's old pullover in the closet. When I came back out, Rosie was nowhere in sight.

"Rosie, where are you?" I called out.

I heard her laugh softly, but I couldn't tell where the sound was coming from.

"Come over here, to the car."

"Here I am," she said, emerging from the shadows. "I was in the lost forest. There are such strange birds in the sky. Black and blind, like clocks."

"Give me your arms." I helped her into the sweater. As usual, I'd stuffed my knapsack with emergency provisions, including a bottle of mosquito repellent. I rubbed the repellent on our clothes— Mimi's old trick. As we set out, an oppressive feeling came over me. It was loneliness. That's what drugs did: they distanced you from everyone. Rosie was light years away, but she'd been that way always, and the drugs were only a neon billboard's flashing bulletin, because over the years I'd managed to forget.

"I'm sorry I got you out of bed," she said.

"I don't mind."

I reached out for her hand and held it in mine so she wouldn't escape again, and also because we couldn't see clearly. It was instinctive, holding hands in the dark; it helped you navigate, and Rosie's gratitude as she moved closer to me made me feel better. The numinous forest on either side of the road was like the entrance to heaven, the entrance to hell. *Halfway through this mortal journey—*

Partway through it, anyhow, we came to the gas station. The light of a single lamppost cast long shadows on the pump apparatus. A good setting for a play, I thought—a stumbled-upon sign of tenuous civilization, in the middle of nowhere, on a summer night.

"I think we're in Oz. Oh, if only I could get into the flea market!"

The letters on the side of the warehouse wavered like hieroglyphics from the underworld. I tried the door, not expecting it to yield, but it swung open, seemed in fact to be hanging somewhat precariously on its hinges. Miraculously, I found the light switch. In an instant, like God's creation, the flea market came into existence. The castoffs of an entire city seemed to lie before us. Attics and basements, the closets of children now married and grandparents now deceased, vacated bedrooms and kitchens: all had been emptied and the contents brought to rest in Marcel's brother-in-law's flea market.

"Maybe Daddy's things are here," Rosie said, "The things he lost—you know."

"No, I don't know. Let's go before you start seeing things."

"I want to stay here. I'll bring him back some plates."

"You can't get those things back," I said, pushing away the apparition of the cashmere sweater in my mother's dresser drawer.

She began strolling down the aisles, collecting dented high-heeled shoes and old wallets.

"We can't take these—there's no one to pay," I said. "We'll come back tomorrow, I promise. You can put them here in the meantime." I handed her an empty laundry basket and she filled it with her treasures. Then she dropped an embroidered pillow on the dusty floor and lay down on her back. She said, "Daddy played the violin, and that's how he survived. They liked his playing. He says he only did it because he thought his parents might be alive somewhere, or his sisters. So he made the effort, because for himself he didn't care. He played, and he forced himself to be half-blind. He found a way not to see, he made everything blurry. And things are still blurry for him. Because he said if he had seen he wouldn't have been able to play, or to stay sane."

"Get up, Rosie. We have to go home."

"He envied the people who threw themselves against the electric fence or found a way to hang themselves. Or volunteered to replace someone during a selection. Some of the people who volunteered were heroes, but some of them just didn't want to live and Daddy wished he could volunteer too. But he thought there was a chance at least one of his sisters was alive because she made it across the border."

"I wish I could phone Patrick," I said. "He'd come get us."

"I can't move. I've been buried alive."

"Come on, let's go." I gripped Rosie's wrists, helped her up, and led her out of the warehouse.

As we walked back, she sang her *Magic Flute* aria about vanishing love. *Nimmer kommt ihr, Wonnestunde, Meinem Herzen mehr zurück. Never again will the hour of bliss return to my heart.*

"It feels good, this stuff," Rosie said when we were back in the house.

"That's the point. That's why people do it. Don't take any more pills."

"I only took one."

"Who knows what's in that stuff! You can't trust the people who make those drugs. Will you stay in your room now?"

"Yes, I'm very sleepy," she said.

I checked the clock in the foyer; it was four in the morning. Soon it would be light. I drew the curtains in my attic room and slept until noon the following day.

There was no one downstairs, and I thought at first that everyone had gone for a drive and left me behind. Then I realized I was the only one who was awake.

I peeked into Rosie's room. Her black hair was damp with sweat and clung to her flushed cheeks.

I had coffee and a banana; I walked to Marcel's store to phone my mother; I walked back; I sat by the lake and read. At four o'clock I opened a can of corn and, standing at the counter Patrick-style, I dug out the starchy kernels. I was starting to wonder whether anyone was ever going to wake up when I heard a soft tread behind me. It was you, Anthony, in bare feet, eyes bleary, unshaven. You were wearing the same trousers, creased now and slightly askew, but you'd put on a clean short-sleeved shirt. Your hair was rumpled and seemed longer today. You opened the faucet and cupped your hands under the cold water, splashed it on your face.

I said, "Rosie took one of these last night." I trailed my fingers through the drugs that lay scattered like candies on the counter. "I had to spend half the night walking with her."

"Really? What did she take?"

"I don't know. She said she only took one, though."

"Well, then, she'll be okay. At least it's all pure stuff. I wish she'd asked me, though. I would have talked her out of it."

"That's why she didn't ask. She didn't want to be talked out of it."

You'd shed some of your skins overnight—for no other reason, I guessed, than that you were exhausted and had come down from whatever you'd been on.

"I'm against drugs," I said.

"So am I."

"It's the fault of the pushers. They're taking advantage of people."

"You're right, Joan. Damn the pusher-man. So, what do you make of my little brother? Figure him out? Pass me some of that superb coffee, please. Instant is my favourite."

"I don't know. He's a bit … removed."

"Removed. Indeed. Now how about we all remove ourselves to a restaurant?"

You stood behind me and slid your arms around my waist, rested your head on my shoulder. "I'll get Pat, you get Rosie," you said. Then you let go and climbed up to the attic, and I followed.

Rosie stirred as soon as I called her name. She sat up, crossed her legs, and smiled. "Hi, Maya … I feel so strange. What's going on?"

"Anthony wants to take us out to eat."

"I'm sorry—I kept you up all night!"

"I didn't mind. How do you feel now?"

"Strange. Thirsty."

"I'll make you coffee while you dress."

Either in celebration or in a mood of contrition, Rosie decided to wear a white summer dress with a gentle flair at the waist, a low U-shaped dip at the back. My mother had made the dress for her; I'd seen the muslin fabric sliding into the sewing machine, but not the final result. With her hair loose and her skin still winter-white, she looked unscathed and somehow motionless, as though she were turning into porcelain.

"Ah, what a ravishing, or shall I say ravishable, sight," you said when you saw her coming down the stairs. You'd shaved and put on your shoes, and your tie dangled untied from your neck. "It breaks the frail heart, that dress. I think my brother is beginning to regain consciousness." You sat down at the dining-room table and fumbled with your tie. "So, Rosie," you went on. "I hear you've been poking about in my wee collection."

"Sorry, I should have asked. Only I knew you'd say no. I still feel strange."

"Never mind. Just don't do it again—this stuff can kill you.
Where is that guy?"

Patrick joined us, groggy and grumbling. "I still don't understand why you had to wake me up," he complained.

You moved the jeep and we climbed into the Mercedes, all four
of us off-centre, though for different reasons. Patrick was half-
asleep, Rosie was half-high, you were on another plane altogether,
and I was worried about Rosie, worried about you. Patrick, I knew,
could take care of himself.

"Ever the old Mercedes," you said. "Famous Nazi war car.
Himmler himself … Hey, remember the Porsche, Pat? Remember
the Moving Phallus? Oh, the hopes Mother Moore had for us!"

Patrick started the car. "Where exactly are we going?" he asked,
as if he'd been told but had forgotten.

"An inn not far from here. Head north, I'll direct you from
there. Remember that seafood place?" You turned to us. "We all
had food poisoning, except for Pat, who doesn't eat seafood. At
least there was someone to drive us to the hospital and stop the car
when we had to vomit. True family intimacy. We almost died, all
three of us. Pat would have been left on his own, a circumstance
beyond his wildest dream, isn't that right, Pat?"

"I didn't want you to die, actually," Patrick said.

"True, true. You were quite the mother hen at the hospital.
Mournful and holy among the beds. Those were the days, my
friend."

We got lost on the way to the inn—you couldn't remember the
route and someone gave us wrong directions. Twice we had to stop
for Rosie, first because she was thirsty and then because she had to
pee. Patrick suggested giving up, but you were insistent and said,
"A last supper is on the agenda."

Finally we found the inn, a gabled, medieval-style château
surrounded by lily ponds and extraordinary flowers: incandescent
orange, piercing blue, drops of ruby light.

"'All night by the rose, rose,'" you recited. "'All night by the rose I lay.' I wish.'"

"They won't let us in here," Patrick muttered.

"Leave it to me, brother mine."

Ignoring the tense look of the desk clerk, you led us through the wide, carpeted lobby straight to the dining room. The maitre d' barred our way at the entrance.

"Je suis desolé, I'm very sorry, sir, no jeans permitted." He meant me and Patrick; you and Rosie were more than presentable.

"Yes, I know—we're on assignment, just dashing through with no time to change. And this is the only worthwhile place for miles." You took out your journalist's ID and handed it, along with a folded fifty-dollar bill, to the confused man.

The maitre d' hesitated, then let us through, maybe because it was early and the restaurant was nearly empty. We were shown to a corner table. Glittering glasses, glittering cutlery, cloth napkins folded into swan shapes.

"Why do you need to eat at this sort of place?" Patrick asked. "We don't fit in, we're just embarrassing ourselves and everyone else."

"Not at all, we look like bohemians and artists, which we are, each in our own way. As for me, I've been spoiled by the fine cuisine of Sir Davies of Mooreland."

Patrick smiled.

"What is it?" you asked.

"Oh, nothing."

"Come on."

"Nothing, nothing."

"Tell big brother Tony."

"I was just remembering—" He chuckled with pleasure.

"That chicken dish with the celery?"

Patrick nodded.

It was an unexpected treat, this sidetrack into intimacy. "What happened?" I asked.

"Oh, we played a trick on Mother Moore. Added several random ingredients to one of our dear cook's creations."

"Well, did she notice?" I asked.

"I think we gave it away by laughing. Mind you, she's easily duped."

"Funny, Patrick said the exact same thing about your mom." I pictured the two of you, giggling from behind a doorway, peeking at your gullible mother. Two cute kids, being mischievous. An ordinary family.

"She said it was an interesting dish and ate it all. We added honey and olives and mayonnaise and apple butter, as I remember."

"And herring," Patrick said joyously.

"How could I have forgotten! Of course, herring."

"How could you forget the herring, man? The herring was the whole point."

"And she ate it? I feel sick just hearing about it," I said.

"She ate anything Davies made," you said. "Think she ever got it on with him, Pat? I wonder. Two lonely souls under the same roof."

"Could we change the subject?" Patrick suggested. "I'm losing what minimal appetite I had."

You laughed, and your laugh was strange and spooky, as if you were inside a cave. "Sorry, sorry. I've always been gauche. It's a terrible liability in my line of work."

Patrick said, "I'd think being stoned out of your mind is a liability. You're going to end up a junkie."

"Never fear. The sight of a needle makes me shake all over. I fainted recently during a blood drive."

"Who would want your blood? The poor guy who got it would wake up from his operation an addict."

"So true."

"What do you do, Anthony, exactly?" I asked.

"Ah, that's the question—what exactly do I do? I write for a financial journal. I report on the gettings and spendings of various regimes. Fascinating, in its own way. Have I sold my soul, Pat?"

"How would I know? You've never showed me anything you've written," Patrick said, sounding almost offended.

"Modesty wouldn't allow it."

"Were the two of you friends growing up?" I asked. You and Patrick seemed very close suddenly.

But you gazed at me blankly, and so did he. Then you cupped my elbow with your hand and said, "You carry a blueprint for utopia in your breast pocket, don't you, Joan? You do have breasts, I assume. If I'm out of line, just kick me."

I leaned over so you could look down my shirt.

"Well, now. Not exactly hills like white elephants," you said, peering in, "but perhaps dunes like white moths. Oh, glorious sight. Be still, my heart."

"Time doesn't exist," Rosie said. "The future, in which we've all died, is already here, and the past, before we were born, is already here. Time drifts in and out the window."

"Very good, Rosie," you said gently.

"Whatever happened to all those people from Bakunin?" I asked. "Mimi, Sheldon, Bruno ..."

"So touching, the faith we had in our capacity to change the world. I don't know. I don't know what happened to them, I haven't kept in touch."

"You had a crush on Olga, I think."

"How adolescent those feelings seem now, in the light of my more immature feelings for Gloria."

"I can't believe I'm sitting here with you and Rosie and Patrick and we're all friends," I said. "I adore everyone!"

"Why?" Patrick asked.

"My brother is so cordial," you said. "I think we should decide what we're having before Joan here makes us all weep. Ever the vegetarian, Pat?"

But after the waiter had come and gone, you floundered, as if you'd lost your footing and were waiting for a chance wave to carry you back to shore. You slumped in your chair, looking despondent.

"Have a drink," Patrick said, and at that moment the two of you could have been dual projections of a single person, each half revealing the unseen side of the other. Patrick's agitated dispassion was a mirror reflection of excitability; your iconoclastic monologues were mirror reflections of harried ideology. You loved each other in spite of everything; I wondered whether your mother knew.

The inn was air-conditioned, and when we came out of the château, the heat seemed artificial for a few seconds, as if we'd stepped onto a movie set.

You said, "Shall we go dancing? Of course, nightlife in these parts is somewhat limited, but the desk clerk suggested an establishment known as Cheri."

"Like in that song, *The Crucifixion*," Rosie said. "Do you like Phil Ochs, Tony?"

"Can one possibly not like Phil Ochs? After you."

I don't remember the drive to Cheri. We were nearing the longest day of the year and it was still light out, but the club was dark and smoky. Other than that, Cheri didn't look much like a bar or dance club; the room was too large, the tables too spread out, the curtained windows too respectable. There was a live band, however, and their electronic equipment was on full blast.

"Look! It's Jean-Pierre!" I yelled into Rosie's ear. The lead singer of the band was the boy with the tanned midriff who'd driven Patrick's Mercedes.

We sat down at a table and shouted our orders—beer for you and Patrick, a double vodka and orange juice for me. I wasn't afraid of alcohol, only of drugs. The effects of alcohol were predictable, and they wore off after a few hours, leaving you exactly as you were before. Rosie asked for water, and you nodded your approval. "Never mix eye of newt with toe of frog," you said. "Maya, may I have this dance?"

"Oh, Anthony! I can't," I moaned. "I have seven left feet."

"I'll dance with you," Rosie said, and the two of you walked hand in hand to the dance floor. You didn't jiggle ecstatically like the others; you held Rosie close, prom-style, as if hearing a ballad. It didn't matter. It was cool to do your own thing, if you knew how to do it. You looked lovely and happy, you and Rosie, and I wanted that moment to be the way things were, always, rather than a brief digression.

Jean-Pierre spoke between numbers, but his French was too slangy or the volume was too high for me to make out what he was saying. Time drifted in and out the windows, as Rosie had said. Suddenly there was a commotion at one of the tables and we all turned to look. A scruffy-looking guy with shoulder-length hair was writhing on the floor, calling for help. He swung his head from side to side and shouted, "Mon Dieu, aide-moi!"

"'Piper, pipe that song again,'" you said. "Now *there's* a junkie. Time to go, children."

But Rosie didn't want to desert the junkie. "Can't someone help him?" she pleaded.

"There's nothing we can do," you said. Patrick paid for the drinks and we left Cheri.

"Poor thing," said Rosie, as we walked to the car.

"Yeah, poor thing," Patrick echoed, but the parody was absurdly out of place in the circumstances, and because I was slightly drunk, it frightened me.

We drove back to the cottage in silence; I think we all felt that our outing had started to come apart at the seams. Though it had grown cooler, when we disembarked you decided to go for a swim, so we all stumbled down to the lake. The moon looked dusty under shredded grey clouds, and in the faint light that reached us from the house we were shadowy figures who could have been anybody.

You stripped and ran into the water with a strange roar. Rosie, still in her white dress, followed you in.

I sat on a blanket and watched the two of you splashing under the unfathomable night sky, with its lonely yellow-grey moon and stars that had burnt out four million years ago.

Rosie waved at me from the lake. "I'm coming out now!" She dragged herself towards the blanket, snuggled up next to me, and fell asleep.

"We have to take her inside," I said. "She's all wet."

"I'll do it," Patrick said resentfully. With surprising strength he lifted Rosie and slung her over his shoulder, as if she were a wounded soldier. I was sure she'd wake up, and maybe that was the intention, but she didn't stir.

You'd found in one of the linen chests a large bath towel decorated with Halloween skeletons, witches on broomsticks, leering pumpkin faces. You draped the towel around your waist and said, "This wayfarin' stranger wouldn't mind a bed either. May I join you, Maya? I don't think I can make it through the night on my own."

I said, "Sure," and we went inside. You lay down on your back on the brass bed. I sat beside you, wide awake.

"What happened with your wife?" I asked.

"Oh, it's a short story. I can't go into it." Your voice was slow and easy; it was the unguarded voice you'd revealed to me when you braided my hair that morning on the beach, when I was twelve.

"How did you meet?"

"At a party."

"Where?"

"New York. I can't really get into it."

"What's she like?"

"Gloria? She's been through a lot."

"What happened?"

You turned over on your side to face me. "No father, mother died when she was two. She was taken in by an aunt who also died, then there was a series of foster homes, if you can call them that—until she found this boyfriend. I couldn't possibly describe him to you. He got her into soft-porn modelling and took her to clubs and that's where we met, at a club. He got all heavy, and I rescued the damsel in distress."

"When did you get married?"

"A month after we met."

"Did she really join the Black Panthers?"

"Someone invited these revolutionaries to a Hollywood party as a showpiece, some Black Panther ripoff group, and they initiated Gloria into the great black cause."

"She's black?"

"Half, I think. She thinks."

"If it's just the group ... she'll get bored with them. Or they'll have a fight. She'll start missing you and she'll come back."

He didn't answer for a few minutes. Then he said, "It wasn't working out anyhow."

"How come? In what way?"

"I don't know, Maya. It was doomed, probably, from the start. Not that I didn't try. We did the whole scene, shuttling back and forth between 54 in New York and pool parties in L.A. It's hard to explain what those things are like. It's not just that it's meaningless, that would be okay, most of life is meaningless. It's that it's so unbelievably malicious. You really get to understand, when you watch status-hungry people, how fascism works—how easily people are drawn into fantasies of power and control, what a thin veneer it all is. Everyone so terrified of not fitting in—fitting in to what? And they'll do anything, and I mean anything, to prevent that from happening. It would be pathetic if it didn't make them so nasty and stupid ... But I went along with all of it for Gloria's sake. It seemed to be what she wanted, even though I didn't think it was good for her. She wasn't like the others, but she wanted something, and she thought that's where she'd find it. I'm not saying we could have made it if we'd been somewhere else. It probably would have ended no matter what. I just couldn't give her what she wanted, whatever that was or is."

"You have integrity."

"You must be joking. You must be joking. You're not idealizing me, are you? Because I was your counsellor at camp or some shit like that?"

"No, you do."

You sat up and said, "You of all people, not to see through that ..." You looked around as if searching for something.

"What is it?" I asked.

"I need a smoke." You darted out of the room and returned with a nearly empty pack of cigarettes.

"Did you really burn your novel?" I asked.

You lit a cigarette and inhaled deeply. You said, "I disposed of it in a less dramatic way."

Your towel was slipping, and without thinking I drew the bedspread around my shoulders. "I'm sure it was better than you thought."

"I'm sure it was worse."

You laughed your spooky, hollow laugh, and I said, "Your laugh scares me."

"Everyone says that. I won't laugh."

"No, it's good, it matches that snazzy Halloween towel. What was your novel about?"

"The struggle of the proletariat."

"Really?"

"No. It was about a guy who bore an uncanny resemblance to myself, living a life uncannily similar to mine. It was stunningly bad, believe me."

"I'm sure it wasn't. I wish you hadn't thrown it out ... Why does Patrick hate your mother so much?"

"Does he? Does he hate her? I think it's just a game they both enjoy playing."

"I don't think she enjoys it."

"No, no—you're right. Enjoyment doesn't really apply in Vera's case. You know, your mother used to call every day at Bakunin."

"Really? No one told me!"

"Mimi took the calls. She'd reassure your mother that you were okay, then after about three minutes she'd start clicking the button and moving the receiver away, pretending they were losing the connection. Your poor mother never caught on. I don't know how you came out so together, living with her."

"My grandmother lives with us too. And I'm not together. You saw how not together I am, when you left me that letter."

"Yes, the story of my miraculous conception. Dad always communicated that way, through letters and notes—even when he was living with us. He'd hide them in books he thought Vera would read, or under her dinner plate ... I guess they couldn't communicate directly—Vera was like on Morse code or something. Dad got really drunk once, when we were up here, and he went out naked in the canoe ... but that's another story."

"Did you ever ... you know, look for the notebook?"

"What do you think?"

"I wouldn't ..."

"You would, if Vera was your mother."

"But Patrick never did," I said. "I hope you don't mind that I asked him."

"Did he know about it?"

"Yes, he knew, but he has no interest in reading it. He says he never will ... Why is Patrick so untouchable?"

You stared into space and ashes from your cigarette fell on the bedspread. "I don't know. He was like that even when he was really young. Once, we were all sitting around the Christmas tree, our grandparents were there too—they flew in from London. Dad was being friendly, and he put his hand on Pat's thigh. Pat jumped as though he'd been electrocuted. He went all white and I thought he was going to strangle poor Dad. Instead he left the house, took a taxi to the SPCA, and came home with Woofie."

"That's strange."

"Yes. He was always easily embarrassed, though. Always shy. Maybe he got it from Vera. I can't remember her ever kissing or hugging us. She probably did when we were little, but I can't remember it. She was nice to us, but it was Dad we went to for affection. We climbed on his lap. At least I did. I remember that, climbing on his lap, inspecting his ears and his beard."

"You know, Patrick pretends the two of you aren't close. But when I see you together ... you act like brothers."

"I never know what he's thinking. No one does, he doesn't open up."

You stubbed out your cigarette on one of the rungs of the headboard. Then you removed the damp towel, which in any case had come loose, and slid under the sheet, lay flat on your back again. Something dark and foreign had flapped around between your legs for a second, before I averted my eyes.

"You read plays together?"

"Yeah, he was a smart kid. I took him to movies, taught him pool ... we did things together. Then Dad left, and I left right after. That was probably hard on him, both of us leaving around the same time. Just him and Vera and that creepy Davies in the huge house."

"Your mother once interpreted a dream for me."

"Really? What did you dream?"

I described the fox dream—the creatures gutted out in the opening shots of a movie, the instruments on the table, the evolutionary progression from creature to creature until at last I was the one on the table, blonde and unfreckled, and then the title of the movie coming on the screen: *The Fox*. I added a part I'd neglected to tell Dr. Moore—the cinema I was sitting in: I was the only one there, and the seats alternated between sickly light blue and primary red, and they were made of a revolting, absolutely revolting, kind of plastic.

"You mother said I wanted to have guts, and fun, and to be foxy."

You shook your head and said, "Poor Vera, she tries so hard, but she always gets it wrong. That dream is about your future, Joan. You're going to be looking inside people, inside yourself. You already do that. You don't realize how different you are—everything with you is on a level most people don't even know exists."

"I know I'm weird," I sighed. "Where's your father now?"

You shrugged. "Who knows? He ran away, he could be anywhere. Vera wouldn't let him in, she wouldn't let anyone in. She drove him mad, in the end. Maybe that's what Pat's so angry about—that she hurt Dad so much. Even though he'd probably be lost regardless. That's just the way he is."

"My mother's the exact opposite. She's nothing but emotions," I said. I, too, lay down, suddenly tired, but I didn't slide in under the sheet. I didn't want to touch your naked body.

"You know, not saying a word, like Vera, and going on and on like your mother—it comes down to the same thing. What I can't figure out is why they decided to stay alive. What's the point of living, if it gets bad enough? Why torture yourself? Maya, can I touch you? Would it freak you out?"

"I don't know."

"Can I try?"

"Yes."

I shut my eyes and sank into waves of pleasure. With my serviceable scarf I'd only ever managed to quell the sensations brought on by dreary homework and imagined rescues. It turned out there was more to it.

You said, "I've never seen anything like this. You were born to come. Here, I'll show you how to do it yourself." And like someone outlining the features of a car, you gave me a lesson in anatomy.

"I didn't know it was so easy," I said.

"The things they don't teach in school ... Will you touch me too?"

I shook my head. "I can't. I'm sorry. I had a boyfriend, Earl—it was such a disaster. We never even kissed."

"It's okay, Maya. Not all women like guys. Are you in love with Rosie?"

"Yes. Maybe we should try. Maybe I should try."

"Be sure first."

"I'm sure. I want to try."

I didn't mind kissing you, it didn't feel like sex. It felt like saying hello, only more intimate. I didn't mind your hand on my body either, or letting you see me naked. But when you tried to come closer to me, you were suddenly as alien and frightening as the reflection in a mirror of someone you know is not there.

I can't change the plot. I can't change that moment. The moment that could have saved you, saved everyone—maybe. When I felt your leg against mine, I moved away involuntarily and, covering my face, I began to cry.

"This is terrible, Maya," you said, drawing the white bedspread around your body as if protecting me from contamination. "Don't cry. Come on, don't cry. Everything's fine."

"There's something wrong with me."

"No, there isn't. There's no plan, there aren't any rules."

"I'm a total misfit in every way! Starting with my height, my family, and now this. I can't even have sex properly."

"I promise one day you will. It just has to be the right person."

"I'll never find that person."

"Of course you will. You're just a kid."

We were silent for a while, though it didn't feel like silence. Then you said, "Let's kiss again. You don't seem to mind that."

You were right, I liked how you kissed me.

"I'd be afraid to do drugs," I said. "Aren't you?"

"It doesn't matter any more."

"What do you mean?"

A strangled sob shook your body. I didn't know what to say. You were suddenly very far away. You sat up, swung your legs over the bed, walked to the window.

"Dark night of the soul," you said in a low voice.

"You're too thin," I said. "You should eat more."

You didn't answer. Then you said, still looking out the window, "I have something to tell you."

"What?"

"I'm leaving tomorrow."

"Where are you going?"

"To find out what Calley did in My Lai," you said.

"Can't you stay a while longer?"

"I don't think so. I thought I could, maybe, but I can't."

"Don't go too far. I think Gloria will be back."

"Even if she came back, I have nothing to give her," you said.

"That's crazy," I said. "That's just not true."

You turned around and said, "You want to connect to others on a deep level, Maya. Most people don't want that—they're too afraid."

"Yes, I like to be close," I said.

You said, "You almost make me want to stick around, just to see what happens to you."

I said, "Yes, you should stay. Didn't you say you have three weeks off work?"

"Let's get some sleep."

"Okay."

I don't know when you fell asleep. I turned on my side and you draped your arm around my waist, as you did long ago in my room, and I dozed off instantly. I dreamed I was planting flower seeds that turned into paintings when they blossomed, and I was mixing them in interesting ways to create the effect I wanted. I was happy. I thought you loved me and that you'd always be my friend.

But if you'd really loved me, Anthony, if you'd cared about any of us, you wouldn't have been so heartless.

I woke up to the sound of voices calling out to us. I dragged myself out of bed and squinted into the morning light. Two cars were parked on the road, a station wagon with imitation-wood side-panels and a small, two-door car—a Fiat, I think it was—that looked like a toy, with its white body and bright red crescents above each wheel. Jean-Pierre, the lead singer with the tanned midriff, was conferring with his friends next to the station wagon. I recognized most of them from the supermarket parking lot and the band at Cheri. They were holding towels and bags of pretzels and bottles of soda water and beer.

I dressed as quickly as I could and ran downstairs.

"Hi, there—we thought to visit," Jean-Pierre greeted me with a shy, cajoling smile. Did he know the shyness was charming, and could only help his cause, or was he really unsure?

"Great," I said. "We're not all up, but why don't you go down to the beach—we'll join you there. You know, we saw you at the nightclub. You were really good."

"Thanks, man."

They dropped the drinks and bags of pretzels on the front steps and made their way down the grassy slope to the beach. I heard them whooping as they splashed into the water.

I was heading back inside when someone behind me chirped, "Let me give you a hand!" A girl holding two tall bottles against her chest trotted up to the porch. "We'd better put these in the fridge, if there's room. We can go on tiptoe, so as not to wake anyone. I'm Karen—Glenn's sister. We're visiting from Toronto—Jean-Pierre's our cousin. Glenn went down with the other guys. They're such frisky puppies."

Karen hadn't been on the joyride with her brother Glenn and the rest of the gang. She distanced herself from hippie culture; she had no interest in it. She was sixteen or seventeen, square-jawed, practical. Even her bare, mosquito-bitten feet looked practical, with their long, ungainly toes. Her auburn hair was tied in a ponytail and she was wearing a denim wraparound skirt and a canary-yellow blouse. Under the blouse her breasts seemed ready for reproduction and children without the complications of desire. Though I'd never met anyone like her, I knew she was the more common specimen, not me. Everything about her was designed to rise above obstacles; life was merely a series of tasks to be tackled with good humour. And I wondered, almost in awe: was it really that simple, after all?

"What's your name?" she whispered, as we picked up the bottles and brought them inside.

"Maya. It's okay, you don't have to whisper. I'm sorry it's such a mess here."

"Oh, this is nothing compared to Glenn's room," she assured me. "I can help you clean up."

"I'll be right back," I told her. I hurried upstairs to brush my teeth and wash up. I didn't want to leave Karen by herself for too long—she was an energy conduit, and I was afraid of what she might do on her own.

She had already started collecting dirty dishes when I came down. "You don't have to clean up," I told her. "You should go swimming with everyone else."

"It won't take a minute. It'll be fun. Is there a broom somewhere?"

Together we collected garbage, piled dishes in the sink, let them soak in hot, soapy water. Watching Karen I understood for the first time the satisfactions of efficiency. It was mesmerizing, the way she lifted rugs, shook them out, then swept thoroughly. Unlike my mother's achronistic campaigns, Karen's tidying had a beginning and an end.

"This house is great," she said, emptying the dustpan into a plastic grocery bag. "Does it belong to Patrick?"

"It's his mother's. How long are you here for?"

"Oh, we always come for five weeks. We pack up as soon as school's over and stay until the end of July. Our mom misses her sister and the family. We have five birthdays close together so we celebrate them all together in a big party. You should come." She began pulling plates out of the soapy water, wiping them with a wet cloth, and setting them on the rack. I wondered why she didn't mind that the dishes on the rack were still dotted with soapy foam.

"Anything around here to dry with?" she asked.

I found a dish towel in one of the drawers and began drying the unrinsed dishes. Maybe the towel would absorb the soap along with the water.

"Thanks for the help," I said.

"It's nothing."

"What's Toronto like?"

"Well, it's not as big and exciting as Montreal, of course. Glenn goes to Seed—that's an experimental school. They have an amazing math teacher there, he's teaching university math to a small group of kids. Glenn's in that group. He's really smart."

"You know," I said, "I'm really glad you guys came. We needed some distraction."

"Are you and Patrick going out?" she asked. "Or is he going out with the other girl?"

"We're all just friends. Patrick's brother is here too, he came by unexpectedly. That reminds me." I gathered the drugs on the counter and dropped them into a drawer.

"Someone here sick?" Karen asked.

"They belong to Anthony, Patrick's brother."

"My brother said Patrick is really nice."

"A bit moody, though," I said.

"I get that way too. Don't I know it—especially at that time of month!"

"That's what my mother says, *that time of month.*"

"She must be tall! Someone in your family must be tall!"

"No, she's just about your height, and I don't know anyone else in my family, apart from my grandmother. I don't even have a photo of my father."

"Oh, sorry." Karen looked away, thinking she'd stumbled on an embarrassing family secret.

A rampant, mutinous urge came over me, an urge that seemed almost physical: I wanted to pull Karen into *there*. Because Karen took reality and shaped it as if it were clay; she made things commonplace, adjusted them so they fit into some preconceived notion of normality. She was the youngest brother who by dint of cleverness and resolve wins the princess, retrieves the ring from the ocean deeps, defeats the fire-breathing dragon. Maybe she'd be a prime moulder of *there* too, maybe she'd cast her ubiquitous aura of confidence and self-discipline on *there*. Let there be light. But what could I tell her? I'd spent so many years fending off my mother's horror stories that I wasn't sure what I actually knew.

"They were all murdered," I explained. "They were tortured and killed—in the war, in Europe."

"Oh, no! How horrible!" Karen's eyes darted around the room. She wanted to change the subject. I was disappointed, but I couldn't stop now. I was on a roll.

"You know those camps they had in Europe? During the war?"

"I'm not sure ... I think I heard something."

"They took people and stripped them and burnt them alive or buried them alive or gassed them to death and made them stir the bodies in like vats, that sort of thing."

Karen had stopped listening. "But lookit, your mother came to Canada, she had you, she must be so proud of you."

I felt repentant—she had tried to be nice to me, and I'd thrown her off-balance for a purpose of my own.

"Yes, she is. Even the bus driver knows about that," I said.

Karen laughed gratefully. "You remind me of our English teacher, Miss Darlene. You're a lot like her."

"I wish I was like you, Karen," I said.

"My goodness, you don't want to be like me! Wait till you see me in a swimsuit." She unclasped her denim skirt and unbuttoned her blouse; like the others, she'd arrived with a bathing suit under her clothes. Hers was a dizzying whirl of pink and yellow and lime-green seahorses trapped in a black sea.

"That's some bathing suit."

She smiled. "My Aunt Céleste gave it to me, and we didn't want to hurt her feelings. Mom says it looks like the devil sent it over from the other side. I don't mind it, though. It distracts people from my figure." But though Karen was not slim, her body was sturdy, and the extra weight suited her.

She opened the back door and stepped into the porch. "This house is really something," she said. "Look, they're playing Frisbee. And my brother has a girlfriend. Wouldn't you just know it."

"Your brother?"

"Yeah, Glenn. Isn't he the limit? There, on the dock."

I followed her gaze and saw this: Rosie in her creased white dress, lying next to a boy with a sweet raisin face. Her head was resting on his chest and she was stroking his arm.

"I thought she was asleep," I said. "I didn't know Rosie was on the beach."

"Isn't he the limit," Karen repeated.

Such a sweet boy! Raisin eyes and dimples and everything wrinkling and crinkling into smiles.

He was lying on the dock in shorts, wet from his swim, and his hair was wet too but still curly because the curls were small and coiled. He was smiling happily as Rosie caressed his arm, softly and lovingly caressed his tanned arm.

Rosie must have woken before us, gone out for a swim. She must have been on the beach when the visitors arrived.

And already she was lying next to one of them. Yet something was different. I'd seen her with boys hundreds of times, but not like this. Her body, its curve, the yielding trust. That's what was missing until now: the trust. Not just with the guys—also with me. She liked me, but I could see now that she held back. You may not know someone is holding back, Anthony, until you see them one day, catch them off-guard maybe, staring at a kite or a sculpture or witty graffiti under a bridge. And then you understand that you have nothing at all, that everything you thought was genuine and generous and loving was a holding back, and at that moment the real possibility emerges and it floors you.

It floored me. Almost like the moment when I first saw Rosie's locker. Her life was not mine. Her life was elsewhere.

Karen scampered down to the beach like a multicoloured rabbit. She called me to join her, but I stayed where I was, on the porch, looking down. Soon she was with the others, splashing and swimming and playing catch. The silver Frisbee spun through the air like a mad bird. Mad with desire and despair. I stared at Rosie and the raisin boy, waiting for something to happen.

"Joan." Your voice startled me. You were always startling me, weren't you, Anthony?

"Oh! Hi."

You were standing slightly behind me, holding a pillow and an empty cement bag. Your worn knapsack was slung diagonally over your shoulder, just as it had been when you arrived. I may have vaguely wondered what you were planning to do with the large bag, but I didn't say anything. My thoughts were elsewhere.

"So, Joan of Arc, how are you this morning? Or afternoon, rather."

"We have visitors," I said.

"So I see."

"They're from the town."

"Oh yes, the town. I remember that little town. I was a frequent visitor there. Callously deserting the cosy family circle. What are you staring at?"

"Rosie."

"The ever-elusive Rosie. Well, Joan, the universe beckons." I thought you meant Rosie.

"Yes," I said absently.

"How I long for love and light. Good night, sweet princess." You kissed my neck, stroked my cheek with your warm hand. Then you went away, into the forest.

Our guests were playing Frisbee in the lake. Rosie and Glenn had slipped back into the water, and they were all shrieking and laughing. They must have heard the sound of a gunshot, but they didn't take any notice, and neither did I. The sound was distant and muffled and could have been anything.

But Patrick heard it and he came running out, pale and wild. "Where's Tony?" he asked.

"I don't know. He was here a second ago. I think he went that way."

"What did he say?"

"I don't remember. What is it?"

"Nothing. I'm going to look for him." And he, too, disappeared into the forest.

I headed down to the water and said, "Hey guys, do you want pizza? We have some in the freezer."

"Pizza—groovy."

So we all came back to the house and sat around drinking and eating. I watched Rosie. Her bits of broken French were like sparkles she threw in the air—everyone tried to catch them. She fit right in; she'd fit in anywhere. Glenn sat on the carpet with his legs apart and she sat in the space between his legs, leaning back against him, reborn.

It must have been close to six when our visitors left. Glenn and Rosie held each other as if Glenn were going off to war.

"Oh, Maya, I'm in love!" Rosie said as soon as they were gone. "Did you see him? What do you think? His name's Glenn."

"He seems nice."

"I always wondered, maybe there was something wrong with me, or maybe I just didn't know what love was, or maybe what I felt really was love, and there isn't anything more—but there is. This is totally different. I can't wait to see him again. He's coming tomorrow and he's going to take me for a drive. He's from Toronto—his mother's French, though. His mother and Jean-Pierre's mother are sisters. He loves music, he plays the flute—he goes to a really small school called Seed—it's alternative, for smart kids who are interested in art or philosophy ... Seed stands for Sharing Experience Something Something—there aren't any rules, even for attendance. I love him so much, I can hardly think about anything else ... Where are the guys?"

"They've gone into the woods, I think. First Anthony, then Patrick went looking for him—I guess they're having a heart to heart."

"When did they go?"

"Ages ago. Before the pizza."

"That's weird. We'd better go find them—they might be lost. Maybe we should take a whistle or something."

"They can't be lost. The forest just goes around the lake."

Like Hansel and Gretel we entered the dark forest. Spruce needles scratched our arms as we brushed them aside. "Patrick! Tony!" Rosie called.

"I'm here." It was Patrick's voice, close by.

We found him sitting against a tree, blank and frozen. As frozen as a block of ice or a statue in a city square. But his eyes were red; he'd been crying, and the tears had streaked his face. A weeping statue.

Beside him we saw your feet and trousered legs. You'd removed your shoes, for some reason. Maybe you thought someone would want them, or maybe you weren't thinking, and you did what people do when they get ready for bed. Black socks tenderly covered your feet, and the bottom cuffs of your suit fell gently on your ankles. The rest of you had vanished—where? It took me a few moments to piece it all together, like some sort of brain-teaser in a quiz book—lampshade or profile? You'd pulled the empty cement bag over your body, you'd hidden your upper body inside it. A quivering cluster of white trilliums with fairy petals breathed softly on the ground beside you.

"What's going on?" I asked, hoping this was some new way of getting high. But another part of me already knew that you had shot yourself and that what you'd had in your knapsack was a gun.

"He's dead. Oh, Patrick—I'm so sorry," Rosie said. She went over and put her arms around Patrick. The girl and the statue, by Hans Christian Andersen.

"Don't be ridiculous," I said. "I just talked to him. He's perfectly fine. Tony?" I crouched down and touched your leg, but your leg had turned to stone, just like Patrick's body. The entire forest was enchanted—our turn would come next.

"How could he do this to Mom?" Patrick shook his head, his breathing uneven. "How could he do this to her?"

"What's he done?" And it was strange, because I was screaming but not making a sound.

"He's shot himself. Didn't you hear the shot? Didn't you hear?"

"Who talked to him last?" Rosie asked.

"I did," I said. I was right about the spell, because I, too, was stiffening, as if an invisible metal beam rising from the ground had attached itself to my body. The beams were everywhere, covered with evil-smelling tar. "He said—I can't remember what he said. I'm sure he's just playing a joke on us. Let's take this stupid bag off."

"I already looked inside," Patrick said. "Don't look."

"Where's his knapsack?" I asked. I was very confused.

"Inside the bag," Patrick said. "He planned everything. The pillow, the gun … he planned it. He used the pillow to muffle the sound."

"It's cold," I said. "I hear something, is that a squirrel? Oh yes, up there."

"How will I tell her?" Patrick said. "After what she went through—"

There was a long silence.

Then someone said what we were all thinking: "Maybe we don't have to tell her."

"We can bury him here. And we'll say he went away."

"To India."

"To a monastery."

"To be a hermit."

"And once a year Patrick can go to India and send a postcard from him."

"No, a letter."

"Will she know from the handwriting?"

"I can do his handwriting. He was always changing it, anyhow."

"It won't be as bad, if she thinks he's somewhere."

"If she knew, she wouldn't be able to bear it."

"At least she'll think he's happy. It's better than nothing."

"We'll have to dig a hole."

"Yes, right," Patrick said. "Let's bury him."

Patrick told us it was illegal to bury a body and not report a death. He said we had to keep it a secret, that if we told someone, it would inevitably get out, because people always reveal secrets that aren't theirs. Then his mother would find out and we'd be charged with committing a crime. Even if we had lovers, he said, or got married, we had to promise not to tell.

He remembered that there had once been a flower garden by the side of the house. He thought that would be the best place to bury Anthony because the top layer of rocks had been cleared. He said the hole had to be deep so animals wouldn't dig the corpse out. I'd never thought of that, of animals digging up human corpses, and that this was why you had to bury bodies six feet underground. It would be impossible to do manually, he said—we'd hit granite—but we could probably manage to dig three or four feet down, and we could cover the grave with a mound of earth and rocks. And we'd plant a tree in the centre, so the mound wouldn't look strange.

Patrick said he had rope in the trunk of his car. Rosie and I went into the house while Patrick watched over you. We pulled a quilt out of the linen chest, a white quilt covered with green and blue leaves. We found the rope and brought it back with the quilt. We wrapped your half-hidden body in the green and blue shroud and then bound you with rope like Inuit cargo. Patrick made a special knot and we tried to drag you out of the forest.

You'd think people brought together by some dire mission would feel close, connected—rescue workers in a war zone, for example—but it isn't like that. The magnitude of what you have to do weighs you down, the nerve and stamina needed to overcome horror—these things narrow your focus, and there's nothing left for communion with the person at the other end of the stretcher or running with you through the flames. All our energies were concentrated on getting through the task; and we recoiled from the task, and from everyone and everything involved in it.

Or is it only grief that makes the world fall away, makes its arrangements impenetrable? Rosie rubbed my back as we struggled with the rope, but the gesture didn't translate into anything other than mechanical pressure on a part of my body. And then there was Patrick, radiating devastation like a natural force, like a hurricane coming our way, and it made us take cover inside ourselves.

They say that memory clings to times of dread. I became aware of a clicking in my brain, the kind people with photographic memories must experience all the time, because it was like the click of a camera shutter. My mind was doing something it had never done before and hasn't done since: it was seeing everything twice, once to observe and once to memorize and store, and I can recall the smallest detail—the angle of the rope, the number of times we twisted it around Anthony's body, the trilliums nearby, white trilliums that had sprung up by miracle in this forest, cascading in all their wondrous splendour, vain and oblivious and generous. I remember being certain, in a hallucinatory flash, that Anthony had moved and then, a few seconds later, that a raven was watching us.

We worked in silence. It wasn't anything new, bodies and corpses and graves, not really; they had always been a part of our lives, the frayed hand-me-downs we inherited from our parents. Only dragging Anthony's body was difficult because he'd grown so heavy and there were brambles in the way. When we reached the house, we laid him down on the back lawn and covered him with a sheet of tarp we found under the porch, in case anyone came. If someone did happen to come, we'd say we'd decided to plant some trees. We took turns, though Patrick did most of the digging and Rosie and I only helped when he stopped to rest. The ground was hard, and farther down it was full of complicated stones. We had to find the edges of the stones so we could pull them out. I know exactly how many stones there were—their shape, their curves, the way the dank earth clung to them when they emerged reluctantly from their tombs and lay on the grass as if stunned because they'd been buried for thousands or maybe millions of years.

The exertion made us thirsty, and we drank the soda water our visitors had brought. Patrick's physical strength, the ease with which he lifted large rocks, dug at hard earth—I'd had a glimpse of it when he carried Rosie. He hid that strength, had no use for it.

We hit granite three or four feet in, as Patrick had predicted. And now we had to lower Anthony inside. We sat on the lawn to gather courage. It makes no difference, what you do to a dead body, everyone knows that, but the suffocation seems ruthless, a treacherous discarding. Rosie reached out, took my hand. I shook her off and said, "I'll get more soda."

Patrick followed me inside and asked if there was any beer left. All I could find was a half-finished bottle on the counter. I offered it to Patrick but he said, "I'm not that desperate."

The sun was setting. We couldn't put it off any longer; it would be even harder, burying Anthony in the dark. We went back out and Patrick wondered whether we ought to remove the cement bag, to help with decomposition. We weren't sure. We talked about it, and in the end we decided to leave the bag but remove the quilt. In the failing light we sliced the rope with a knife and the quilt unravelled and the cement bag crept up Anthony's body. Patrick half-retched and we were afraid he'd pass out but he didn't.

We lowered Anthony inside and covered him with earth. "Poor Tony," Rosie said. "Poor Tony." But if she was merely producing from her storehouse another morsel of solicitude I told myself that her selflessness was an absence of self, and it allowed her to stand apart, untouched and unharmed.

His rage depleted by exhaustion, Patrick sighed and said, "Okay, I'll try to find potting soil—I think I saw some outside the nursery."

"I'll come with you," I said. "Rosie, you'd better stay here, keep an eye on things."

She was afraid of staying alone, I knew she was afraid, but everything had changed. Heartlessness is contagious, that's what Anthony didn't take into account. It's catching, and I'd caught it from him. And Rosie, whom I thought I'd shield forever, was now at the mercy of mine.

She nodded and I avoided her eyes, the sad eyes that all this time I'd seen and not seen.

In the car Patrick said, "We used to talk about what if. What if you went blind, would you kill yourself? What if you had to choose between killing yourself and killing an innocent person? And then about how we'd do it, if we had no choice, if there was a nuclear war and it was better to die fast."

He rubbed his eyes with his left hand as he drove, the way men do, without thinking, without tears. A mime of misery.

It was dark by the time we reached the town. Everything was closed, and the nursery lot was fenced in by wire netting, but in the light of a streetlamp we could make out large bags of earth and a row of potted firs near the wall. The gate was unlocked; it was only a question of tracking down the owner. Go dig my grave, make it wide and deep—

Patrick stopped someone on the street and asked him who owned the nursery and where they lived. We followed the man's directions to a farmhouse. In front of the house, like oversized lawn ornaments, a scattering of tractors were being their usual tractory selves, and it didn't matter that Icarus had fallen into the sea. À *louer*, the sign said. Patrick rang the front doorbell and asked whether he could pay for the bags of earth and one of the fir trees. They didn't ask why we needed them, they didn't seem curious or baffled. Who knew what hippies from the city did, or why? We returned to the nursery and loaded the car. We brought the bags to the cottage and then we made a second trip.

On the way back with the second load I asked Patrick to stop the car. "I'm going to be sick," I said. I rolled down the window and waited for the nausea to pass.

"Fucking bastard," Patrick said. "He brought the gun with him, he planned everything. Fuck him."

Rosie was sitting on the steps of the front porch, like a child waiting for her parents. I didn't ask her if she was all right.

We ripped open the bags and poured earth on the grave. There was always less than we thought once we poured it on the ground. But the grave was deep enough now, with the new earth lying heavily on top of it. We planted the fir tree in the centre and we covered the space around the tree with heavy rocks, a last precaution against predators.

"It looks like a grave," I said. "Marcel will know."

Patrick said, "No, it would never occur to him."

I said, "What if your mother comes up here?"

He said, "She never comes here. And if she did, she'd think we planted a tree. It looks like a tree, that's all it looks like."

Patrick said, "We should have a service—something."

We went inside, to the bookshelf, and took down anthologies, searched for a paragraph or a poem to read at Anthony's grave. I suggested Housman, but Patrick said, "All that angst," and Rosie suggested "Dover Beach," but we both said, "All that angst," and Patrick suggested "No Man Is An Island" and I said, "Too pedantic," and in the end we settled on "Fern Hill."

Patrick read the poem and his voice broke several times. We tried not to cry so that he wouldn't cry, because we knew he didn't want to. Then he left to sell Anthony's jeep.

We were covered with dirt. "I need a shower," Rosie said.

"Go ahead. I'll wash in the lake," I told her.

"I'll come with you."

"No," I said. "No, I want to go by myself."

"I know what you mean," she said, not knowing at all. "I need some time to think too. It's so sad."

But she wasn't sad at all. She was exulting in the manifold delights of requited love. Anthony's death was nothing but a temporary inconvenience, like fog on a rainy day. And now the fog had lifted and she could get on with her new life.

It was very dark by the lake. I stripped and washed the earth off my arms and legs. Then I submerged my jeans and shirt in the water, washed them too.

If I were Karen, I thought, there would not have been suicide, and if someone died because of an accident or because they were sick, there would be a funeral and mourning and forgiveness and recovery. There wouldn't be deception. If I were Karen, I would have given myself to Anthony and loved him the way he wanted to be loved. That's what I thought then. But now I know that I was mistaken about that, too, because no one is immune, not Karen and not anyone else, and what I assumed other people had—a simple life—no one has.

I hugged my knees and buried my head in my arms and cried, furiously. Nothing would ever be the same, and I didn't want it to be the same. They were both wrong about my dream, Vera and Anthony. I was gutted out—that was what the dream meant. I was watching myself lying on a table, my insides removed, and I didn't much care. And it would be that way from now on.

Patrick still hadn't returned by sunrise. Rosie slept downstairs on the sofa, and I climbed into the bed Anthony had crashed on the night he arrived. I wanted to go back in time; I wanted to breathe in all that was left of him. Rosie had caught on—how could she not—and she didn't try to talk to me, not even to ask what ignorant sin she'd committed. She thought I was upset, and that soon everything would be as it was before; soon she'd be kissing me hello and goodbye and I'd tell her everything and love her fiercely.

And Glenn would understand that I was her best friend, and he'd be happy for her, because you can be devoted to more than one person.

But a mountain of crushed glass had risen between us. As I watched her sleeping on the sofa, I knew I'd refuse to see her again, once we were back in the city, and I told myself she wouldn't mind, because I'd never been important, I was only another fan, another hanger-on. And she'd been waiting all along for the prince, and the prince had come.

Patrick crept in some time in the morning, but only came as far as the front porch, and neither of us heard him. He left us a note on the porch floor, next to a tin: *There's money for you in the coffee tin. I've notified Marcel that we're leaving. Take a taxi home. Marcel will close the house.*

I opened the tin and counted two thousand dollars. I knew by the time I'd finished counting that Patrick was buying us off—that he, too, was going away and not coming back.

Rosie didn't want the money. "He left it for you, Maya," she said. She wanted to even things out; she wanted us each to have a gift, and though it wasn't even, because money is only money, at least it was something. She tried to hug me, but with the expertise that comes of years of practice, I eluded her.

She asked me if she could call Glenn, if that was okay with me, and I said yes, of course. "I'll never tell him," she promised. "I'll keep the secret, even from him." It was a sacrifice I was in no mood to appreciate. Oh, the blunders of our sad, stupid souls!

We walked to the gas station and phoned him. We told him that Patrick had been called back to town because of a death in the family, and Glenn said he was on his way. We waited by the flea market, our backs pressed against the hot metal. Glenn arrived ten minutes later in the little white car with the four red crescents. He'd told his aunt, Jean-Pierre's mother, about the emergency, and she insisted he bring us over to their place.

When we stopped at Vera's cottage to collect our things, Rosie and Glenn moved in a pas de deux, their hands touching whenever they passed each other, a festive mating dance. I couldn't find anything of Anthony's, apart from his tie and the drugs. I'd forgotten about the drugs. I dumped them in the trash and draped the tie around my neck. I wanted to bring back some of Vera's books. No one would read those books here, no one would come back for them. But I didn't have the heart for it. We dumped our things in the car and drove off, with Glenn at the wheel.

Hunched in the back seat, I considered Patrick's bequest. I'd be able to move out now. I'd go to Cégep, which was free, and work in the evenings. Start a new life.

The cool layout of plans sustained me all the way home. But when I walked through the doorway of our duplex, everything in it bore down on me—the sallow carpet and brittle furniture and dejected canals trapped in hideous gold frames—and above all my mother, my mad mother, who was propelling herself towards me with her usual gasping and wheezing and thrashing.

I turned on her. "It's your fault, it's all your fault—you've ruined my life!" My voice was shrill, hateful. Her eyes glazed over, her body went limp. I didn't care—on the contrary, this was exactly what I was trying to say, that she tricked me always out of my life, and even now was trying to trick me out of my moment of reprisal. "You ruined everything, and now look at me, look at what's happened! I hate you, hate you, hate you!" I wondered, as I lost control, what would hold me back, and why. I wanted to strike her.

Instead, I fled to my room, slammed the door, threw myself on my bed—Anthony's bed—and sobbed. Between bouts of weeping I was aware of a great deal of movement and clattering outside my room, mostly in the kitchen. When I came out some time later to make myself coffee, I saw that Bubby and my mother had prepared, in an urgent, intimidated hush, all my favourite dishes.

Mourning drains you. I sat down at the table and let my mother pile food on my plate.

—has your heart been broken in love mamaleh—

One might as well be good to one's parents, I thought. Nothing comes of hurting them except more reasons to feel remorse, unbearable remorse. We were all stuck inside the city of refuge—not just me.

"Yes," I said. "My heart has been broken in love."

*—poor mamaleh—*she muttered, stroking my hair—*such a world such a world we live in—*

The next day I set out in search of a place to live. Plateau houses were not yet attracting the affluent professionals who have since claimed the neighbourhood, and within hours of apartment-hunting I'd found a beautiful, inexpensive flat—a raft in the midst of calamity.

I longed for beauty. Anthony's suicide didn't prevent me from yielding to passion; I wasn't planning to reduce myself to an automaton. On the contrary, I wanted more than ever to plunge myself into the world of pure, seductive aesthetics—dance and theatre, museums and music, objects and books. Here were finished products with endless possibilities, here were the embowered tapestries the poets liked to imagine when they wrote about art. *There she weaves by night and day*—I would remain in that bower, not weaving but watching, and there I'd be safe from the unconsummated work-in-progress, the appalling muddle that intimacy turned out to be.

Only my mother wasn't impressed by the Plateau apartment. She stood on the balcony and shook her head. Who were my neighbours? What if they were delinquents, drunks, criminals? Who would hear me if I cried for help? And the plumbing—the electric wiring—the toilet would overflow, the sockets were unsafe. But Bubby approved, and when we came home after signing the lease, she chose the best linen and blankets for me, the best towels, and stacked them on my bed.

We hired someone's cousin to move my things: the sleigh bed, my desk, two chairs, a lamp, dishes, books. My mother's card-playing friends donated other odds and ends: an old sofa, a bridge table, more lamps, and, as if I were not only moving but also losing access to the usual resources, bags of useless clothes.

My mother helped me unpack and subjected every available surface to her soapy sponges. But her efforts were symbolic, for the Greek family who'd lived in the flat before me had scoured it from top to bottom. They'd even left me a tiny cross in the kitchen drawer, for good luck.

I managed, eventually, to send my mother home. I walked her to the bus stop and promised to phone that evening and go over for supper in three or four days. After she left, I took a long bath in the deep claw-foot bathtub. Then I lay in my bed in the strange, lonely flat. Its empty rooms felt as foreign as another language, the prowling remnants of someone else's story. Between the cool ironed sheets, amidst the smell of apples and soap, I was free to reinvent Anthony's exit. In my fantasy I turned away from Rosie, asked him why he was carrying a cement bag. I went with him to the forest, talked to him, stroked his arm, hugged him, told him all would be well. *You can have love and light here,* I said. I made him open his knapsack and fling the gun into the lake. He'd be back in L.A. by now, and Rosie would knock on the door of my new place and come in, and I'd make her tea in a glass. She'd tell me about Glenn and I'd tell her about my plans and we'd hang out.

It was a good deed, and a bad one. I'm not sorry. We saved Vera, and also Gerald, anguish. But at a cost to ourselves, or to myself, at any rate. Because Rosie could take cover in her newfound love and Patrick could take cover in his intransigence, but I was naked in the icy wind.

—but this is all wrong! Rosie was as windswept, as alone as I was, and I punished her for things that were not her fault. The truth is that I didn't want that part of myself any more, the part that had loved Rosie and been loved in return, because if not for me, Anthony would be alive.

The eighth year of
the new millennium,
common era

∽

These days my mother lives with Gustav, her former suitor and present husband, in an apartment complex in Côte St. Luc. Squat, brutal, stubbled with concrete balconies, these cement monstrosities appear to have been inspired by an H.G. Wells dystopia—human dwellings for when machines take over. But as soon as one enters the apartments themselves, a magic transformation takes place, and the Fort Knox doors that line the tenebrous halls give way to small oases of comfort and light.

I visit once a week. Gustav and Fanya both greet me with enthusiasm, help me take off my coat, usher me in. An addict of low-volume television, Gustav was a limousine driver in his pre-retirement days, but his passion was the moonlighting he did, and still does, at The Workmen's Circle. He's a slight, tidy, swarthy man with accommodating eyes and a steady disposition. I've never seen him eat anything other than Mandelbrot—a relative of biscotti—dipped in tea. Though he's never been interviewed, he is, remarkably, one of the few children from Korczak's orphanage who survived the extermination camps.

The minute I enter the little sanctuary, a profound lethargy spreads through me. I sink down on the plush sofa, and my mother enumerates all the items on the Levitsky menu. I nod submissively. At some point during the procession of dishes, I fall into a limp, dreamless sleep. When I wake, I take the elevator down to the pool to swim laps. Sometimes I'm joined by Max, a hollow-chested man who before going into the water dons, with the shamelessness of the elderly, a white spandex bathing cap and state-of-the-art scuba gear. Then I head back upstairs for another carbohydrate-enriched meal, while on the television the mysteries of woodwork are unlocked by a man we can't exactly hear but who inspires confidence. My mother continues to recount stories of sedition on the part of manufacturers—she calls them corporations, these days—

and her victories over them. But Gustav has succeeded in shifting her base of operations, and her narratives are now confined to the present. She no longer mentions the war.

Everyone else mentions the war; the silence has been lifted, replaced by a flood of memory and monuments. A search for information on the Internet yields millions of sites.

I'm interested, now, in my mother's past, but having trodden those merciless waters for so many years, she's better off on shore, and I let the past be. Instead, I tell her and Gustav about my life— the sort of people I meet at Sororité, the dramas I watch from the sidelines or hear about at my table. I'm considered a good listener, a safe repository for confessions of harboured resentments or infatuations. "I'm the on-site Mother Superior," I say, and they chuckle. They chuckle at all my stories; I make them funny. Since I'm not involved in any of them, it's no effort to take a lighter view. But about Tyen I haven't breathed a word. I don't know yet where, among the *dramatis personae* of this mystery play, she'll be cast.

In the evening, I return to my place. I bought this triplex with the war reparations that for years had been arriving regularly from Germany. My mother never touched those payments; she thought they were a trick, and that if she withdrew so much as a dollar, uniformed Nazis might spring from behind the counter at the Bank of Montreal and take her away. But a few years after I moved into the flat, the building went up for sale, and I persuaded my mother to release the money for two down payments: the triplex for me, a condo unit for her and Bubby.

Fanya resisted at first, but the Bedford Street neighbourhood had deteriorated, and one evening hoodlums snatched her famous alligator purse. Mrs. Blustein came to my mother's rescue once more; there was an apartment for sale in the Côte St. Luc building where she lived. Pleased with its immediate availability, the security features, and the idea of a friend close by, my mother overcame her fear of moving house. She gave me custody of her account and asked me to go ahead with both purchases. When the last papers had been signed, Gustav insisted on treating us to a meal at Ruby Foo's, famous for Cantonese egg rolls, boisterous celebrity diners, and the beautiful silk-clad woman who sold cigarettes on a tray. Bubby, as always, preferred to stay at home, but she was happy about the move, and while we were at the restaurant she baked us an apple cake. That evening we all gathered around the kitchen table in the Bedford Street flat for the last time.

Bubby is gone, of course. If she were alive, she'd be well over a hundred. She was sick for a week, unable to swallow or eat. I came to Intensive Care and said her name, held her smooth, round hand, now shiny and slightly waxy. If she felt my hand on hers or knew I was there, she didn't respond. An hour later the nurse told me it was over; she'd stopped breathing.

I remembered a story my mother used to tell me. I'd lost the story inside the maelstrom of my mother's memories and my resistance to those memories, but it resurfaced now. When my father was a baby, my grandmother had taken him with her to visit friends in the country. She left him in the garden, under a tree in bloom. My father lay on his back in his baby carriage, looking up at the white and pink blossoms. Miriam was indoors, having tea, biting into a cookie, when all of a sudden she cried out, *He can't breathe*. She ran out to the pram and saw that two petals had fallen on my father's nose and mouth, and she was right, he couldn't breathe, he was suffocating.

Her sixth sense gave him sixteen more years that were good, before the war came. Her sixth sense gave me life.

I phoned my mother from the hospital and told her Bubby Miriam was gone. There was no funeral; my grandmother didn't want one. No one in her family, other than my father, had had a funeral: everyone else had been thrown onto piles. My mother, under the influence of Gustav, behaved well. Every day I thank the good angels for bringing Gustav into our lives.

As for the Michaelis, Glenn moved in with them that September. My mother, who kept up with developments from her post at the dry cleaners, informed me that Glenn's high school, Seed, had allowed him to complete his last year by correspondence. Rosie was taking music at Cégep and Glenn accompanied her to her classes. I was at Cégep, too, but not the same one, as the last thing I wanted was to see the Eden gang. I enrolled at a more offbeat, inner-city campus, a converted St. Henri factory, not far from the Camp Bakunin pickup spot, as it happened.

That winter, Mr. Michaeli died; my mother called to tell me, and I considered going to the funeral, but in the end I came down with the flu and couldn't make it even if I'd wanted to. Sheila had also gravitated to the St. Henri Cégep, and sometimes we ran into each other in the college's lounge, where between classes we lazed about on red and grey ottomans. Sheila told me that Glenn had been accepted by the Math department at Harvard. They were all moving to Boston: Glenn, Rosie, Mrs. Michaeli.

"How come you're not in touch?" Sheila asked. "You used to be inseparable."

I shrugged. "Things change." Rosie had left several messages for me with my mother, but I never answered and she'd given up. I did hear from Mrs. Michaeli, though. The trip to Paris had whet her appetite for travel, and she joined a trekkers' club. At regular inter-vals, my mother and I received postcards from her of desert dunes, children in holiday costume hugging shaggy llamas with oddly anthropoid legs, sci-fi peaks of aquamarine glaciers. *The world is larger and more diverse than anyone imagines*, she wrote.

Dvora is in touch with Rosie—she's in touch with everyone. Two days after high school, Dvora found work as a waitress at a seafood restaurant, and there she met an Australian obstetrician who was in Montreal for a convention. When he returned to Australia, she went with him. They have five children and a horse farm, or maybe not exactly a farm, maybe just a large field that allows them to keep horses and enter competitions. Banished, as she puts it, to antipodean Australia, Dvora maintains contact via email with what she likes to call "life on the outside." She mentions mutual acquaintances from time to time, but the information is skeletal: Rosie's had three children, all boys; Earl and his wife are real estate agents in Toronto; Avi is a lawyer. A catalogue of lives.

Sheila phones me once in a while, or I phone her. She teaches at a high school in Vancouver; I gather that she's popular with her students. Her two marriages ended in divorce, but she has a son, currently studying at Stanford, from a third liaison. Last year, her father fell off a ladder at work and died shortly afterwards. Her mother is at a nursing home in New Brunswick which is run, conveniently, by one of Sheila's sisters. In her usual wry, dry way Sheila explained why she didn't attend her father's funeral and hasn't been to see her mother. "My mother wouldn't recognize me, and my father wouldn't have, either." She's invited me to visit her in Vancouver, but I can't leave Sailor. In any case, between semesters I find I want only to vegetate on the sofa under a mohair blanket and watch movies from La Boîte Noir.

Anthony has a child. Gloria came looking for him in late August; she'd had a change of heart and was looking forward to a happy reunion—especially in light of the good news that she was pregnant with Anthony's child. Patrick had already absconded, and Gloria, scrounging for information about her husband, asked to see me, so I went round to Vera's to meet her. Vera left us to ourselves.

I don't know exactly what Anthony saw in her; we hardly ever know. To me, she seemed unengaging, but maybe pregnancy had made her placid, flattened an alluring intensity or hunger that had been there before. Or maybe I was too distraught to see her clearly. I gave her a truncated version of our last encounter: the restaurant, the nightclub, Anthony's intimations that he was leaving soon, though he didn't say where. My voice almost betrayed me, but Gloria didn't know me well enough to identify as out of the ordinary the irregular pitch and halting syntax.

She nodded as I spoke. When I'd finished, she said, "We fought, you know. We fought over nothing. He was trying to protect me, I guess, and I kept saying, you're being patronizing. But he wasn't, I don't think. Anyhow, he was right about those guys I went off with. All they wanted was for me to make them coffee and sandwiches. Women's rights, that's just lip service. They weren't a real group. There's power in sticking together, not in dividing up again and again. And sisters have to stick together if we're going to get anywhere."

It was my turn to nod.

I felt small, physically, I felt I was shrinking. Lying had shrunk me. I made my excuses as soon as I could and ran down the street, disoriented and ashamed. At the water's edge I caught my breath. The lake's soft beauty, its gentle desolation in the ethereal light of dusk, shifted me back into place. Anthony's reach was long, but it weakened in the face of such distractions.

I worried about Gloria, pregnant and husbandless, and I was relieved to hear that two months after her fruitless visit she moved in with a famous New York theatre director. Vera bought an apartment in Brooklyn Heights so she could help with the baby. Gloria sent me news of the birth on a postcard of the Manhattan skyline. She'd had a boy on December 11, his name was David. *If you hear from Tony, tell him we miss him*, she wrote.

At first, Vera phoned me every few months. Skimming was not her style, and her conversation drew on unanswered, and unanswerable, questions. She assumed there had been a romantic entanglement up at the country house—heartbreak, unrequited love, perhaps a triangle that had driven us all apart. She asked if I'd heard from her sons. No, I said, we weren't in touch. Facts are elusive, she said; they serve to hide more than they reveal. Like language itself, she mused. And did I know that Patrick was in

Alberta in a small northern town, working as a shipper? He phoned her on Sundays but didn't have much to say. He seemed to like the job and the people he worked with. He was on the defensive, she told me, torn between concern for her and resentment. She hoped he would find a way out.

The shipping stint lasted two years. Then Patrick had a fight with a new manager and quit. He continued westward to Vancouver—"even farther from me," Vera commented, with her usual stricken composure. He decided to go back to school and study library science. And it was at the library that he met a woman who was translating a thesis on the medieval Jewish commentator Abravanel. Or Abrabanel. Or Abarbanel. That was the difficulty that brought them together: the many spellings of the commentator's name. She was separated and already had a child; Patrick moved in with her, and they married when she became pregnant again. Their daughter is nineteen now, or maybe twenty. "It would be good if he found some balance," Vera said. "Adar initiated the relationship, I think. She is the expressive, vulnerable self he longs to release but can't. That can spell disaster." As for Anthony, he was still at the monastery in India. "Searching for something, just like his father," she sighed. She heard from him once a year, she told me; he sent her long letters. He was doing well; he liked the life he led; it was peaceful. Gerald, on the other hand, had returned from his travels. Did I want to come for supper and meet him?

I declined. It was hard enough lying to her on the phone; I couldn't imagine maintaining the deceit for an entire evening, making small talk with Anthony's parents while images of his freakish burial forced themselves on me like a movie reel spinning out of control. And Vera, who had struck me as a mind reader when I first met her, would notice at once that something was awry. No wonder Patrick had left.

Three months ago, I ran into Vera at a bookstore. She wanted to buy a gift for her grandchild, Anthony's son. He liked biography, did I have any ideas? In her billowing beige windbreaker she looked like a sad old owl. She was glad to see me, and we talked about my job, my mother, the weather. Then suddenly she peered at me and said, "I think you know where Tony is. I think you know and don't want to tell me."

"We promised not to tell," I said uneasily.

"Ah. Well, as long as he's happy with that sort of life. I thought it was a phase that would pass. But as long as he's happy. It's too bad for David, you know. Still, Wallie is a loving father to him." And then I imagined that she looked at me suspiciously.

I looked away.

A few days later her heart, a frail bird's heart, gave way in her sleep. Gerald phoned for an ambulance and then he phoned Patrick. The funeral was private, but there was a column in the newspaper about Vera: her work as a child psychiatrist, the books she'd written. I called Patrick and suggested we get together. "It would be nice to see you," I said, "after all these years. I'd like to meet Adar too."

I was aware, as I left the house, that I was excited—it was the sort of pleasurable excitement I'd feel if I were about to mount a major exhibition, or see a photo of my father. Patrick was after all a link to something, and maybe he had the key—though I hardly knew what I might be trying to unlock.

Patrick introduced me to Adar in the noisy brasserie. I saw almost at once that his marriage was not a success, and during the next few hours I was privy to a discouraging close-up. Patrick's self-protective irony had strayed into the arena of offhand nastiness. He had become cruel—maybe against his will and without his approval, or even his recognition. Subtly he disguised a frozen rage, detached himself from his behaviour. Only when he spoke about his daughter did he step back, or away, as he had when he'd communed with Woofie, all those years ago in his attic apartment. His face lit up, and I saw that he was a loving father. But the rest of the world was as deadly as ever, and he had become deadly in return.

Adar—astute, fragile, sensitive—felt sorry for him. Her compassionate plan was to reinterpret the cruelty, hand it back to him transformed. It was a doomed project, and the only outcome was intimidation. She was afraid of Patrick, and I wanted to save her. Anthony would have said that the blueprint for utopia in my breast pocket was still impelling me, still defeating me.

I often wonder: did Anthony plan our fraud? It occurs to me that he counted on us to conceal his death, bury him, read a poem over his grave. He thought we were up to it, and that he wasn't important and that we'd be fine, we'd move on, and if we were unhappy, well, people were unhappy; there was no avoiding that. He was wrong about everything.

Yesterday I wrote to Dvora and asked her for Rosie's current email address. As always, Dvora was happy to hear from an old friend:

Hi Maya! Great that you guys are connecting! Rosie always writes to me from her hubby's address at Harvard (makes me feel important to see the address on my inbox) but actually I haven't heard from her since last spring. I'll look around in my files (you know me, I never throw anything out) and see if I can find her letter and I'll forward it to you. Guess what, I'm going to be a grandmother!!! Help!!! Emma's expecting twins—probably girls but they aren't exactly sure, could be boys with small (for now) willies. I'm attaching a photo of the whole gang. Phil as you see has gone grey and no wonder! He might retire next year as delivering squelchy babies in the middle of the night is getting to be a bit much for him. Our Beautyshop Quartet had to disband because Janet's getting chemo. We've probably all gone croaky by now anyhow, though we placed sixth last year which isn't too bad. I'm still doing the donkey rescue work, not that those bad-tempered grouches ever bray a word of thanks. OK gotta run, fab to hear from you!

An hour later, she forwarded Rosie's letter:

Hi Dvora, I'm very glad things are working out so well for you and that your multi-family Passover dinner was a success. It's obvious that you're very

popular in the community and no wonder, you were always so kind and generous to everyone and funny. Remember all those toffees you snuck into the pool for us? Yesterday Glenn bought a Wii for the boys, they're very excited about it and making a racket. Did I tell you, there's an immense man, he must weigh three hundred pounds, he runs the coffee shop a few blocks away and I want so badly to be his friend. Not that we ever say more than a few words to each other, but I wish I knew him better. He's so unhappy! I brought him some tulips from the garden but I think I only made it worse. I dreamed we were lovers. Glenn reads *The Prophet* to me every night. Remember Kris gave me that book at the surprise party my parents and Maya organized when I turned 15? I keep dreaming that I'm swimming and I discover I have no arms, only tiny fins. It's a very scary dream. Sometimes I imagine the whole room is teeming with people, half-dead, half-alive. I guess I'm actually dreaming but it feels so real! Do you dream?
xx

I've read and reread the letter, trying to find in this distressing text—what? exoneration? a way out? or maybe a way in ... though one thing does strike me with cathartic force: the shackles that held our parents to their unspeakable past, those shackles seem to have multiplied through some sort of process of spontaneous generation—and now it's our own past that thwarts us, and we are flailing with tiny fins, trying to move on, but a great, cumbersome weight holds us back.

I clicked on "compose," typed in Glenn's address—how wonderfully simple it is, these days—and wrote:

I've been thinking about you, Rosie, and feeling sad that we lost touch—I hear news about you and your family from Dvora, but it's chatty and superficial. I remember your sad eyes. Please write. I guess you heard that Vera died. She never sold the country house—an artist she knows has been living there for many years. Maybe we could drive to the house one day and visit the grave. Or meet in New York and see Anthony's son, talk to Gloria. I'm sorry about everything. I want to see you. Maya.

Glenn replied almost immediately:

Dear Maya, I was so pleased to receive your letter, which I read. I hope you
don't mind, but you addressed it to me so I assume you wanted me to print
it out and give it to Rosie. Rosie has been unwell. I don't know how much
you know, but the problem seems to stem from depression. Maybe if you
came, she'd feel better. I don't want to put you out of your way. You have
your own life, I know. It's only that I'm at my wit's end, and I know you were
once close. If you come, we have a big house and a guest room and you'd
have all the privacy you need. Or we'd be happy to put you up in a b&b.
Have you ever been to Boston? I think you'd enjoy seeing the sights. Well,
that's about it. I have a meeting and I have to run. Thanks for writing.
Sincerely, Glenn.

We think we aren't important; we tell ourselves that because we
were helpless and ineffectual once, this is who we are, and our exits
don't matter—no one will miss us. I told myself that Rosie had
Glenn. My desertion was a way of mourning through imitation, a
way we have of re-enacting the worst traits of whoever it is we've
lost. For those tangled reasons, and others, I did to Rosie what
Anthony did to me.

Of course, I don't know why she's in trouble. I only know I
haven't been there to help out. And I also know something else
now that doesn't occur to us when we're young, and when what we
have in common with our fellow-travellers is being young, and it
seems as if it's easy to find friends. It only dawns on us later, as
people drift away, that friends are in fact hard to come by, hard to
replace.

I've already bought my plane ticket and arranged for a dog sitter.
I leave tomorrow morning. The past is irretrievable. I will never be
in Eden again, trailing after Rosie, helping her gather up her
books. I'm waiting, as Anthony did not, to see what comes next.

Eikah

Yes, I said
when they offered me a blanket
they gave me a blanket
I sat in the back of a truck
there were folding seats on the side walls
I sat on the seats with my back leaning against the wall
you could choose
without concealing that you were choosing
without hiding
that was what freedom was
not having to hide
the Russian drivers were full of good humour
they laughed and hit each other in play
sang out of tune
my thoughts were very narrow
I barely noticed the weather though I remembered later
that it was a sunny day with blue skies and a chill in the air
I was planning my future
everyone was in a stupor
everyone's thoughts were narrow
they'd been narrowed
if I made it to Prague I'd look for Katya
find out if they were all in one piece
Katya's father could help
if he was alive
he liked me
he knew people once
I wanted to continue my studies in Canada
I imagined horse-drawn wagons
hands hidden inside fur muffs
fields of snow

fireplaces
sparsely populated cities
fresh eggs
eggs were part of my future
if I found Katya I would eat two lightly salted poached eggs on
    buttered toast
I'd wear a dress
I'd listen to the radio
everyone had diarrhoea
there were seven people in the truck and the driver had to stop
    constantly
we pounded and the Russians laughed and stopped the truck
no we didn't pound
we tapped on the glass window between the back of the truck and the
    Russians
but was there a window?
or was it only a metal wall?
it must have been a window
how else would I remember the Russians
laughing and slapping each other's shoulders
I was half-asleep when the truck stopped suddenly
ten kilometres from the city
we all froze in panic
maybe it was all an illusion
maybe they were back
maybe some parts of Europe were still under their control
anything sudden did that to us
the mind gets trained in one direction
learns to protect itself
but there was no one there
only a little girl sitting by the side of the road
dressed in strange clothes that didn't fit her
the Russians had stopped for her
but no one moved

the Russians were waiting for one of us to climb down and get her
but no one had the strength for it
I was afraid the truck would move on
the girl would be left behind
she was half-dead like the rest of us
any minute she'd stop clinging on
and her death would be our fault
worse than our fault
when we weren't selected
because we didn't choose
only hoped
some of us hoped
but here we had a choice
it was very hard
I staggered up
undid the half-door at the back
someone helped me with that
I got out of the truck and took the girl's hand and led her up inside
the girl sat on the floor
she thought she had no choice
she didn't know the war was over
I said the war is over
she didn't seem to understand me
it was impossible to tell what language she knew
if any
she had a devious face
like a small demon
she'd lost her mind
she clutched my shirt with her small dirty hand
the shirt the Red Cross gave me
I guessed she was between seven and fourteen
hard to know with everyone shrinking
and looking so old
one British soldier thought I was an old woman

he said to someone bring the old lady over here
the way the girl clutched me was closer to seven
her eyes were closer to fourteen
but even two-year-olds had those sad old eyes
in the ghetto
and fourteen-year-olds clutched
we all lost our ages
the truck reached the city
the Russians offered us cigarettes
Prague was impossible
nothing had changed
nothing had changed
it was all the same
there were broken windows from the riots
heaps of rubble
but apart from that it was the same
we were the nightmare
intruding on the city
the Russians let us off the truck
we dispersed
the girl wouldn't let go of my shirt
and anyhow there was nowhere for her to go
the Russians were returning to the DP camp
they could take her
I couldn't leave her with the Russians
I'd have to take the girl with me to Katya's
everyone stared at us or looked away
afraid
the first few days we'd slept in a field
wrapped in blankets from the Red Cross
a tall man hovered above me
repeating over and over I killed him, I killed him
he dangled the rope he'd used to strangle an officer in front of me
then he moved on to someone else

dangled the rope in front of them
we'd all lost our minds
it was only a matter of degree
I had ways to hold on to sanity
I studied the human mind
sadism
torture
starvation
group behaviour under threat
I pretended to myself that I was doing research
undercover
now I was encountering revenge
the German officer he'd strangled was lying face down in a ditch
no one cared
we were tired
it began to drizzle and we were taken in trucks to a train
British soldiers gave us sardines
sweet lemon juice
the sun shone in through the open doors
I tried to tell the soldiers that if we ate more than one sardine at a time
and more than one tin in a day
we would die
I tried to warn people
but two men and a woman ate too fast and died in great pain
I slept on the train and then I slept five or six days at the American
    post
I heard that a Russian truck was leaving for Prague
and I managed to find it
now I had to find Katya's house
I was lucky
someone took pity on us
and gave us a ride
the girl was still clinging to my shirt
the driver talked about the riots

I wanted a bath
he let us off at Katya's house
I looked up and saw the red curtains of her apartment
Katya's apartment
the curtains were a good sign
the driver told us that two thousand people were killed in the uprising
Katya and her parents could have been among them
I wanted a bath
and eggs
and to be rid of the girl
my own baby died on January 14, 1942
he was shot on the way to the ghetto, in my husband's arms
along with my husband
it was worse for other parents
that realization came to me in the months that followed
the realization that given the choices, it was worse for those whose
   children were still alive
I rang the bell
I could hardly stand on my feet
a maid I didn't know opened the door a crack
she kept the chain on
she called out: refugees
an old man and a girl
old man
I laughed at that
my first laugh in the new world
Katya came to the door
she undid the chain
she said we don't have much
I'll see what I can find
I said it's Vera
I'm not old and not a man
I'm Vera
this is a girl we picked up

I don't know anything about her
Katya let us in
we sat in her living room
the maid prepared tea
Katya said what can I give you
we have four eggs
I made bread this morning
I said I'd like poached eggs on buttered toast
and hot milk with cocoa
the girl should have a soft-boiled egg and as much milk as you can
    spare
nothing that's hard to digest
Katya hurried to the kitchen to tell the maid
I was laughing
Katya was crying
I said let's have some music
Katya put on the radio and a classical piece came on
Fauré I think
the little girl let go of my shirt
walked to the middle of the room
began dancing ballet
precise ballet movements
she kept it up for half a minute or a minute
then she fell to the floor
and began shrieking
piercing
demonic shrieks
she peed on the carpet
and Katya's father walked in
alarmed
there was an old man on the sofa
a girl shrieking in a puddle of urine on the floor
when the girl saw the man she stopped shrieking
terrified

ran back to me
clutched my shirt again
Katya said it's Vera
her father said I know who it is
he sat down next to me and kissed my hands
Jan? he said
I shook my head
Jan and the baby were shot on Jan 14, 1942
just as well I said
considering
considering what was coming
I said I want to go to Canada
can you arrange that?
can you get me a visa?
I want to study there
even if I have to start over
I want to start over anyhow
the eggs were ready
the girl clutched my shirt in one hand and held her spoon with the other
we tried various languages
with the help of dictionaries
I was back in a world that had dictionaries
damask
paintings on the wall of children on a sled
finally we had some luck with Italian
the girl understood Italian
I asked for a bath
Katya said the water was only tepid but she'd add hot water from the
  kettle
I undressed
the girl didn't let go of my shirt
she sat on the floor holding the shirt
I got into the water and lay down
the water turned dark brown

we changed the water four times
Katya vomited
she was too thin to be pregnant
it was seeing me naked that made her vomit
the girl refused to be bathed
Katya wiped her with wet towels
Katya was afraid of her
but to me she was ordinary
her demonic shriek in the living room had been ordinary
it was this life that was out of the ordinary
I wanted to sleep
Katya gave me her bed
the girl slept with me
we slept for days on end
slept and ate
our cells regenerating
with remarkable speed
the human body was remarkable
the human mind was even more remarkable
how had I not gone mad?
how?
I didn't know
even my memory had survived intact
another mystery
Katya asked a friend who spoke Italian to come visit
he tried to find out more about the girl
where she came from
she didn't know
Katya's father managed to get me a visa
he pulled the usual strings
he wrote to McGill University
they were willing to take me
I'd have to start over
my period returned

my tissues repaired themselves
my hair began growing back
the maid took a liking to the girl
went out walking with her
the girl had a wild look in her eyes still
but she was well-behaved
she was learning Czech
if you studied the mind several lifetimes you still would not understand
    more than a fraction
there was endless oddity about us
at night I returned to another world
nightmares you'd call them
Gerald
but they were memories
replaying themselves in my mind
during the day I could control my thoughts
I controlled them
but at night
at night they returned
but if you hold me tonight
maybe I'll sleep better
with you I feel safe
is that what you mean when you say you love me
I feel safe with you
Gerald
for me that's enough
for me that's enough
do you understand?
can you understand?

Acknowledgments

David Davidar, my publisher, inspired me with his humanity, spirit of generosity, and unwavering integrity. David will never know how much I owe him for his faith in my work; creativity cannot thrive without the sustenance of such faith.

It was a joy to work with my editor, Nicole Winstanley. Nicole's unfailing good humour, patience, energy, and insightful comments were a gift. The entire Penguin team has been incomparable. A special thanks to copy editor Heather Sangster for astute and thorough scavenging.

Joan Deitch, who lives in London, is a brilliant, devoted editor as well as fab friend and confidante, sweet and funny and unstinting with her time and expertise. Her encouragement was invaluable; she held my hand through all the panicky middle-of-the-night worries and entertained me with her lovely letters.

Penn Kemp came up with many imaginative, sensitive, and poetic suggestions. I am very grateful to Derek Fairbridge for his careful reading and numerous helpful comments. I am obliged to John Detre for making time to answer questions about the 1960s and for generous professional assistance. It was, as usual, fun plying Ken Sparling with musical questions; apart from providing scintillating answers, Ken always had a wise and intriguing word for me.

I was deeply moved by the heartfelt responses to the manuscript of Tom Deitch, Cesar Garza, and Ruz Gulko.

Marsha Ablowitz, who was so kind to me when I was five years old, reappeared in my life and was as kind as ever. Her contribution is deeply appreciated.

For unending support and quota-free listening as I made my way through all the stages of producing this book, and for enthusiasm about my writing these past forty years, I thank, inadequately, Shirley Rand Simha.

For expert help with many hurdles, I am grateful to Chris Heap.

Joan Barfoot understands everything. I can't thank her enough for her thoughtfulness and magnificent books.

Many thanks to Mindy Abramowitz for the open line.

I am fortunate to have fellow-artists Richard Cooper and Margaret Wolfson on my side. I am most grateful to Andrea Levy for providing a loving second home for Larissa, and much else.

For technical help my thanks to Lisa diLanzo Brombal, Ze'ev Gedalof, Hélène Hampartzoumian, Howard Johnson, Peter F. McNally, Charles Stevens of Cottage Blooms, West Falls, and the staff at the wonderful Guelph Library, whom I kept busy and who were so very accommodating. I was extremely lucky to find the superb Tel Aviv photographer Shlomi Bernthal and gifted Israeli actor Shir Shomron for the cover photo, which was beautifully adapted by the inspired Penguin design team.

I would not have survived the demands of a sixty-hour workweek without the unrivalled sports therapist Johanna Thackwray.

I am humbled by the many heroic death-camp survivors in my life and family. In the end, there are no words with which to tell their story and no way to understand what they experienced. This silence hovers at the edges of the novel and of all our lives. We give it meaning by living with love and striving for justice.

This book is dedicated to my daughter Larissa, whose radiance transforms my life every minute of every day.